Alyssa felt the touch of Sue's lips travel directly to her heart, which suddenly felt even more full. It had been so long since someone had taken care of her.

Sue rose almost effortlessly, dropped Alyssa's hand and looked out across the water. A few puffs of cloud had bunched along the horizon, their edges turning pink as the sun lowered.

Alyssa wanted to move to Sue, to kiss her and feel her touch like that shaft of sun.

"So," Sue said, "do you think the risk would be worth it?"

It's happening! Alyssa took a deep breath. "What risk?"

Sue didn't move, but Alyssa could feel the energy coming off her in waves. "You know what I mean," Sue said. "I haven't misread this."

"No." Alyssa didn't move either.

"No, it isn't worth the risk? Or no, I haven't misread this?" Sue stared at the water.

Before Alyssa figured out what to say, Sue placed a palm where Alyssa's shoulder curved into her neck. Alyssa could feel the rhythm beating there, hard. Then she felt Sue's hands slide around her, and Sue lowered her lips to Alyssa.

Alyssa welcomed her, tasted her. Desire cascaded through her body. *Uh-oh*. Was she ready for this, now?

Alyssa felt Sue's lips leave hers, moving across her jaw. Sue's breath rushed near her ear, twisting her passion even tighter. She turned her head to find Sue's lips again, and her quiet moan delighted Alyssa.

I could have her in bed tonight if I wanted to, Alyssa thought. And she wanted to. *We would touch and make love. I could relax.*

Visit

Bella Books

at

BellaBooks.com

or call our toll-free number

1-800-729-4992

guarded hearts

HANNAH RICKARD

Bella
BOOKS

2004

Bella Books, Inc.
P.O. Box 10543
Tallahassee, FL 32302

Printed in the United States of America on acid-free paper
First Edition

Editor: Christi Cassidy
Cover designer: Bonnie Liss (Phoenix Graphics)

ISBN 1-931513-99-6

Dedication

To Devon, because I promised

Acknowledgments

I am grateful for the many people who supported my work on this book. Erin, Amelia, Rhoda, Carla, Al, Bill, Julie, Chris, Cindy and Trisha read it and kept me enthusiastic. Several dog trainers and police officers shared details about their specialties—any errors did not come from them but from me. Also, Jennifer Crusie Smith provided astonishingly generous and wise mentoring. My editor, Christi Cassidy, made revision fun. Finally, thank heavens for my family who said, "Write," for my dogs who taught me about the peace of the woods and unconditional love, and for Jen who led me to the courage to let this be what it needed to be.

Chapter One

"And another thing," Alyssa Norland's boss said. "Get a dog."

She followed him and his golden retriever down the steps from the cottage that served as their office. "Wait a minute, Marcus. Can we at least talk about the class size?" Alyssa could see her students—eight puppies and twelve people—gathered in the center of the training field, waiting.

Marcus Dixon stopped so abruptly she almost ran into him. He used his thumbs to hitch up his sagging khakis and leaned close to her. "No. Remember, it's Dixon's Obedience and Guard Services." He touched the logo on his purple polo shirt. "I'm Dixon."

Yeah, Alyssa thought. *Me Jane.*

"So, if I say you have to up the number of students to twenty, we don't need to talk about it." He pushed his graying hair back from his forehead.

"But it's too many. Without an assistant, they won't learn—"

1

"Alyssa."

His tone stopped her. She swallowed.

"I hired you last September because the American Canine School said you were the best." He hitched his pants again. "I've watched you work. They were right."

Alyssa shrugged and dug the toe of her running shoe into the ground.

"If anyone can train twenty puppies at once, it's you." Marcus grinned. "You're dedicated beyond belief."

"Thanks, Marcus, but—"

"But DOGS has to make money to pay your salary, honey." His face flattened, lips tight. "And Alyssa, please. Whoever heard of a dog trainer without a dog?" He shook his head. "It's been ten months since you got here. I know you like to use Hendrix for your demos, but it hurts your credibility. Get your own dog."

Alyssa tilted her head to one side, stretching her neck to release the tension growing there. "I don't have time for—"

"Make time. Raise the class size. And find some more private clients while you're at it. It's July. We should have more business. We *need* more business or I'll have to reconsider whether or not I can afford to keep you on."

Crap. Alyssa didn't want to lose this job. She loved her students. And she owed it to Vinnie. "Okay, okay," she said as he turned toward the parking lot. She had a background in public relations. She could do this. "I'll work on it."

Marcus pointed at the waiting group. "You're late for class."

Double crap. "Right. Sorry. I'll see you tomorrow."

As Marcus and Hendrix got into his van and left, Alyssa trotted over to her students.

"Hey, everybody." She waved.

The people greeted her and began to disentangle their puppies from what had been an epic wrestling match.

She checked her watch: 7:32 p.m. Just a few minutes late.

"Let's circle up," she said, "so we can talk about any problems you've had this week." While her students moved into a semicircle, puppies bouncing into place at their sides, Alyssa rebanded her wavy hair into a tight ponytail.

"Can you start here, dear?" Delia Watkins, who neither looked nor acted her seventy-two years, waved frantically. "I'm in despair."

As if to prove his master right, Delia's collie puppy bounded forward, yanking the leash from his owner's hand. He zigzagged around the other people in excited freedom, shaking his rope toy as if intent on killing it.

"He just zips away," Delia said, going after the pup, her frizzy gray hair fluttering about her head.

"Don't chase him, Delia. That's his game." Alyssa watched the puppy's brown eyes roll sideways toward his owner. "Wait and think. What's he want?"

"For me to chase him."

"Right. So keep it his game, but turn the tables on him. You make the rules," Alyssa said, watching the pup dance around the others. "If he wants to play, he has to chase you or the game ends."

She instructed Delia to call the dog, then run away from him instead of toward him. When her dog ran after her, she should bend slowly to touch him. If he dodged, she had to stop running and disengage from the game.

"Whoo-hoo, Tango," Delia sang, jogging in the opposite direction.

Sure enough, the pup dropped his toy and raced after her. In seconds Delia held her dog by the collar.

"Miraculous, darling!" the older woman cried as she fumbled with a bright pink leash. "First you turn my thug Teddy into a guard dog and now this."

"Teddy's a great Rottweiler," Alyssa said.

"Only because you came along." Delia smiled at her puppy.

"Anyone else struggling?" Alyssa asked the group.

A small hand rose into the air. "Miss Norland, can we talk about last week's lesson?"

Alyssa turned to her youngest student, eight-year-old Adam Braeburn, who looked up at her with a freckled face and bright blue eyes.

"You mean the down-stay, Adam?"

"Yes." He nodded and glanced at his father who stood off to one side reading a newspaper.

Why couldn't the guy ever pay attention to his kid? *Well*, Alyssa thought, *at least he's here tonight.* The Braeburns were summer residents of Radley and, like many others, the husband spent weeks working at home while the wife and kids lived here. He must have taken the week off.

"I can't do it," said Adam.

"Sure you can." She smiled at everyone. "Let's all practice the down-stay individually. I'll come around and check on each of you in a minute." They set to work and Alyssa knelt beside Adam and his twelve-week-old Doberman. "So what's up?"

"Well—" The boy swallowed. "Mom says Buck has to be well-trained or Dad's gonna buy a fence and we'll have to keep him outside."

Alyssa wanted to march over and ask the man if he knew that thieves stole dogs from outdoor kennels, sold them by the pound to research labs scrounging to save a dollar or two. They'd open any fence, throw away a collar with tags, even cut off an ear if it held an identifying tattoo.

Like Vinnie.

She sighed. She wouldn't march or lecture. She would need Calvin and Samantha Braeburn to help her find more clients. Calvin, an investment broker, had a lot of influence with the wealthy summer population. And Samantha knew simply everyone. She hung around every afternoon with the summer regulars at the Blue Seahorse Bar and Grill. The best thing Alyssa could do was smile and help their son train the pup. Then they'd recommend her to their friends.

"Show me what Buck's up to," she said.

The boy chattered as he demonstrated. "Well, I know what you taught us to do. Make him sit first, and he does that, see? But when I try to get him to lie down, he just stands back up. See?"

Alyssa pulled a liver treat from her pocket. "Try dragging your treat along the ground more slowly. Keep his nose following it and your hand on his butt, and he'll lie right down." The puppy flopped onto his belly and she gave him the treat. "You try."

Adam repeated the gesture, and the puppy again went onto his belly. "He did it!" Adam shouted. Buck leapt into the boy's face, licking in frantic joy. "Dad, Dad! He did it!"

" 'Bout time," Braeburn said without looking up from his paper.

Not the response Alyssa had wanted, for herself or the boy. "Nice work, Adam. High five." She offered the boy her palm and he smacked it with his. "Keep it up."

Next, Alyssa helped a teenager with a shaking Chihuahua and then bent to pet Melanie Sybesma's puppy, a chocolate Newfoundland pup that had flopped over, its too-big feet splayed to one side.

"Any problems with Nestor, Mel?"

"Just keeping him awake." Melanie laughed, gently nudging the pup's foot. "And keep him from chewing on my badge if I'm too tired to find a hanger and toss my uniform on the floor." She rubbed the shiny badge pinned over her breast. She was a Department of Natural Resources cop and a good friend. "Do the teeth marks show?"

"No." Alyssa laughed. "Let's see what he can do."

As she stood, Alyssa heard tires crunching on the parking lot gravel behind. The black Subaru station wagon was unfamiliar. She would have remembered a roof rack like that. As it pulled up to the training field fence, she tried to see the driver but only made out a moving shadow.

Someone unexpected. She took a deep breath. *I'm safe here. This isn't Chicago.*

"Who's that?" Melanie asked.

"Don't know." She glanced at her students. No one seemed to recognize the car.

"You got a new client?"

"That'd be nice, but not that I know of."

Melanie bent, trying to lift her dog into a sitting position. "Would someone just drop by this late?"

Alyssa shrugged and watched as the passenger door on the driver's side swung open. A wiry German shepherd leapt out, took three steps, then sat, watching the puppies intently.

Next, a tall, broad-shouldered woman wearing jeans and an oversized forest green T-shirt unfolded from the car. Her brown hair curled over her ears and forehead as she bent to talk to the dog. She scanned the group as if looking for someone, then lifted herself easily onto the hood of her car, evidently prepared to wait.

"Know her?" Melanie asked.

"No. You?"

"No." Melanie poked her in the ribs. "But you should. I would make it a point, if I weren't already married. And if I were gay."

Alyssa glanced toward the parking lot again. In her previous life she would have wandered over, introduced herself and asked such a good-looking newcomer to chat over a drink. But not now.

"The dog looks well-trained," Alyssa said. "Maybe she wants personal protection training." That was probably it. Just a new client without the sense to call ahead. Not dangerous.

"Okay, I'll consider the subject changed." Melanie kissed her pup on the forehead. "Come on, Nessie, wake up and show off your obedience." The puppy shifted groggily into a sitting position. "Okay, Alyssa, he's up. Did you bring that tab leash for us?"

Alyssa rolled her eyes. "Sorry. I'll get it from the office."

"You can borrow mine, Officer Sybesma." Adam moved to unsnap the four-inch strip of leather from Buck's collar. His crush on Melanie showed all the more when she came to class like she had tonight, wearing her conservation officer uniform, complete with badge and gun.

"Thanks, Adam," Alyssa smiled, "but I've got one for her." She turned to the group. "Anyone else need a tab?" No one did, so Alyssa jogged to the cottage and bounded up the back steps two at a time.

Where's my mind? Late for class, forgetting stuff, letting some unknown woman make her nervous . . . she had to get some control. This wasn't doing her image any good.

As Alyssa grabbed the tab from atop a stack of papers on her desk, the phone rang.

Alyssa hesitated, wanting to get back to class. *Still, maybe it's another new client.* She answered.

"Dixon's Obedience and Guard Services."

She heard a strange sound, like the flipping of a heavy blanket over a newly made bed. Then nothing.

"Hello?"

"Miss Norland."

She didn't know this scratchy voice. "This is Alyssa Norland. May I help you?"

"Yes." He drew the word out. "Miss Deborah Norland. You will."

Alyssa's heart thumped.

"You see, I know what you haven't told anybody about Covington Enterprises and how you lost your job. If you want me to keep the secret, you'll give me what I want."

Alyssa tasted the tang of adrenaline. "What do you want?"

She heard the disconnection.

Who the hell was he? A reporter? Or had Covington's people finally found her?

She struggled to absorb it all. It had been fourteen months. She had started to believe she'd escaped the horrors—the lies she'd exposed, the threats, the shooting. She closed her eyes against that memory. She had run, hidden, hoping it would end.

A sharp pain in her palm drew her attention to her hand, clenched tight around the tab. The brass buckle bit into her flesh.

I know what you haven't told.

She hadn't run far enough. She should just get in her car and drive away. All night. Anywhere. Just away.

But that woman in the lot. Alyssa'd have to walk right past her to get to her own car. And if the woman had a gun . . .

Alyssa drew a deep breath. *Okay, get real. That isn't going to happen again. Not with Melanie out there in full uniform.* She was safe. She could think about it later. Right now, she had to get back to class.

Class ended right on time with a quick handout for the week's homework. Alyssa forced herself to smile as her students said their good-byes.

"Don't you leave here tonight without her name and number," Melanie teased as she dug in her jacket pocket for her truck keys. "Long tall beauties don't show up too often in Radley, even in the summer. Make your move before every other lesbian in town does."

Alyssa wished she could tell Melanie about the phone call, but she forced a smile. "Are there any other lesbians in town?"

"You mean besides you and Delia?" Melanie tugged the leash gently to urge Nestor out of another nap.

"I heard my name," Delia sang, joining them.

"Well, I'm off. Got a big day tomorrow at the Crystal Lake public launches," Melanie said.

"Doing what?" Alyssa asked.

"Visibility, mostly. When a town of eight hundred swells to two thousand eight hundred in the summer like this one, well, the summer folks need constant reminders that this isn't just their play-ground. They gotta behave, just like at home."

"Good," said Delia. "Maybe they'll stop double-parking with their blinkers on in town. Like their blinkers make it okay when I want to pull my truck around." Delia jostled Tango in her arms like an infant. "And always with Illinois plates, too."

"Usually." Melanie nodded. "See you ladies later." She joined the rest of the students meandering to their cars. No one, Alyssa noticed, spoke to the woman.

"Alyssa, dear." Delia ruffled the fur on Tango's head. "I've had an exciting few days, and—"

Movement drew Alyssa's attention toward the parking lot.

The woman had begun to walk toward them, the dog heeling by her side. She didn't wave or call out, just headed over with long, fast strides.

Alyssa's heart leapt. Something wasn't right. The woman moved too fast. "Hang on a sec, Delia."

She turned to face the stranger, breath coming quick and short, stomach tightening. What to do? She didn't want to turn off a new client. But what if she had come from Chicago, worked for Covington? The last time she'd dealt with someone linked to Rodney Covington, the bitch had shot Vinnie.

That oversized T-shirt didn't hide the strength of this woman's arms and shoulders. *Hard to outmaneuver*, Alyssa thought. Still she stepped between Delia and the approaching stranger.

If this woman were a reporter, Alyssa would try to keep her from saying anything in front of Delia. But if she worked for Covington . . . well, she'd be damned if she was going to let Covington's people hurt her again.

As the stranger approached, her shepherd, unleashed but in heel position, eyed them eagerly. Alyssa didn't think he looked like an attack dog, but he certainly had them in his sights.

"Be careful, dear," Delia whispered.

Ah, Alyssa thought, *Delia senses it too*.

Without so much as a twitch in warning, the dog bolted toward them, his ears flattened, mouth open, white teeth flashing.

"Zero, come!" the woman called, chasing the dog.

"Delia! Do *not* move!" Alyssa shouted.

"Right."

Alyssa spread her arms wide, shaking her hands back and forth. "Zero! Good dog, Zero!" She sidestepped several paces to the left.

The dog glanced once at Delia and Tango, then veered toward Alyssa. His jaw opened, looser, tongue flapping.

The dog barreled closer. *Too close*.

Alyssa moved too late to avoid the dog, who ran into her chest and knocked her backwards onto the ground.

"Zero! Damn it, get over here!" came the owner's voice.

Zero ignored his owner and returned to stand over Alyssa. He looked down at her, his red and black ears at full attention, his brow wrinkled in concern.

He sniffed her cheek, then barked a high-pitched yap.

"I'm not dead," Alyssa muttered to the dog, reaching up to grab his collar. "That's quite a game you've got going there, my boy. We'll have to change that."

"Bravo!" Delia clapped, still holding Tango. "This makes me feel so much better."

Alyssa wondered how long it would take her bruised tailbone to feel better.

"Sorry." The woman arrived holding a leather leash. "You okay?"

"Yes, I'm fine." Alyssa sat up and held the dog's collar toward the woman, who snapped the leash on.

"Sit," the woman said, and Zero sat. "You're a bad dog."

The shepherd's head drooped.

"Not now he isn't," Alyssa said.

The woman stared at her. "You're flat on your butt because of him."

"That doesn't matter. You told him to sit and he did." Alyssa could tell from her face that she didn't understand her point. "What do you think you're teaching him by scolding him when he obeys?"

The woman laughed once. "Don't give me that. This dog knows exactly what he did wrong."

"Who are you?" Alyssa asked.

"A terrific catch, Alyssa, dear. Really!" Delia walked around Alyssa to pat Zero on the head. Then she turned to the woman. "And at least we know it isn't just me tottering off balance."

"Delia, what are you talking about? You don't totter." Alyssa began to rise.

"Here." The woman offered a hand to Alyssa, but Alyssa stood on her own.

"Alyssa will have you handling Zero like an expert in no time. Just like me and Tango." Delia patted the woman on the forearm and leaned forward. "It isn't all about strength, you know. Brains too.

You've got to think like your dog. Turn the tables on them. Get them to play by your rules."

"That's a stretch for some people," Alyssa said, looking up into the woman's dark eyes. At five eight, Alyssa stood taller than many women. This one must have been nearly six feet.

"I'm Sue Hunter." She offered her hand again, and this time Alyssa took it firmly. "I'm looking for Ms. Norland."

A bolt of anxiety zipped through Alyssa. "I'm Alyssa Norland. Why are you looking for me?"

A half smile crossed Sue's face and she pointed to Alyssa's shirt. "You're a dog trainer. My dog needs one."

Alyssa forced her gaze to remain steady. Maybe she really was just a new client. "I train people, Ms. Hunter. Owners train their dogs."

She saw Sue's jaw tighten then release into another half-smile. "I don't think I need it. I know the commands. He just doesn't obey them all the time."

Alyssa had dealt with dog owners like this before. Unwilling to take responsibility for their dogs' behavior, they never got anywhere with training. She needed clients, but not ones doomed from the start.

"I don't think I can help you, Ms. Hunter."

"Oh, Alyssa, of course you can!" Delia put Tango down, and the puppy ran up to Zero and flopped over onto its back. The big dog bent to lick the pup's face. "I already told Sue you would."

Alyssa rubbed one hand over her aching tailbone. "What's going on here, Delia?"

"This is what I've been trying to tell you. Sue will be living in the apartment over my detached garage this summer while Carolyn's in Vienna working on that grant." She looked at Sue. "Retired my foot."

Alyssa saw Sue's barely contained smile. It looked like warmth, not derision. Good sign.

Delia turned back to Alyssa. "Teddy and Tango love them, and Sue can help out around the house, while she works—" Delia paused. "What is it you do now, Sue? You haven't told me much since you quit—"

"I design Web sites now." She looked from Alyssa to Delia and back. "Free-lance."

"Right. Well, anyway, dear, she just arrived last weekend, but Zero has knocked me flat a few times already." The dog looked up when she said his name and swished his tail in the grass. "I don't need that kind of risk on my old bones. So I told Sue she'd just have to get the dog trained." Delia drew a breath and turned to Sue. "I was working Tango so hard, I didn't even see you there in the parking lot. Did you tell me you were coming tonight?"

"Nope." Sue reached down absently and rubbed Zero's ears. "The water was too rough for the kayak, so we thought we'd stop by."

"Good. Not losing my memory yet." Delia grinned at Alyssa. "And since Zero knocked you down too, I guess I'm not losing my balance either!"

"Delia, Zero could knock down a football player with the hit he gave me." Alyssa looked again at the shepherd who grinned up at her, his tongue lolling. Harmless. Just willful.

"Miss Norland." Sue tunneled her fingers through her short curls. "I want to live here this summer. So." She looked down at her dog. "So here we are. My time is valuable, so I would appreciate working with an expert."

Alyssa glanced toward the nearby dunes. Given that phone call, she wanted to know a lot more about this woman before working with her. But maybe landing a new private client would get Marcus to ease up on increasing the size of her puppy class.

"Please, dear?" Delia smiled at Alyssa expectantly.

Alyssa didn't like the idea of Delia alone with this uncontrolled dog, even if he was sweet. She should do it to help Delia. And the dog. Zero had potential he would never reach if left to his owner.

"Okay." *What the hell*, she thought. *Help people, help dogs.* That's why she'd gotten into this after all.

"I think private lessons would be best," Sue said. "I can't commit to a class. I have to stay flexible to meet my clients' needs."

A chill skittered up Alyssa's spine. That meant they'd be alone together and she still knew little about her.

"Marvelous!" Delia kissed Alyssa's cheek. "I'll leave you two to work it out. Gotta get some of my chores done tonight and tomorrow. Friday night is the third Friday of the month, old gals' night at the Twelve Point, and I have a hell of a lot more fun knowing I've gotten the laundry done."

"The Twelve Point?" Sue asked.

"The tavern," Delia said. "For us townies. Open year-round too. Not like that fancy-pants Blue Seahorse Bar and Grill." She made a face.

"The Twelve Point is smoky and dark," said Alyssa.

"But it has the best pizza and cheapest drafts in the whole county," Delia said. She nudged Alyssa. "You need to loosen up and get out more."

"I've been there a few times," Alyssa said. She didn't want Sue to think she was a stick-in-the-mud.

"Not enough." Delia winked at Sue. "You come along sometime. We close the place down."

"I'm sure you do," said Sue with a straight face.

"Of course, most of us drink pop. Come on, Tango." They watched as she headed toward her bright red extended cab pickup and lifted the puppy in.

As Delia drove off, Alyssa studied Zero, whose colors shone in the amber light of the low sun. Golden eyes, with black markings highlighting his nose and forehead. Just like Vinnie.

I know what you haven't told.

She had to be careful until she found out what was going on.

"I look forward to meeting your dog," Sue said after Delia's truck had disappeared. "Impeccably behaved, I'm sure."

"Vinnie died a year ago May." Alyssa swallowed. Or did she already know that?

"Oh. Sorry." The lines stretching from Sue's eyes softened. Alyssa wondered how old she was. About thirty-two, her own age.

"I need to lock up," Alyssa said. "We'll schedule an evaluation session as soon as possible."

"I'm finishing a project for a client tomorrow. How about Friday?" Sue's dark eyes creased upward at the corners when she smiled. "I'm planning to leave Saturday morning for a short camping trip in the U.P."

"Fine." Alyssa began to walk toward the cottage. "Four o'clock. I'll see you then." She strode to the office without looking back.

She didn't like this at all but she didn't want to overreact. She needed information. Maybe tomorrow she could convince Melanie to check out Sue without having to reveal anything about the phone call or Chicago or why she'd changed her name. If that got out in Radley, she could kiss her hope of finding new clients, and her job, good-bye.

Chapter Two

The next day passed full of the sunshine and eighty-two-degree breezes that made northwest Michigan such a summer paradise. Alyssa drove the five miles from Radley to Beulah to conduct two private lessons and grab some lunch. Then she went to Interlochen to temperament-test a litter of six-week-old labs.

"I wish I had information on this to give to my customers," the breeder told her. "Then they'd understand why I won't sell them a puppy that I think would be a bad match."

Alyssa promised to write a flyer for her in the next day or two, provided the breeder would recommend Alyssa as a trainer to her customers. She grabbed a quick dinner on the way home then decided to swing by Melanie's house for a chat.

When she stepped up onto the Sybesmas' porch, she heard a woof and a crash from inside.

"Oh, Nestor!" Melanie's voice came through the open window.

"Hey, can I come in?" Alyssa asked. "I need to ask a favor."

"It's open."

Inside, Melanie was righting a framed picture on an end table near the living room sofa. Her husband, Brian, called the dog.

"You startled Nestor out of his beauty sleep," Melanie said.

"Nothing broken though," Brian said. "Lucky boy."

The bulky brown dog wagged his tail, then stood with front feet on the sofa seat. He struggled to grab hold with one of his back feet but failed.

"Here." Brian placed a flat hand against the dog's rear end and pushed. The pup settled against a pillow and closed his eyes.

"Pushover," Alyssa said.

Brian grinned. "You trainers. No mercy for a little baby dog." He crossed the living room and hugged Alyssa. "Long time no see."

"Yeah. How's Jeff?" Alyssa hadn't seen their son in over a month.

"Scooping ice cream in Glen Arbor, which is flooded with tourists and their teenage daughters." Brian folded his hands. "Heaven for a seventeen-year-old."

"So I've interrupted a quiet night alone for you two." Alyssa turned toward the door. "I'll leave right now."

"No you won't." Melanie grabbed her friend's arm and pulled her to the couch, seating her next to the snoring puppy. "Brian brought stuff home from the office. Didn't you, honey?"

Alyssa swung her gaze to Brian, who nodded slowly.

"We have girl talk," said Melanie.

He made a face. "I'm outta here. If Jeff comes home before you finish, tell him he can seek refuge in the testosterone-laden atmosphere of the den." He winked, then left, shutting the den door behind him.

"I still can't imagine you two as the parents of a teenager."

Melanie laughed. "Thanks. We were young, but we were in love." She edged forward on her chair, grinning expectantly. "Speaking of which, what's her name?"

"Whose?"

Melanie pursed her lips then slapped Alyssa on the knee. "The long-legged wonder's! Who do you think?"

"Sue Hunter," Alyssa said.

"Is she gay?"

"I need to get to know her better. That's why I came."

"You need to borrow some clothes for a date?"

"No!" Alyssa never borrowed anyone's clothes. "Why would I do that?"

Melanie stared at her. "Because we're friends."

Alyssa blinked. "Yes, we are. So, I'm hoping you can get me some information about her."

Melanie's eyes narrowed. "Why?"

For a moment, Alyssa considered telling her everything. But Melanie was a cop, after all. So she shrugged.

"She wants private lessons for her dog. I'd just like to know a little more about her before I meet with her tomorrow."

"So ask her. Do you know how to reach her?"

"She's staying with Delia." Alyssa looked down, stroking Nestor. "I don't know. It feels funny."

"So you want me to check on her? It's that weird?"

Alyssa stood. "Yeah. Will you?"

Melanie hugged her. "Look. If you've fallen instantly in love with this woman, good. Just practice safe sex."

"Spoken like the mother of a teenager."

"And proud of it." Melanie stepped back. "But if you think there's something fishy, don't be stupid. Warn Delia. Tell Sue Hunter to find another dog trainer. You don't need it."

"No, no." Alyssa felt a warm rush of guilt. She didn't want to unjustly ruin another woman's reputation. "Really, she hasn't done anything. I'm just curious."

Melanie squinted at her.

"Besides," Alyssa said, "right now I'd take her as a client if she were a space alien. Marcus told me yesterday that I have to double my client list or I'm out of a job."

"What?" At her shriek, Nestor opened one eye and raised his head. "That jerk." Melanie bent to pet the dog. "Go back to sleep, baby."

"He says we aren't making enough to cover my salary."

"You believe him?"

"Why would he lie? He says I'm doing a good job."

"A great job! He'd never find anyone as good as you who'd want to live up here in the boonies."

Alyssa smiled. "Okay, then. So why make me miserable if it isn't true?"

Melanie crossed her arms. "Maybe he's taking advantage of you, to make more for himself."

"Look, Mel, he gave me a great opportunity right out of dog school, he pays me a living wage—"

"Barely!" Melanie said.

"Well, it's more than a lot of new trainers make. I have a nice life here. I'd like to keep my job."

"Honey," Melanie said. "I want you to stay. But not if it means you get screwed."

"It'll work out." Alyssa fingered her car keys. "So will you get the scoop on Ms. Hunter for me?"

"Okay." Melanie grabbed a pad and pen from the kitchen.

"The dog's name is Zero. She's supposedly a free-lance Web designer. That's all I know."

"Okay," said Melanie, writing. "I wish I'd gotten her plates." She chewed on her pens. "But I can always find an excuse to run into her at Delia's. And this'll give us a start. I should be able to call you sometime tomorrow."

"Thanks."

Melanie tilted her head. "You sure we shouldn't have drinks and chat some more?"

"Thanks, no." Alyssa shook her head. "I need to get rolling on this private client thing for Marcus, so I should get home and strategize."

"I suppose." Melanie sounded doubtful.

"Say hi to Jeff for me." Alyssa opened the front door. "And tell Brian it's safe to come out now. See you."

After a night of interrupted sleep, the Friday morning sunrise made everything seem brighter to Alyssa. She walked from her airy cottage to Lake Michigan's sandy beach. As she stood with the waves whispering over her feet, Alyssa felt silly for overreacting to that phone call Wednesday night. After all, the caller just implied he knew a secret. No specifics. Probably just a prankster. Everyone had something to hide, not just her.

Today she'd just let it go and get focused on her goal: more clients. She needed to get the word out. So, she spent most of the day driving to visit vets and pet stores in a three-county area, including Traverse City. She left her business card everywhere but got no firm leads on new clients. At 3:50 p.m., she pulled into the DOGS lot between Marcus's van and Sue's Subaru wagon. Sue stood latching the yard gate behind her. She looked the same as Wednesday, relaxed, short curls moving in the breeze, wide shoulders stretched underneath a T-shirt, though this one was red.

"Hi," Alyssa said. She felt a twinge of guilt that she'd asked Melanie to run a check on her.

"You said you had things to teach me." Sue stood relaxed, her weight shifted to one leg. "I'm here to find out if it's true."

"Oh, it's true, Ms. Hunter," said Alyssa as she pulled the pen from the clipboard she'd brought from her Jeep. She smiled at the dog. "Hello, Zero."

The dog opened his mouth to pant.

"Today, Ms. Hunter, I'm going to conduct an evaluation to find out what you and the dog know and how well you work together. That helps me understand how I can best help you."

"I thought you had that figured out Wednesday night. And please, call me Sue." She stood holding the dog's leash, her weight still on one foot. Her other leg jiggled inside her jeans.

19

Nervous? Impatient? Alyssa wanted to win her over so she'd commit to lessons. "Okay, Sue. I'd like to begin by watching you work your dog. Just put him through his paces. You know, heel, sit, down, stay, whatever tricks he might know."

Sue stepped up to her, put the leash into her hand and pulled the clipboard away. "Actually, since I'm paying for this, I'd like to watch *you* work Zero. I'm evaluating whether I want you as my trainer or if I'd rather work with your boss. There is another dog trainer here, right?"

"Yes. Marcus Dixon is in the office now, if you'd like to—"

"No. Don't give up like that."

Alyssa straightened, her spine stiffening. "I'm not giving up on anything."

Sue smiled. "Good. Because I didn't say I wanted him. I said I wanted to evaluate you. Does that make you nervous?"

"Of course not." This woman was something else.

"Good." Sue sat in the grass, legs crossed, clipboard beside her. "Go ahead."

Alyssa looked at the shepherd who looked up at her, his wide pink tongue lolling to the side. This was a good way to find out what the dog could do with clear guidance.

"Sit," she said, and the dog plopped his rump down immediately. "Good boy." Zero wagged his tail. "Heel." She stepped and the dog followed, his shoulder even with her hip. She led the dog through a broad figure eight pattern in the yard. "He heels beautifully. He doesn't even lag around the turns." She stopped walking and Zero stopped but stood looking up at her. She scowled and dropped her vocal pitch as she snapped on the leash. "No. Sit."

Zero sat and she grinned.

"Good boy, Zero," she said, her tone high and celebratory. The dog wagged in delight.

She heeled the dog forward again, and after a few steps, stopped. This time the dog sat immediately, and she praised him.

"Do you ever feel schizophrenic when you switch from the angry voice to the happy voice?" Sue asked.

Alyssa laughed. "It does sound goofy, doesn't it? But, hey, dogs respond to it. I bet it would work on kids too."

"Or on lovers," Sue said.

She wasn't touching that one. If she had a ten-dollar bill for every time someone thought they were funny asking if she could train their spouse, she could buy her own business.

"You'll have to learn to do it too," Alyssa said, "if you want him to respond to you as well as he does to me."

"How do you know he doesn't?" Sue asked.

Alyssa led the dog up to his master. She dropped the leash into her lap. *Time to turn the tables.* "Show me." She raised her eyebrows. "Or does that make you nervous?"

Sue blinked those warm brown eyes, then stood, stepping just a fraction too close. "Do I seem nervous?" she asked.

You seem annoying, Alyssa thought. "Would you like to approach this training in a different way, Ms. Hunter?"

"Sue." She handed the leash back to her. "And no. I want you to show me what you know. For starters, you held the leash in a funny way. Why?"

No one ever noticed that. Alyssa looked at Sue again. Her hands rested against slightly rounded hips, and her dark eyes seemed relaxed and fluid, like the rest of her, but aware. She squinted in the sun and her crow's feet angled upward. Her jaw squared off a wide face.

"That's a great question, and one of the first rules of dog training," Alyssa said. "The leash is the starting point." She stepped next to Sue and tucked the loops of leather into their proper spots on Sue's hands. "Now hold your hands together, like you're swinging a baseball bat, and keep them here." She pushed Sue's wrists up against the button of her jeans and her knuckles brushed the other woman's stomach.

21

Taut. Like a trampoline. Alyssa felt a tug low within her and backed away. *Think about the leash*.

"There. You look ready. Go ahead and heel him around. Just remember to praise him when he's good."

They worked for half an hour on Sue's heeling techniques.

"It's crucial to get this," Alyssa said. "Heeling establishes you as the leader. It sets up everything else. Next we'll work on the sit."

Sue's brows furrowed. "He can sit," she protested. "You saw him do it."

Alyssa folded her arms. Was everything going to be a battle with her? "What's his favorite toy?"

"A squeaky purple dinosaur."

Alyssa liked that Sue didn't look the least embarrassed when she said it.

"Okay, so say you're playing fetch with the squeaky purple dinosaur. You throw it and Zero takes off after it. If you called 'sit,' would he?"

Sue laughed, and she saw large white teeth behind her curved lips. "Oh, right. Like any dog would."

Alyssa had had just about enough of Sue's excuses. "A well-trained dog would. And if Zero would, then you could order him to sit whenever he bolts like he did before."

Sue scratched her head, disheveling her curls. "That sounds nice, but I don't believe it can be done."

"Then you'll fail to do it," Alyssa said. "And there's no point wasting your time or money." She snapped the pen back onto the clipboard. "Thank you for coming, Ms. Hunter."

She turned and walked toward the office. *I'll just have to find someone else tomorrow*, she thought.

"Wait a minute." Sue came after her and Alyssa stopped and turned.

"You know, Ms. Hunter," Alyssa said, "that's another order. Stop giving me orders."

Alyssa saw something in Sue's gaze shift.

22

"How did you get to be a dog trainer?" Sue asked. "Did you just decide one day or what?"

Alyssa's stomach tensed again as she struggled for polite words. "No, Ms. Hunter. There are a handful of nationally recognized dog-training schools in the country. I went to one of them for my certification."

She nodded, still studying Alyssa.

"Was there something else?" Alyssa asked.

"Yes," Sue said, holding her body still. "I'm thinking that I would like to arrange for private lessons with you. You can start Zero and me however you see fit."

Alyssa stifled the smile that threatened to spread. "Okay. Plan on bringing Zero to the puppy obedience class at least once," she said. "The one you saw the other night meets again tomorrow morning at eleven. It would be a good distraction for Zero to practice with."

"I can't," Sue said. "Going out of town."

"Right. Camping. Wednesday then?"

"Fine." Sue nodded. "I'll see you then."

As Sue walked Zero toward their car, Alyssa headed into the cottage to report on her day—and her new client—to her boss.

Chapter Three

It was almost ten p.m. before Alyssa got home. After a late lesson with a beagle mix, she'd worked another few hours preparing hand-outs and gathering tools for her demonstration Monday morning at the kids' camp. One less thing to think about this weekend. She fixed herself a chef's salad, ran a load of laundry, then hunkered into her overstuffed sofa to read the new issues of her dog-training journals.

She loved her cottage in the dunes. When she'd moved to Radley, a tiny town almost forty miles from Traverse City and just south of the Sleeping Bear Dunes, Delia and Carolyn had told her about it. The owner lived year-round in Florida now and wanted someone responsible to occupy the place. Sliding glass doors faced west, revealing magnificent sunsets. At night, the Point Betsie light a quarter of a mile away striped the sky in regular circles. No one else lived within sight.

This space had become her sanctuary. Here, for the first time in many months, Alyssa had found a place to live unafraid. She had dropped her first name, started a new career, built a new life she loved.

Just after eleven, the phone rang. Alyssa went to the kitchen and picked up the cordless receiver. She didn't touch the button to connect, but waited for her answering machine to pick up on the sixth ring. She wished she'd committed the few extra dollars a month to caller i.d.

"Alyssa? Pick up."

Alyssa pushed the talk button. "Hey, Melanie. What's up?"

"Hello to you too. And I'm fine thanks, though I ought to be in bed."

"Why aren't you?"

"Well, we had a poaching apprehension that created unbelievable amounts of paperwork. I'll be up for hours. I just got home and thought I'd call you before I dug into the rest of this."

"You know, Sue Hunter came by the office today. She's going to take private lessons."

"How private?" Mel's voice had a suggestive swing in it.

"Melanie, she's kind of a jerk."

"So what? She's gorgeous. You can put up with a little bit of jerk in a really gorgeous woman."

Alyssa shook her head even though her friend couldn't see her. "I don't know. Everything's a battle with her. She's not much fun."

"But is she gay?"

Alyssa thought about it. Sue seemed single—Alyssa hadn't noticed any rings—and Delia had invited her to stay. And there had been that moment when Sue had stood just a little too close. "I think so."

"Well, look, gay or not, if she isn't any fun, you're better off alone."

"Sure. I guess so."

"So, listen. It seems your client is thirty-four years old and has a permanent address in Detroit. She licenses the dog according to law. No driving infractions."

"Not even a speeding ticket?"

"Nope." Melanie paused. "Which isn't too odd considering that until two years ago she was a cop."

Surprise. Alyssa leaned against the counter. "No."

"Yes, for about twelve years. She joined right after college."

The woman who had shot Vinnie had worn officer's blues. Had she been a real cop? They'd never found her.

"Sue told me she did free-lance Web design," Alyssa said. "She never mentioned being a cop. I wonder why?"

Melanie laughed. "I'll bet she makes more money working on the Web. And telling people you were a cop tends to stall conversations. Bad dating technique."

"Mel, seriously."

"I am serious!"

"Why would someone quit the force mid-career?"

"Well," Melanie said, "for one thing, I'll bet she's home in bed, asleep right now, instead of getting information on people for her friends. There's injury. Family. Starting up in private security. Lots do that. Better money in it."

"Okay." Covington had always hired private security and paid them well.

"Anyhow, nothing criminal came up. I've already made a few calls to see if I can find any connections to her old department, someone who knows what happened. I'll let you know as soon as I hear anything."

"Thanks, Mel."

"No problem. Hey, she checks out okay. Now you can sleep tight, huh?"

"I'll be up a while myself if you hear anything," Alyssa said. "Good luck with your paperwork." She hung up and set the phone back in its cradle on the counter. She wished she had thought to ask Delia about Sue. How much did she know about Sue Hunter's life between the police force and coming to Radley? She had to be sure Sue didn't work for Covington.

Alyssa knew she wouldn't fall asleep now even if she went to bed. Her busy mind kept replaying snippets from the last three days. More clients. A creepy phone call. Sue.

She decided a hot bath might relax her enough to get some sleep. While the tub filled with hot lavender-scented water she checked her calendar for the next day. Class at eleven, then a private lesson at one. She should get to the office by nine to get everything all set.

She had just stepped out of her sweatpants when the phone rang. Melanie must have heard something new. Thank heavens she hadn't already gotten into the tub.

Alyssa sprinted into the kitchen to grab the cordless receiver then turned to take it with her back to the tub.

"Hello?"

The second of silence that followed snapped through her like a spitting electric line. She froze in the middle of the living room.

"I know your secret, Miss Deborah Alyssa."

Alyssa's heart scrambled, and her ear burned beneath the receiver. *The same scratchy voice.* "Who is this?"

"And I know what you've been up to tonight. Did you enjoy your reading? Your chat on the phone?"

Alyssa's head jerked up and twisted toward the glass sliders.

"No use looking for me," the voice said. "You can't see me in the dark. I've made sure of that." He paused. "Aren't you chilly? I'm chilly out here, though the view is luscious. Maybe I should come in and get warmed up."

He could see her.

Her heartbeat throbbed in her neck.

"What do you want?"

"You. Shall I call you Miss Alyssa?"

Without moving her head again, Alyssa slid her gaze toward each window, then the doors. She saw herself reflected in the black glass. "That's my name."

"If you give me what I want, I'll keep your secret." His voice sounded slow now, less scratchy.

Think. He still hadn't said anything specific. He could just be a weird prankster. "What secret?"

There was silence. Then laughter. "Bad girl, Miss Alyssa. Playing games with me." When he spoke again, his voice was pinched with rage. "Don't play games with me!"

She flinched. "This isn't a game to me."

"Good. We'd hate to have to punish you."

She waited for the demand. With Covington there had always been demands.

But none came. "I'll be seeing you again," he said, his voice relaxed. "All of you. Up close. Personal."

Her legs crawled as if covered with spiders. "What do you want from me?"

"Just behave, Miss Alyssa. We know what happens to bad little girls. Remember Vinnie." The phone clicked into silence.

Alyssa leaned against the counter that separated the kitchen from the living room. With a shaking finger, she turned the receiver off.

She stood still and waited, listening, nerves sharp for any nearby movement.

Silence.

But she knew he lurked out there somewhere, watching her. She felt as if someone had taken a bite out of her soul.

She took a deep breath. *At least I can wreck his view.* She pushed away from the counter and stood squarely on her bare feet. The house remained silent.

She went to the floor lamp near the couch and switched off the light.

Surrounded in darkness, Alyssa waited for her eyes to adjust. Covington or his men could be anywhere. Not just tonight, but tomorrow, and all the days after that.

She strained to see any movement outside. *What will I do if he shows up on the other side of that glass?*

Without thinking, she closed the blind on the nearest window. It felt good to do something.

She moved to the next window, pulled that blind, then crossed the room, and closed all the blinds. She turned to the west wall, and for the first time regretted that she did not have blinds or drapes for the sliding glass door.

She sat on the couch, the nubby fabric biting her bare legs. From here she could see both the front door and the slider. The blackness outside was punctuated by a sky filled with stars. The glass seemed such a fragile barrier between her and everything else.

The caller's probably home in bed by now.

She knew she'd never get to sleep after this. Absently, her hand drifted over the arm of the couch into a basket of odds and ends. She felt smooth leather, thick but creamy with use, and pulled it toward her.

Vinnie's leash.

Remember Vinnie.

She traced the rounded edges, smelled the Amish-cured leather, felt the weight of the brass coupler. She remembered how the dog's ear had pricked up in excitement each time she handled the leash.

Tears formed behind Alyssa's eyelids as the vision invaded her head: Vinnie's lithe, black side turned upward toward the sun, his one ear scooping the grass, his motionless legs stretched as if he were still running. A small black spot marred the patch of bronze hair where his neck met his shoulder, and crimson blood seeped into the grass below.

She'd saved him once from the labs at Covington Enterprises. She'd saved him again from the pound when no owner could be found. But in the end, she could only kneel helplessly by.

In Chicago, the caller had warned her to drop her testimony against Covington or else. But the prosecutors had promised protection and she'd exposed her employer, Covington Enterprises, and her mentor, Rodney Covington, for using stolen pets as lab animals. That had turned out to be the tip of the iceberg of unethical and illegal practices at the research and development facility. Covington had hired her to improve public relations, but in the end, she ruined his company.

When his corporation shattered, Covington cut a deal that allowed him to keep most of his personal fortune and serve minimal time in prison. She thought it would all end when he began his two-year sentence. But then some woman dressed as a cop had shot her dog. Another phone call promised Covington hadn't forgotten her. They'd never identified the cop or the caller, never been able to do anything to stop them. So she ran, dropping her first name, starting a new career, hoping to escape any connection with the case. Just a month ago she'd found out he'd been released early because of end stage cancer. She'd tried to convince herself he'd be too sick to think about her. But now she knew he was after her again.

Alyssa shuddered, the skin on her legs cold. She couldn't call the police. After all, so far she'd just had a couple of harassing phone calls. If she told them more, her arrest for stealing the animals would come out, though the charges against her had been dropped. Even the slightest connection to a robbery could hurt her as a guard dog trainer. She had access to too much private information. It definitely wouldn't help her get new clients.

She wished Vinnie were here right now. His sensitive nose and ears would sense someone approaching long before hers would. Looping the leash around her hand twice, Alyssa forced herself to relax and settle in for the six-hour wait until sunrise.

The next hour passed slowly for Alyssa in the darkness. The green numbers on her microwave marked each taut minute. Waves rolled onto the beach and the Point Betsie light rotated in regular rhythm.

She told herself the watcher must have gone away. She hated sitting, doing nothing, waiting like a sitting duck. So she got up, pulled her sweatpants back on and, with a wistful look toward her bedroom, went back to sit on the couch.

Another half-hour passed. Shortly after one o'clock she heard a car approaching.

She sat up, her arms and legs tense, the leash stretched between her hands. The car pulled up to her cottage, the brightness from its headlights sweeping the floor in her entry. When the car's engine switched off, so did the lights.

She heard a footstep on her wooden porch.

Alyssa stood, then froze, listening. Yes, outside, another step, but this one very quiet.

Trying not to be heard?

Someone had come after all, just like in Chicago.

Alyssa felt sick and energized at the same time. He would come through that door at any minute. The doorknob lock wouldn't keep out anyone determined to get in. She didn't have time to run into the bedroom and look out the window. Besides, no one she knew would come out this late without calling first.

She scanned the two-room cottage. No place to hide, even in the dark.

I have to fight. She snapped the leash in her hands as her thoughts whipped around. *How can I surprise him?*

She thought she saw a shadow on the side of the house, caught quickly in the Point Betsie's turning light.

He was circling the house.

Okay, Alyssa thought. *I need him in here, on my territory. I'll have the advantage*. She'd simply lure him in.

Alyssa stuffed the leash into her pocket and picked up the coffee table, silently placing it in the middle of the entryway, a few feet in front of the main door.

Then, with a silent prayer, she gently opened the door. He must be on the other side of the house. Good. She knew she had a clay pot of geraniums nearby. Alyssa stuck her foot out. If she could just reach it.

With a thunk, the pot tipped over and rolled off the porch. Just enough noise to make someone think she'd run for it. Leaving the front door slightly ajar, Alyssa backed into the hall closet, leaving the door open just a crack to peek through.

She barely had time to untangle the leash from her pocket when the front door swung open and someone came inside her home.

31

Chapter Four

The intruder stood quietly inside the door and Alyssa willed herself to breathe and keep her knees bent.

It's just like controlling a violent dog. Balance and timing. Wait.

His slow footsteps sounded heavy and sand scratched under his shoes. His breath told her he stood just in front of the closet.

Take just another few steps, she willed.

He took one and the dark hulk of his shoulder passed in front of the crack. He was taller than Alyssa, stronger.

For a moment, her courage wilted. *This is no dog. It's a man. He may have a gun. Just stay here and keep quiet. Maybe he'll go away.*

He stepped again. Then paused.

Alyssa held her breath.

She knew he would not just go away.

He took two more steps, then Alyssa heard his shin thud against the edge of the coffee table.

Now!

Her brain registered his sharp intake of breath and his bent posture as she leapt out of the closet with the leash before her. In mid-stride she adjusted her body, then landed on top of him, looping the leash around his neck. Behind her the closet door crashed into the open front door and something snapped.

He dropped down, his hands on the floor and his head on the coffee table. Alyssa heard a clatter as something metal hit the floor.

Her body on autopilot, Alyssa wrapped her legs around his narrow waist, then folded the slack of the leash over itself and twisted. She hoped he would black out from lack of air, and she had to keep out of his reach until then. He was thin but had long legs and arms. She hoped she could hold on.

Supporting himself with his head against the table, he reached up, struggling to loosen the leather from his neck. Then he threw his arm back, trying to reach her feet, but she kicked it out of the way. With all her strength she twisted the leash even tighter.

Alyssa held on as he reached again for the leather around his neck. Then she felt the muscles in his back weakening under her thighs.

He kept struggling, groping again toward her right leg. She slung it out of his way, then heard his hand fumbling on the floor. Too late she realized he might have a knife, but she couldn't see well enough in the dark.

Suddenly, a small light clicked on, pointing toward his crimson face squashed against her coffee table.

Sue Hunter.

Alyssa dropped the leash and fell backwards off her, a slice of wood biting into the palm of her right hand.

Sue gasped for air, then snapped the light off. "Thanks." Her voice was little more than a croak.

"For what?"

"Letting me go."

They sat in silence for a few seconds, before Sue lit her tiny flashlight again and pointed it at Alyssa. "You wanted to kill me."

Alyssa held up her hand, blocking the sharp light. "Not you personally. Turn that thing off, though, or it'll get personal."

Sue clicked the flashlight off and Alyssa stood and snapped on the hall light.

Sue rubbed her head in her hands, unwrapped the leash from her neck and looked up at Alyssa. "You've got a hell of a trap set up here. Who were you expecting?"

"The jerk creeping around on my front porch!" Alyssa grabbed the table and carried it into the great room, ignoring the pain in her hand. As she set the table down, she noticed a bloody palm print. She looked at her hand. A slice of her closet doorframe appeared dark in the ragged flesh beneath her thumb. She'd deal with that in a minute. "What the hell were you doing out there anyway?"

"Delia sent me because she couldn't get through on the phone," Sue said. "Her house was robbed tonight."

Alyssa couldn't believe her ears. "Oh no! Delia? Teddy?"

"Both fine." Sue shook her head as if trying to clear it. "In fact, Teddy was still on guard when Delia came home, so she didn't notice anything wrong at first. But then she discovered some jewelry missing. She called the police then tried you. Couldn't get through, so she sent me."

"I trained Teddy." What had they done to him? He was topnotch.

"That's why Delia wants you there with her during the police interview."

Alyssa's throat tightened. *Police.* She didn't want to talk to the police. But the thought of her friend, alone and scared, set her in motion. "Of course. I need to change. Do you want to go ahead?"

"No way. She sent me to get you and I'm not going back without you."

Sue stood slowly then stumbled. Her shoulder caught the wall and she stared at Alyssa.

"Oh, for God's sake, sit down while I change," Alyssa said, gesturing toward the couch. "You look like you're going to pass out."

❧

Sue swallowed several times. "First, you'd better—" Still leaning against the wall, she drew several deep breaths and the lightheaded feeling began to fade. "You'd better get that hand cleaned up."

Alyssa looked at the blood dripping down her fingers, and without a word went into the bathroom to run water over her hand.

Sue followed. *This woman clearly has issues.* She'd never had anyone take her down so completely, not even on the force. Sue had been curious before, but now she really wanted to know what Alyssa's issues were.

"You need an ambulance?" Alyssa asked as Sue entered the bathroom.

"You're not that good." But in fact she was. Alyssa could have killed her. Where had she learned that move?

"You look like I'm that good." Alyssa turned her hand under the running water. "You've got pieces of my closet door in your hair and one hell of a set of welts around your neck."

Sue felt the burning flesh near her throat where the leash's brass coupler had bit in. "I can't pass them off as hickeys?"

"No way." Alyssa picked at her palm. "Crap. I can't get this piece of wood out."

Sue moved beside her and reached toward her hand. "Do you want me to—"

"No! Don't come near me." Alyssa drew back. "You walked into my place without knocking or saying who you were. I should call the police."

Sue blinked against another wave of lightheadedness. She hated to see such fear in another woman's eyes. Alyssa must be into something really ugly. "Look. When I pulled up, I saw your phone line had been cut."

"What?" Alyssa turned off the faucet. "Cut?"

"That's why I thought I'd check around. Then I heard a noise on the porch, saw the pot knocked over and the door standing open." She wouldn't mention the note. Not yet. "I thought maybe you were being burglarized. So I came in. To help you."

Alyssa studied her a moment. "Let me by and don't move." She left the bathroom and returned seconds later with the cordless receiver in her hand. "There's no dial tone."

"I have a cell phone if you want to call the police."

Alyssa paused. "No. I have to get to Delia and Teddy."

Alyssa watched as the blood again welled from the gash in her hand. It wouldn't stop bleeding until she got that wood out. She opened a vanity drawer and pulled out tweezers. Her left hand fumbled.

She looked at Sue. "I'm only trusting you now because Delia does." She held out the tweezers. "Would you? I can't with my left hand."

Sue took the tweezers and drew Alyssa's hand into the light. "Don't blame me if I hurt you," she said. "You drove this in deep."

"Do you ever accept responsibility for anything? Like breaking into people's homes?"

Sue looked up, tweezers poised just above Alyssa's open flesh. "Don't ever aggravate a woman who has a sharp metal edge this close to your skin." She poked at the edge of the wood. "Piss me off later if you want, but not now."

"Right."

Sue pulled the first slice of wood out. "So, you want to tell me what's going on?"

Alyssa jerked her hand away. "What do you mean?"

Sue looked at her steadily. "I mean, your phone line is cut and you hid in a closet and attacked me when I came in."

"You came in without saying anything!"

"You were hidden before that, remember?" She slowly reached out and took Alyssa's hand.

Alyssa didn't draw back. "The car came. And no one knocked. It's the middle of the night. Anyone would protect themselves."

Sue nodded. "Okay."

She allowed Sue to tug her hand back into the light and pull out the rest of the wood, then bandage the gash.

"That should hold as long as you don't use it much," Sue said. "No yanking on dog leashes for a while."

"I never yank," Alyssa said, heading for her bedroom. She didn't want to think about the phone line. First, she had to find out what happened to Teddy. He'd never let someone past his guard without a fight. She took less than two minutes to slide into jeans and an oversized gray sweatshirt and to scoop on her socks and running shoes.

She walked back into the entry where Sue waited. "I called the house," Sue said. "Let them know we got delayed but we're on our way."

"Good. Let's—" The sight of the mess in her doorway made Alyssa stop.

Sue stood behind her. "You kicked some ass here."

Alyssa couldn't believe it. She'd swung the closet door open so hard it had smashed into the open front door, cracking both in several places.

"I can't lock the house now."

"Nope," Sue said.

Alyssa felt the fine hairs on her neck tingle. Did she dare leave the house open wide with that caller lurking around somewhere? Had he cut her phone line, trying to isolate her? What would have happened if Sue hadn't come just then?

"I can fix it for you first thing tomorrow," Sue said.

"What if—" Alyssa paused. "What if an *animal* gets in while we're gone?" An animal who made phone calls.

"I'll bring you home and check the place out, okay?" Sue placed a wide, warm palm between Alyssa's shoulder blades and pushed gently. "Now let's go, or Delia will send a search party for both of us."

With all this commotion, the caller's probably long gone. Alyssa drew a resolved breath. "Okay. I need to see Teddy and figure out what happened." With Sue close behind her, Alyssa stepped into the night.

Since the moment Alyssa burst out of that closet and nearly killed her, Sue had felt hyperaware. At first she figured it for oxygen deprivation. Now she recognized it as lust.

"Slow down," Alyssa said from the passenger's seat.

"No." Sue wrestled the steering wheel to the left for the next curve on the shoulderless road through forested dunes. She wished she could slow down her desire.

"Be careful!"

The right front tire bumped off the lip of the road, scattering a mix of gravel and sand before Sue regained the lane.

"I can handle it," Sue said.

"Can you?"

"You know," Sue said, steering back to the right, "I can handle a lot more than you seem to think." That's why this lust thing bothered her so much. Got in the way of clear thinking.

"Right. Let me remind you of our first meeting." Alyssa held up her fingers as if counting. "Uncontrollable dog. Not leashed. Around puppies. Knocking down elderly ladies."

"You are not elderly," Sue said.

"I meant Delia." Alyssa wriggled her fingers.

Long, strong fingers, Sue noted. From handling big dogs. Her arms too. Short, but muscled.

"Plenty of reasons for my opinion of you," Alyssa continued, "and there's more. I'll start with no visible means of support."

That caught Sue off guard. "I'm a Web designer."

"Yeah, I heard what you told Delia. Free-lance. Name a client."

"Why?"

"You aren't going to stiff Delia for the rent, are you?"

"No!" She followed another curve to the left. Somehow she had let Alyssa turn this around.

"The drive's just ahead on the left." Alyssa pointed.

"I know. I live there, remember?" Still, Sue could barely see the dirt drive among the trees. The car bounced over the ruts. *We live out in the boonies*, Delia had told her. *No distractions while you figure things out, my dear.*

She'd been here a week and had been plenty distracted.

Sue glanced sideways at her passenger, who rubbed her injured hand. *Tough lady.* Keeps a lot of secrets. Was she afraid of getting hurt? Or of getting caught?

Sue reached down and touched her jeans pocket. The note was still there. She wanted to tell Alyssa about what she had found, but not until there were no distractions.

They emerged from the trees and ahead lay Delia's enormous log cabin, built to look old and weathered. The understated lighting glowed amidst the landscaping, but bright lights from inside the house pierced the darkness. Sue drove past a detached garage with four stalls and the second-floor apartment where she lived. She pulled up behind a green Department of Natural Resources vehicle parked next to a county sheriff's car.

"Why would the DNR be here?" Sue asked.

"They're state peace officers," Alyssa explained. "Melanie must have been the nearest cop on call." They climbed from the car and headed up the walkway. A small area of the front yard had crime scene tape around it. "In a town this tiny, without local police, the nearest county deputy can be a half-hour away. So DNR cops help out."

Sue hadn't realized DNR officers had such broad duties. That intrigued her.

Alyssa stepped in front of the glass storm door and knocked so hard that her auburn hair bounced against the neck of her sweatshirt.

Sue rubbed her neck. She still couldn't believe Alyssa had gotten the jump on her. Alyssa's jeans wrapped around all her curves, and she wasn't big, though she was nicely shaped.

She shook her head. *Stop it.*

"I don't hear the dogs," Alyssa said, bouncing on the balls of her feet.

A female DNR officer appeared in the hallway and opened the door. Sue recognized her from class the other night.

"Hey, Alyssa. Delia's been asking—" she began.

Alyssa walked by her. "Mel, where are they?"

"In the camp room," the cop called after her as Alyssa disappeared around a corner. She turned back to Sue. "I don't believe we've met."

Sue extended her hand, reading her nameplate quickly. "I'm Sue Hunter, Officer Sybesma."

"Ah." She smiled. "The renter. With the German shepherd."

"Yes." Sue nodded. "You were in puppy class the other night, with a big brown pup."

"Right. I'm Melanie." She stepped back so Sue could enter the house.

Just talking to another cop made Sue feel more relaxed and on the ball. "So, you've worked with Alyssa for a while?"

"For a few weeks with Nestor. And I helped train the guard dogs. Why?"

"I'm doing private training with Zero. She seems a little nervous to me. Just wondered what you thought."

"She's great." Melanie studied the welts on Sue's neck. "Something happen to your throat?"

"Allergic reaction to some laundry detergent." She rubbed them. "Should've been gone by now." She shrugged. "Show me in?"

Melanie nodded, and together they headed into the house.

Chapter Five

The "camp room"—a family room decorated with rustic furniture—faced west, overlooking Lake Michigan. Alyssa noticed the water was a deep black beyond the glaring glass. In front of the window, Delia perched on the edge of the leather sofa. The tallest man she had ever seen, dressed in a sheriff's uniform, paced in front of her. Teddy the Rottweiler lay at Delia's feet, moping.

"Oh, darling, it's just awful!" Delia leapt up, crossed the room in two light steps and flung her arms around Alyssa. Delia sniffled, then lifted her head from Alyssa's shoulders. "Thanks, Sue, for bringing her."

"No problem." Sue spoke from behind her.

"Who are these people, Officer Sybesma?" The deputy's voice boomed in the big room.

Delia spun and answered. "These are my friends. Alyssa Norland trained Teddy with my housemate, Carolyn. She can answer your questions, I'm sure." Delia reached out to Sue, pulling her forward. "This is Susan Hunter, an old friend. She's renting my apartment for the summer."

An old friend? Alyssa would have to ask Delia more about that later.

While he took their addresses and phone numbers, Delia turned back to Alyssa. "Deputy Strunk called Marcus when I couldn't find you. He wants to talk to a trainer tonight. What happened?"

Alyssa hesitated. She hadn't prepared to face Marcus in all of this.

"Her line's out," Sue offered, glancing her way.

Alyssa nodded.

"Probably an animal," Delia said with a tsk-tsk. "You can't stay out there without a phone."

"I'll loan her my cell until her line is fixed," Sue said. "No problem."

What a great conspirator she'd make, Alyssa thought.

"You have to look at Teddy, dear." Delia's eyes glinted as she tugged Alyssa onto the couch. "Something has to be wrong."

"I'll check him out. It'll be okay." Alyssa hoped she sounded more reassuring than she felt.

"If only the dog could talk, Miss Norland," the deputy said. "I'd have a lot fewer questions to ask you."

"Before we begin, Deputy," Sue said from her spot near the entry, "could you introduce yourself?"

Alyssa watched the big man stiffen. Score one for Sue.

"I'm the county sheriff's deputy in charge of this investigation."

Alyssa knew a bully when she met one—canine or human. She hated them.

Sue arched an eyebrow. "Well, someone with duties that impressive must want us to know his name."

The deputy laughed. "C.J. Strunk, Ms. Hunter." He raised his hand to scratch his high forehead, shadowed by jet black hair. "So, Ms. Norland. I'd like to know what you think happened with this dog tonight."

"I don't know enough to even guess." Alyssa turned to Delia.

"I came home," Delia began, "and Teddy was on guard. I released him right away and thought maybe he'd had an accident or something, because he looked a little guilty, you know, with his head hanging. But the house looked okay. Tango barked his head off, but he always does when we get home."

"Where's Tango now?"

"In his crate. Less bothersome. Anyway, then I headed for bed—"

"And discovered several items of antique jewelry missing," said Strunk.

"Right out of my dresser." Delia's voice rose to a squeak. "Can you imagine?"

"Someone got past the dog," said Strunk. "I'd like to know how you think that happened."

"Let's see Teddy first." Alyssa knelt and rubbed his soft, square nose. "Hey, boy. What happened?" He blinked at her, his ears flat against his skull. "He's stressed."

"And you know this because—?" She felt Strunk's gaze follow her movements closely.

"Because of the position of his ears and tail. How his jaw is set," Alyssa said. "Stressed and confused, I'd say." She rubbed the dog's body. "I don't feel any bumps from an injection or anything. When will you have the vet report?"

Her question caught Strunk off guard. He stepped closer to her, his huge frame towering over her. "What do you mean?"

"She means, has the dog been compromised?" Sue explained. "Injured? Drugged in any way?"

Alyssa appreciated having an ally in the room. But Strunk did not.

"Officer Sybesma! Everyone in the county is standing in this room right now except a vet. Why haven't you gotten one here?"

"I'll call for one right away, sir," she said, her face blank. She turned and left.

How does Melanie stand that? Alyssa wondered.

"Now that we're checking on the dog," Strunk said with a weak smile to Sue, "let's consider what else might have been compromised." He turned toward Alyssa. "A fine choice of words by Ms. Hunter, don't you think?"

Before Alyssa could answer, another man's voice called from the entryway. "Delia? Anyone home?"

Marcus swung into the room, leading with his belly, brushing past Sue. "Delia," he said. "Are you all right?"

"We're fine," she said. "Where's Hendrix?"

"I left him at home." Marcus dropped to his knees next to Alyssa and Teddy. "Teddy, good dog," he crooned, stroking the dog's flattened ears. "I'm so glad to see you. Here, boy, have a cookie." He looked up and nodded to the deputy. "I'm Marcus Dixon, owner of DOGS. My firm trained this guard dog and I take full responsibility for his failure here tonight."

"Hold on, Marcus," Alyssa said. "We don't know that Teddy failed to guard. We don't know what happened."

"Now, Alyssa," Marcus said, voice smooth, "we'll discuss it later."

She wanted to discuss it now. But she also knew better than to further confront her boss in public.

"I agree, Mr. Dixon," said Sue.

She would take Marcus's side, Alyssa thought.

"With Alyssa," Sue continued. "She makes an excellent point. We don't know that the dog failed in his training."

Marcus rose slowly. "Have we met?"

"I'm Sue Hunter. A new client. Just signed on for some extensive—and expensive—private training with Alyssa."

"Alyssa's training Zero," Delia said, her hands fluttering. "She's the best dog trainer there is."

An uncomfortable silence fell over the room and Alyssa felt her chest grow hot. She couldn't imagine how thieves had gotten past Teddy. Could her training have failed? He seemed rock solid when she trained him.

"I have great confidence in her abilities as a trainer," said Sue.

"I've seen her do amazing things." She shifted her gaze from Marcus to Alyssa.

"Her abilities. Yes," the deputy boomed. "That is why I am particularly interested in what she thinks happened here tonight."

"I need some more information, first," Alyssa told Strunk, then turned to Delia. "You're sure Teddy was on guard when you left tonight?"

"Oh yes, dear, absolutely. I put him on guard when I went to the Twelve Point." She looked at Strunk. "Usually Carolyn handles Teddy. She's the one who insisted on a guard dog. She's in Europe for the month." She waved the details away and shrugged. "Anyway, Carolyn made me promise I wouldn't leave the house for anything without putting Teddy on guard." Delia shrugged again. "So I did."

"For all the good it did."

Melanie entered the room. "The vet will be here in about thirty minutes."

Strunk nodded.

"I'm going to go out and make a cast of that footprint," Melanie said.

Strunk nodded again and Melanie left. The deputy looked at Teddy, who lay with his head on his forelegs. "Ms. Watkins didn't lock her front door. Trusted the dog. He doesn't look like much of a guard dog."

"Well, I never lock the doors with Teddy here on guard. That's the point, isn't it?" Delia laughed and shifted her voice to baby talk. "You protect Mommy's stuff, don't you Teddy-bear?"

The dog's stump wagged.

Strunk cocked his head. "When the dog's on guard? Sometimes he isn't?"

"That's right," Delia said.

"Because—" Alyssa began.

"Training," Marcus interrupted. "The best area guard dogs aren't vicious at all, but obedient, even-tempered animals. You teach them a command to guard a certain area just like you teach them to heel or lie down."

Sue had begun to bounce on the balls of her feet. *Why is she so antsy?* Alyssa wondered.

"A dog who knows how to heel on command," Marcus continued, "doesn't do it all the time. Likewise, a well-trained guard dog isn't guarding all the time. He waits for the command."

"So, if you gave him the command now, he'd attack me?" Strunk's attitude toward the dog was distinctly less skeptical now.

"Of course not," Alyssa said. "He'd just go after anyone who tried to enter the building. He's not an attack dog. Delia can't send him out for a bite."

Alyssa saw Melanie go past the room, bucket in hand, then heard water rushing into the bucket from the kitchen sink.

"Hell of a thing if you have guests," Strunk said.

"Oh, he loves company!" Delia bent and stroked the dog's head. "Come on, boy. Perk up."

"But I thought she said he'd attack," said Strunk.

"Only if he had his working collar on and the proper command," Marcus said. "If his collar's off, or if he hears his release word, he's just a pet."

"Works like a charm. Collar on, command, he's on guard. Release command, collar off, he's just a dear playmate for Tango." Delia appeared unconcerned that this evening it hadn't worked.

"Well, he wasn't so charmed tonight," Strunk said. "Or we wouldn't all be here. Someone got past him."

"People don't just walk past a guard dog," said Alyssa. "That's why I was so glad to see Teddy here. Usually thieves slit their throats."

"Oh!" Delia clasped her hands to her neck and sucked in her breath. Alyssa placed her hand on her friend's knee.

"Killing them is the only way," Marcus said, "assuming they've been properly trained."

Alyssa felt her face flush. "Teddy was properly trained," she said through clenched teeth.

"I'll vouch for that." Melanie paused near the doorway with her bucket. "I acted the role of criminal during his final training exercises." Her eyes widened. "Scariest thing I've ever done in my life. To see a hundred-pound dog like that flying at you full tilt, mouth wide open and full of teeth." She shuddered, then smiled. "It was impressive."

"Yet you have all your limbs," Strunk said.

"She wore a protective sleeve," Alyssa said. "Hard plastic, covered with fabric. The dog attacks that."

"The hit knocks you back," Melanie said. "Like shooting a semi-automatic for the first time. Wow."

"So you don't doubt the dog's training?" Sue asked Melanie.

"Not from what I saw. He bit me with all his pearly whites and he's known me since he was a pup."

"So that issue seems cleared up, doesn't it?" Sue said to Strunk.

Alyssa felt mild surprise at Sue's support.

"For now," Strunk agreed. "Still, someone got in and took—how much do you guess, Ms. Watkins?"

"Forty thousand dollars' worth of jewelry."

Marcus whistled.

"You keep that much in the house?" Sue asked.

"Well, dear, I have a guard dog." The explanation seemed to make perfect sense to Delia.

"So someone got in, took forty thousand dollars in jewelry. And didn't bleed on the carpet from a dog bite, or even ransack the house, for that matter." Strunk rubbed his forehead again. "So, what do you make of all this, Ms. Norland?"

"It's terrible," she began. Her chest felt tight. Why was he asking her?

"Surely some other people know how to—uh—turn this dog off?" Strunk asked.

"Out of the question." Marcus stepped forward, his stomach almost touching the deputy's hip. "My business would carry enormous liability if that were the case. It's ridiculous."

Strunk looked at Alyssa for what seemed a very long time. He turned toward Marcus. "Tell me about avoiding liability."

Alyssa jumped in. "Ethically, most information remains confidential in dog training." She swallowed. Her heart pounded so hard she could hear it inside her head. "Of course, I know Teddy's release word because I helped Delia and Carolyn train the dog."

Strunk smiled at her like a cat ready to pounce.

"But I could never use it." Alyssa barreled ahead before he could interrupt. "Because the dog is trained to accept the release command from the person who put the collar on and gave the guard command."

"We could demonstrate if you'd like," Delia said, her voice as energetic as ever. "You could be the criminal."

From the corner of her eye, Alyssa saw Sue bite her lip to keep from grinning.

"No, thank you," said Strunk, staring steadily at Teddy. "Ms. Norland, I'm interested in this confidential information you spoke of." He shifted his gaze back to her. "Where is it kept? In a file?"

"No!" Marcus stepped forward again but Strunk's glare silenced him.

"It wouldn't be too confidential in that case, would it?" Alyssa said.

"It should be if you had a guard dog to protect it," said Strunk.

Jerk, Alyssa thought.

"Where is it kept?" Strunk demanded.

Alyssa pointed to her head. "Here." She stretched her neck from side to side.

"That's a lot of trust people put in you," Strunk said.

"A guard dog trainer must have a spotless reputation," said Marcus. "Absolutely above reproach or they'd never succeed."

Alyssa remembered the caller's threats. The room seemed hotter and smaller and her nerves sprang to alert. How could all of this be happening at once? "Of course," she said, "the clients know the information too. And anyone the client tells would know."

All eyes shifted to Delia.

48

"No one except me and Carolyn," she said.

Strunk made a few notes in a small pad. "So who knew where you kept the jewelry?"

Delia considered, her lips pursed. "Carolyn, of course. Maybe some of the girls, you know, gabbing about putting on the finishing touches before a night out. And, Teddy knew, of course."

"The dog knew?" Strunk looked like this was all getting to be too much for him. "How could the dog know?"

"Because that corner of the bedroom was one of his focus areas," Delia said.

Strunk lowered his pad and pen. "What the hell is she talking about?"

"A focus area—" Alyssa began, but Marcus cut her off.

"Area guard dogs usually work in pairs," he said, "one covering the front of a house, one the rear. But since Delia and Carolyn have one dog, the standard procedure dictates training the dog to cover places in the house where valuables are kept. The dog will guard the focus area nearest the intruder." He looked around the room. "There could be a focus area in here. I wouldn't know. I didn't train the dog."

"But Ms. Norland did, didn't she?" Strunk's voice grew so loud it seemed to echo off the room's picture windows.

I knew, thought Alyssa. Her stomach began to burn. She didn't want to wind up in jail again. She'd spent one night there and it was enough. She knew what it had felt like for the dogs in Covington's lab. Cages too small for animals or humans.

"Forty thousand dollars would supplement your income nicely, wouldn't it?" Strunk nodded to her bandaged hand. "And I can't help but notice you have a fresh injury there. Would you be willing to have a doctor examine it to verify it isn't a dog bite?"

Her throat so dry she could barely speak, Alyssa nodded. "My doctor's name is Thomas Connick. I'll see him as soon as possible. I had nothing to do with this."

"You'll forgive me, Miss Norland," Strunk said, "but I've heard that sort of thing before." He swallowed, then grinned with a fake compassion that failed to cover his suspicion.

Chapter Six

Twenty minutes later, Alyssa left the house. Though Melanie walked beside her, she still felt completely alone. She could hear Delia, Marcus and Strunk still talking inside, but panic buzzed in her ears.

"He suspects me!" she said. "He'll ruin me. No one wants a dog trainer accused of theft."

"Nonsense, Alyssa. Strunk's fishing. It's a big case and he'd love to pin it on someone the first night. We'll be talking to the cleaners and the lawn service people too. Relax."

"Delia doesn't have housecleaners. And I knew everything. The jewels. My fingerprints will be all over the house and Teddy's collar. And I was home alone. No alibi."

Melanie nudged her side. "Hey. The guy's an intimidator. He's got nothing. The footprint I took tonight was a man's."

Alyssa grabbed her friend's forearm. "Melanie, I cannot go to jail." Tears jumped to her eyes.

"Whoa, Alyssa. Slow down. You're way ahead of yourself there, girlfriend." She hugged Alyssa. "It's gonna be okay. We'll deal with it tomorrow. It'll look better in the daylight."

Alyssa shook her head to stop the tears. "Is that what you tell Jeff?"

"Yeah, when he was four years old." Melanie hugged her again. "But you look about as tough as he did when he'd wake up from nightmares."

That's what this is, Alyssa thought. *A nightmare.*

"Go home and relax. Take a shot of whiskey or something, snuggle up in your bed and get some sleep."

Alyssa thought of her broken door and wanted to weep. Her shoulders felt as if they'd slip from her body.

"Seriously, Lyss, get some sleep, okay?"

Melanie looked concerned, so Alyssa smiled more brightly. "Yeah. I'll sleep."

"Good." She looked at the cars parked near the house. "You need a ride home?"

"No." Sue came up behind them, gently touching Alyssa's arm. "I'll get her home."

Melanie looked at Alyssa, the question subtle but there.

"It's okay," said Alyssa.

"Come on," Sue said.

"I'll talk to you later," Melanie said, then went back into the house.

Alyssa started down the walk with Sue, whose hand felt warm and gentle.

As Alyssa sat in Sue's wagon, she realized again how tired she was. Her ribs felt wobbly and disconnected from her spine. "Home, Jane."

A soft lick on her left ear made her sit forward.

"Zero's coming too," Sue said. "In case there are animals."

"Hey, boy." Alyssa rubbed the dog's soft nose and settled back into the seat. Maybe she would get some sleep after all.

Sue drove, intrigued by Alyssa's unbroken silence. She'd proclaimed her innocence to Strunk but hadn't said anything to her, so she just let her stew. Sometimes that was best.

As Sue turned into the driveway Alyssa finally spoke. "It's four-thirty in the morning." She sounded as if the life had drained from her. "I have to teach a class at eleven."

Sue pulled her car up behind Alyssa's. The outline of the front doorjamb stood out stark and white against the deep shadows of the splintered door.

Alyssa was holding her head in her hands. "How can so much have happened in such a short time? My life turned over in just four hours." She started to giggle, then looked up. "It's crazy."

Zero shuffled forward in the deck of the wagon to check on her.

"Look at my door," she half sobbed. "I don't know if it will ever be okay again."

Sue had seen people react this way before, after a crime or an accident. They'd hold it together for so long, then a piece would drop out. Soon the rest would fall. Most of them picked it all back up and moved forward. "It's just a door. It can be replaced. Things'll work out."

"I notice you didn't say 'work out for the best.'" Her eyes were heavy-lidded and bright, her lips full from sobbing.

She's beautiful. The realization surprised Sue.

Alyssa wiped a tear from her cheek. "Hey, thanks for sticking up for my training ability tonight."

"Did I?"

A tear trace glistened near the outside edge of one of her eyes, and Sue felt a sudden urge to wipe it away. She held herself still, however.

"I wasn't sure why you did it, though," Alyssa said. "I mean, you haven't worked with me much."

"I've seen enough to know you can train a dog to do anything you want."

"Thanks, I—" She paused. The fullness of her lips disappeared as she tightened her jaw. *"Anything I want?"*

She'd figured it out. *Good.* "We might as well talk about it," Sue said.

"You think I did this!" Alyssa twisted in the seat and leaned as far away from Sue as she could. "You weren't protecting me. You were setting me up! You—oh!" She got out and slammed the door behind her so hard the car rocked.

Sue got out of the car and let Zero out as well. She grabbed her small duffel and joined Alyssa where she stood on her front porch, staring at the broken door.

"Get back in your damn car," Alyssa said quietly, "and get away from my home. I don't want you here."

"I'm supposed to check for animals, remember?"

"Get out."

Sue dropped the duffel. She could hear Zero sniffing in the dune grass near the corner of the house and waves in the distance. Otherwise, silence. "Nope."

"I don't need your kind of protection. 'Her training's impeccable.' You finessing jerk! Have you already told Strunk you think I trained Teddy to let me into the house?"

"Hey, at least I believe in your talents. It's more than you can say for your boss."

"Screw you," she said, her face alive even in the darkness. "Marcus has to protect his business. What are you trying to protect?" She slapped her head in mock stupidity. "Oh, right. Some weird cop honor, I suppose. Helping old Strunk out, right?" She turned away, but did not step through the doorway. "Quite a team."

So, Sue thought, *she knows I was a cop and she doesn't like it.*

"Look," Sue said. "I'm not a cop anymore. And frankly, you're above slandering law enforcement in general because of your friend Melanie."

Sue saw Alyssa's shoulders fall as she exhaled.

"And," Sue continued, "I do have something to protect, something very important to me. Delia."

Alyssa turned back toward Sue. "I could never do anything like this to someone I loved." Her voice came low and slow.

"Good," Sue said, "because she adores you. But I'll tell you what. I think you are connected to this burglary somehow." She bent to pick up her duffel. "So I'm staying. Call the police if you want. I'll loan you my cell."

"Are you protecting me or protecting Delia from me?"

"It doesn't matter. I'm staying."

"I don't get it. Why don't you go home to protect Delia?"

Even in the darkness, Sue could sense Alyssa's fright. Her hand drifted to her pocket. She hadn't told Alyssa yet about the note she'd found.

"Are you going to plant evidence in my house?" Alyssa's voice was cold with fear and Sue felt sorry for her.

"Look, can we just go in? I should get you into bed." Sue put her hand near Alyssa's elbow, but Alyssa drew back, her eyebrows arched.

"You think I'm a thief and you still want to get me into bed?"

Sue chuckled. "Nice. Even terrified, you still have a sense of humor."

"It keeps me sane."

"I just meant you must be exhausted."

Alyssa nodded absently as she reached out and ran long fingers down the crack in the door. "It seems like this happened days ago."

"Not to my neck."

She drew her hand back. "Sorry. I don't like to hurt people. Even if they break into my house."

"I didn't break in, but it's okay. Worth it, actually, to see those moves." Sue's body pulsed with the memory of Alyssa wrapped around her. *Not now.* "Zero, come."

The dog trotted up and leaned against Sue's knee.

"Tell him he's good," Alyssa said.

Sue watched Alyssa go inside and snap on the light. The shadows curved around her hips, swallowing the shape of her lower legs. Sue remembered the power she'd felt in them when Alyssa had jumped her.

"You coming?"

The strained pitch in Alyssa's voice drew Sue's attention. *She's afraid of something here and she doesn't even know about the note yet.* Sue looked at Zero. "Better look around out here, huh, boy?" To Alyssa she said, "I'm gonna check out a few things here first. You got a bigger flashlight? The one I used earlier is pretty small."

Alyssa dug a yellow lantern out of the entryway closet and handed it to Sue. It cast a broad beam into the dark. "Why do you want to check out there?" She narrowed her eyes, clearly tense.

"Habit. See if anything else has been disturbed besides your phone line. Just take a minute." Sue made eye contact with Zero. "Sit." The dog sat. "Stay."

"Tell him he's good," Alyssa said, "when he does what you ask."

Right. "Good dog." Sue turned to her. "You too."

"Don't give me orders. I'm not your dog."

Sue just nodded and swept the light over Alyssa's Jeep, noting the intact windows, the hood and trunk latched tight, the tires inflated. In daylight she'd have to crawl under there and have a quick look at the brake lines.

Sue had circled the house earlier, after she found the note. But that was without using a light. Now she directed the beam along the foundation of the house. No obvious tracks, not even her own. Tracks wouldn't hold up in the sand and wind. She swept the light out across the ridges of dune grass to the west. Nothing. A lighthouse flashed in the distance.

The south side of the house also seemed fine. Still, she couldn't really tell. After all, someone had been here. Someone with a knife.

Back on the porch she was surprised that Zero hadn't moved. She released the dog and they entered the cottage.

Alyssa still stood in the entry, gazing into the darkness of the living room. She jumped when she heard their steps.

Sue felt her chest tighten. She couldn't bear to see a woman this frightened no matter who she was. "Everything's okay outside," she said softly. She couldn't find a wall switch to light up the darkened room. "How about in here?" Zero went to Alyssa and nudged her hand.

"I'm not sure."

Sue stood beside her and could see her eyes darting back and forth, straining to see into the dark. She didn't even respond to Zero's prodding.

Sue needed light. She moved through the room and kitchen, turning on every light she could find. Everything looked as they had left it.

Alyssa stepped into the living room with her hands crossed in front of her stomach. Her wide green eyes focused on Sue. "I don't want to be afraid in my own home."

"You won't be. I'll fix the door tomorrow."

"I thought you were going camping."

Sue shook her head. "Not after this. I'll stay to take care of your door and make sure Delia's okay." She'd had a hell of a night. "Get some sleep. You'll feel better in the morning."

"That's what Melanie said."

"Melanie's right." Sue stepped forward, wanting to hold her. Maybe kiss the creases of fear from her forehead. But she didn't reach out.

Alyssa stared at Sue for a long second, then turned aside and waved toward the dark hall. "Could you check the rest of the house? You know. For animals."

"Sure." Sue looked over the bathroom, even behind the soft fabric shower curtain woven with a pattern of summer leaves. Not the same as the two-dollar liners she picked up at the grocery store every month or so. She loved the way this one fell in soft folds against the white porcelain tub. The tub was full of clean water. A moss green rug and matching towels muted the effect of the white tile walls. They were dry to Sue's touch. Had something interrupted

Alyssa last evening when she'd been about to take a bath? The pedestal sink looked original to the cottage, but clean. A faint scent of lavender hung in the room, the same scent she'd noticed on Alyssa.

Sue strode into the bedroom and turned on the light. The queen bed had been turned back but not slept in that night. The ivory sheets looked smooth beneath a down comforter encased in a duvet cover of ocean blue. Four pillows in matching blue and ivory were piled against the simple dark wood headboard. *Enough for two.*

Alyssa's highboy dresser matched the headboard and provided no hiding places. Framed photos on top showed an elderly couple. Probably her parents, Sue thought. A one-eared German shepherd. *The dog she lost.* A few earrings lay in a small bowl atop a cedar box.

The hardwood floor underneath the bed harbored no strangers, and no balls of dust or hair. No dogs live here, Sue thought, envisioning the wreaths of hair that had scooted around her own apartment in Detroit.

She opened the double doors to the closet, hung mostly with jeans, khaki pants and DOGS polo shirts in a variety of colors. Three pairs of cross-trainers, all white and blue, were lined up neatly on the floor. A few shoeboxes sat behind them. Alyssa's scent reached from the clothes like an embrace. Not perfume, but the essence of her hair and skin.

In the back portion of the closet Sue found several business suits and two fancy dresses. She gently fingered one, garnet-colored and sheer, draped from a hanger. She imagined how Alyssa's cinnamon hair and green eyes against this fabric would draw the attention of every man—or woman—who saw her.

"Sue?" Alyssa's voice came from the other room. "Everything okay?"

Sue backed out of the closet and shut the doors. "Yes." She left the lights on and returned to the living room. Alyssa sat on the couch, Zero beside her, his ears pricked with attention. "I even checked the closet floor. No raccoons or coyotes. Not even a mouse."

57

"Thank heavens." Alyssa drew her hands through her hair. "I'm exhausted."

"Go to bed. I'll sleep here on the couch."

She laughed. "I can't go to bed. I have to keep an eye on you and make sure you don't plant evidence in my house."

"What're you talking about?" *Plant evidence!*

"Oh, don't look at me like that," Alyssa said. "You think you're the only one trying to protect Delia?"

"What do you mean?"

"The fact is, I don't know about your innocence any more than you know about mine."

"What do you mean?"

"Well, let's start with what I know." Alyssa absently stroked Zero's neck. "I'm minding my own business, then you arrive, and next thing, Delia gets robbed. I wouldn't do it because it would wreck my career." She smiled. "You, on the other hand, have no career to ruin. You already quit the police force. I wonder why?"

Sue stiffened. "None of your business."

"That makes me curiouser and curiouser. And you don't have a real job now."

"I told you—"

"I know. Free-lance Web design. I'd like to see some of your work. It might help me believe that *you*, in fact, are not the big danger to Delia right now."

"How would I get past the dog?"

"I don't know. I don't know how anyone did."

They stared at each other, neither of them moving.

Finally, Sue sighed and lowered herself into an easy chair across the room. "Okay," she said, settling back against the soft cushions. "If this is what you want."

"I want you to go home," Alyssa said. "So we can both sleep."

"No way." Sue shook her head. "Not with that door broken." *And the phone line cut. And the note.*

Zero stretched out at her feet. "At least he'll get some shuteye," Sue said.

"Sunrise isn't far off," Alyssa said. "What then?"

Sue didn't know. Sitting here staring at her didn't seem like a good option. Especially since the angles of the light on her cheeks and hair were making her even more attractive. She looked at the dog. "Maybe we could do some dog training."

Alyssa laughed a little. "Okay, then. Here we are."

Yep, she thought. Here we are.

It was after six, and Alyssa couldn't stand it much longer. She wanted to call a truce. She was stiff and she needed to go to the bathroom. But she wasn't going to flinch first.

Zero solved the problem by stretching his legs all the way down to his toes and yawning with a high-pitched squeak. He rolled from his spot on the couch beside Alyssa and stretched, lowering his chest to the ground and raising his haunches high. He wagged his tail at Alyssa and walked over to greet Sue with a happy lick to the hand.

"I hope you enjoyed your night's sleep, boy," Sue said, rubbing the dog's neck.

"It's nobody's fault but your own if you didn't sleep," Alyssa said. God, her neck hurt.

"I wasn't complaining. It's been a long time since I've watched a sunrise." Sue nodded to the sliders. "Even the western sky celebrated this morning."

Sue's turn of phrase pleased Alyssa. The sky had looked like the decorations for a giant party, purple streaked with gold and pink. She couldn't think of anything to celebrate, but the view had lightened her mood.

"I'm gonna take him out," Sue said, pushing herself up from the chair with a groan. "Oh, man. I haven't spent the night in a chair since—" She stopped and rubbed her face awake. "Well, since I was a lot younger."

Okay, Alyssa thought. *She moved first. Now I can too.* She needed the bathroom. "I'm gonna take a shower." She made eye contact with Sue, as if warning a misbehaving dog. "I'll only be a few minutes. You won't have time to plant evidence or anything. Got it?" Actually, she'd thought about it for the last hour and a half and decided Sue couldn't plant evidence and get away with it. After all, Delia knew she was here.

Sue shook her head. "It's not even six-fifteen. Can't we wait until after breakfast to start this? I'm not awake enough yet."

Alyssa grabbed some clean clothes and shut herself in the bathroom.

She angled her body so the hot shower could pound on her sore neck. Why was she having such a hard time deciding how she felt about Sue? With dogs, her instinct never failed her. She'd met supposedly vicious dogs, but by watching them for just a few minutes, she could tell if they snarled from aggression, or fear, or confusion, or something else. Once she knew what troubled the dog, she could calm the nasty behavior.

But her instinct about people never worked as well as her sense about dogs. She'd misjudged Covington. But she'd been right about Delia, and Melanie. And she'd studied Sue for the last several hours, and nothing there indicated true aggression toward her. She just never felt very sure when she found someone attractive.

She sudsed her hair with lavender-scented shampoo. Of course, she didn't have a good track record. She'd struck out dating in college. Todd, with his flamboyant car and clothes. Too self-centered. Lou, the thoughtful musician, brilliant and funny. He'd become a Catholic priest. Too celibate. Then she figured out she was gay and met Karen, who'd taught her things about her own body that she'd never even read about. Fun, but no real depth. She'd ended it and sunk herself into her public relations career.

Alyssa rinsed the shampoo. Sue looked good and seemed smart and had a no-nonsense approach to most things, except for a blind spot or two where her dog was concerned. She turned off the shower and reached for a towel. Maybe she just needed to relax.

She changed the bandages on her hand. No signs of infection. Truth was, her instincts had sent her a clear message the last few days: *Fight for yourself.* She might not know exactly what to think of Sue Hunter, but she needed to trust that message. She needed to keep training dogs. Proceed as normal. She had a class today, then a private lesson. After that, she'd hunker down and make a plan for drumming up more clients. If she didn't act guilty, then people would believe her.

She tossed on a polo shirt with a sweatshirt, jeans and thick rag socks against the morning chill, then pulled her damp hair back into a ponytail. It curled more if she didn't blow it dry, and she liked it that way. She glanced in the mirror, wished her butt was flat and decided she could face the world.

She was feeling pretty good when she returned to the living room, but she felt a whole lot better when she saw Sue standing barefoot in the kitchen, a red and white plaid towel draped over one shoulder and a carton of eggs in hand. She also smelled coffee.

"You've got eggs," Sue said. "I can make a dynamite omelet out of just about anything. What do you say?"

Alyssa couldn't remember any woman ever cooking breakfast for her, other than her mom. Not even after spending the night at Karen's. She waved toward the refrigerator. "Help yourself."

Sue squinted at her. "You trust me not to drug your food?"

Alyssa shrugged. "I guess so." She watched Sue dig through the refrigerator. She'd changed and her blue T-shirt set off the highlights in her chestnut hair. Her back stretched as she reached for an onion, the outline of her shoulder blades rippling the shirt. She looked great.

Maybe, Alyssa thought, *maybe I should just enjoy it.*

61

Chapter Seven

Alyssa's admission of trust caught Sue off guard. She opened a few drawers in silence until she found a knife and cutting board and began to chop the onion. Why couldn't she ever think of something clever to say on the spot?

She scooped the onion into the warming pan. She was just out of practice. She needed to think like a cop. Build Alyssa's trust up further. She clearly feared someone and Sue just couldn't let that go. She had to convince Alyssa to let her help, or she'd have one long wakeful night after another.

Maybe if I show I trust her a little, Sue thought. It made her nervous, but what did she have to lose?

"I haven't cooked breakfast for someone in ages," she said. "And certainly not for someone who watched my every move."

"When was the last time?"

"Home. In Detroit." She topped the onions with another pat of butter.

She heard the stool scrape against the hardwood floor as Alyssa sat. "Does this mean you're going to tell me where you came from and what you're doing here?"

"Sure." She turned the onions with a spatula.

"Why now? Why not during the empty hours of the night?"

Sue looked at Alyssa over her shoulder and noted her wry smile, even though her eyes narrowed with suspicion. "Because," Sue said, "I don't want to go through another night like that last one. And you would." She turned back to the pan.

"Damn right." The stool creaked as Alyssa shifted her weight, settling in. "So, why'd you quit the police force?"

Sue sighed. She didn't want to go into too much of this now, or ever. "My partner felt my job endangered me. And her. And our potential family."

"Your partner?"

Sue didn't say anything.

"Oh!" Alyssa said. "Not on the force. In life."

"Yep. She wanted kids. Told me to choose either the force or her. So I quit the force." Sue broke four eggs into a bowl, adding some half and half. "She wasn't banking on that. She already had someone else. So a few months ago, she left anyhow."

Sue stirred the eggs, surprised when the familiar pain in her chest didn't come.

"Why didn't you rejoin?"

"I thought she might be right, at least about cops and family life not mixing so well. My father—" She paused in her stirring. "Well, my dad was a cop for a while too. He quit for similar reasons." *A young, lonely daughter without a mother*. "You got any more questions?" Sue slid the eggs into a second pan. " 'Cause this is your chance."

"Why did you come to Radley?"

"I'm a Web designer. I started that after I left the force. I can pick my own hours, live anyplace with a cable line." Sue turned to face her and leaned against the counter. "I kayak and camp whenever I can, so I wanted to be near lots of water and woods. This is the perfect place."

"And Delia?" Alyssa asked.

"My parents knew Delia and Carolyn. We summered here when I was little. Kept in touch over the years. My parents are gone now, but this seemed a good place to come." *For recovery.* "Getting involved in this was *not* part of my plan."

"Mine either."

"So, do you want copies of my tax returns to verify my income source? A copy of my gun permit? Zero's dog license?"

"You have a gun?"

Sue smiled. "Not here." Sue turned back to the stove and slid the simmering onions onto the cooking eggs, then added the ham and some shredded cheddar cheese.

"Would you really give me all of that?"

"Yep."

"Why?"

"So you'll trust me."

"And why do I need to trust you?"

Here we go, Sue thought, as she folded the omelet in half and turned again to face Alyssa. "So you'll tell me what's really going on around here. Do you trust me enough to do that?"

"What makes you think there's more to know?" Alyssa asked.

Sue dropped the knife, pulled a piece of paper from her pocket and placed it in front of Alyssa. "This."

Alyssa unfolded it. It was a note, written in a crooked hand with red felt-tip pen. "Be a good girl and I will keep your secret. Give me what I want." She could almost hear the caller's uneven voice speaking the words. Energy drained out of her.

"Where did you get this?" she asked.

"Hang on," Sue said, touching her hand briefly. "Coffee's coming up."

Alyssa almost grabbed her hand just to have someone to hold on to. But Sue pulled away too fast.

Sue poured her a cup and added cream. "I thought so."

Alyssa accepted the cup. "Thought what?"

"That you're into something bad here. You just went pale, so don't try to tell me otherwise. If there's one thing I've learned about you, it's that your face gives you away. You'd be lousy at poker."

Alyssa took a sip, and Sue turned back to the stove.

"Want to tell me about it?" she asked.

"No, I do *not* want to tell you. When and where did you find it?"

"Last night. On the porch floor. Under that flower pot." Sue's eyes never left Alyssa's. "That's really why I let myself in so quietly."

"Why didn't you tell me?"

Sue turned the burner off. "I thought you had enough to deal with." She ran hot water into the onion pan. "Wanna know what I think? Someone knew how to get past that dog. You're the likely candidate. Normal thieves would have killed Teddy, or picked another house altogether. That points to you too, because while you might burgle a house, you wouldn't kill a dog."

"Now I know why you're an *ex*-cop," Alyssa said. "You're lousy at this." She hoped her bluff worked.

Sue turned to face her, omelet pan and spatula in hand. "Want to straighten me out?"

"No." *You can't trick me that easily.*

"Okay. It points to you. Except, there's the phone line, the note and the fact that you're scared to death." Sue split the omelet in half and eased it onto their plates. "You aren't the criminal type. Not on your own. But maybe if you were forced. Blackmailed. Threatened."

She felt Sue's dark eyes look into hers.

"You should be scared. You're isolated out here. And whoever left you that note was on your front porch. So somebody got damned close."

Too close. Alyssa's skin crawled.

"So I figure that note's reminding you to take the blame for the robbery because someone is holding something over you." Sue's gaze didn't waver. "Am I right now?"

"I don't want to talk about it." If Sue knew Alyssa had stolen dogs from the Covington labs, she'd surely think Alyssa had something to do with the robbery. Thank God she'd changed her name. A casual Internet search wouldn't pull up Alyssa Norland.

Sue looked at her for what seemed a very long time. "Okay. Then pass the salt."

Alyssa watched as Sue salted her eggs and began to eat. Could she be giving up that easily? She drained her coffee and held out the mug for more.

Sue poured her another cup then filled her own. She pointed to the eggs with her fork. "Not bad, considering what I had to work with. Eat. The protein will keep you on your toes."

Alyssa looked at the omelet. Maybe Sue would drop it now. Despite her nerves, the eggs smelled fabulous and she was hungry.

Sue pointed to Alyssa's calendar on the counter. "So, what's up for today?"

Alyssa held the fork steady. "Why?"

Sue glanced up from her plate. "I'm just making conversation?" She swallowed. "No, you wouldn't buy that. How about I'm debating whether or not you need me to keep an eye on you."

Alyssa started to protest, but Sue cut her off.

"For protection. Not because I think you're going to burgle someone's house again." Sue winced at her own words. "Sorry. I didn't mean you did it the first time."

Alyssa held her fork over the plate. "I can take care of myself."

Sue smiled. "You know, I'll be mightily insulted if I have to feed your half of that omelet to Zero."

The dog, who had been lounging in the sun by the glass doors, stood.

"No," Sue said. "Zero, down."

The dog lay back down. Sue took another bite.

"Tell him he's good when he behaves," said Alyssa.

"Eat something." Sue nodded toward the food.

Alyssa took a bite. It tasted incredible.

"Good dog," Sue said, making eye contact with Alyssa before glancing at Zero.

"You're an ass," Alyssa said.

Sue laughed.

She hadn't meant to be funny, and she wanted Sue to know it. "But I should have known. I've seen that side of your dog. Like owner, like dog." The eggs melted in her mouth. She would never have guessed Sue could cook.

"Is that Vinnie's picture in the bedroom?"

When had—? Oh. When she'd asked Sue to search the place last night. "Yes. Vinnie. For Van Gogh. One ear and all."

"Another German shepherd fan." Sue swallowed the last bit of egg and placed her fork on the plate. "How come one ear?"

"I adopted him. He'd been stolen and evidently had an identifying tattoo in his ear. Probably the thieves cut it off."

Sue's face twisted. "Why bother? Wouldn't thieves just dump him if he had an i.d.?"

"Oh, they didn't want to dump him. They wanted to sell him to a lab. And labs can't work on animals with any marks of ownership. That's why people get their dogs tattooed in the first place, you know, to prevent thefts. But the crooks carry garden shears now."

Sue leaned onto her elbows. "Don't labs usually raise their own animals, for control and so on?"

"Often. But some have other priorities." That was the most polite way Alyssa could think to put it. "It's cheaper to buy dogs than raise them. And cheaper dogs are more attractive. Some labs buy them from pounds and shelters for vivisection. Some buy them from thieves."

"I see." Sue glanced at Zero. "So should I get him tattooed?"

"Yes, but not on the ear. On the abdomen. Then it can't be cut out without killing the dog, and there's no point in stealing him. Put a tag on him too, one that says he has a tattoo."

"Where can I get it done?"

"Dr. Lindsey, the only vet in town, can do it."

"I'll call him today." Sue stood and picked up her plate.

The morning's not a complete loss, Alyssa thought, finishing her omelet.

"I need to talk to him anyhow," Sue said. "About Teddy's blood test results."

Alyssa pushed her empty plate toward Sue. "Why would he tell you?"

Sue picked it up. "You may have forgotten, but Delia has asked me to help her. She sent me here for you last night, remember?"

Alyssa nodded.

"She trusts me, even if you don't."

It wasn't that she didn't trust her. When Sue had touched her a minute ago, Alyssa had trusted her completely. She was just so confused.

"Your argument doesn't work, Sue." Alyssa stood. "After all, Delia trusts me, and you don't."

Sue wiped her hands on the towel. "I changed my mind last night. I don't think you're trying to hurt Delia. I think you're trying to protect yourself."

"But you think I'd hurt her to protect myself?" Anger flared in Alyssa's chest. "That's how much you trust me?"

"People do it all the time," Sue said. "It's natural when you're in danger."

"Well, not me!" Alyssa leaned forward, bracing herself on the island. "It may make sense to you in your ego-centered world-view, but it doesn't make sense to me. You can trust that I would *never* do anything that would endanger one of my friends, even to protect myself." She stood straight again, the anger draining. "I've had it done to me. I wouldn't put anyone else through it."

Sue studied her. "Well, okay then."

"That's it?" What game was she playing now?

"Yep. I believe you. You're very convincing. Plus, your neck gets red blotches when you're mad." Sue turned and began to rinse the dishes. "As opposed to when you're trying to hide something."

Alyssa jumped when Sue's cell phone rang, then she remembered. It couldn't be the caller. How would he know to use that number?

Sue wiped her hands and answered, listened for a second, then passed the phone to her. "Marcus."

Alyssa took the phone and walked into the entry for more privacy. The cracked door looked even weirder in the daylight. She decided to be positive. "Good morning, Marcus."

"Not for you, honey. Your one o'clock canceled. And two people from your class called to say they wouldn't be in."

His coldness startled her. "Did they say why?"

"No. But what do you think?" She could hear him tapping the desk in the office, his worst nervous habit. "News must be all over town by now."

Crap. "How? The paper hasn't—"

"Don't kid yourself. Half the town monitors police calls."

"Marcus, this will blow over."

"Maybe. You've got until a week from Monday to prove it."

"Ten days?" She couldn't help shouting. "I need at least a month!"

"I can't keep you on for another month with a bad rep. It'll rub off on me. People need to know you aren't hiding anything. Show me you can still get some new clients and we'll talk about it."

"It's not enough time."

He exhaled into the receiver. "It's not up for discussion, Alyssa. You've got free time today. Get started on a plan or visit potential clients. Or find a dog. Remember, you need a dog. People'd be more likely to believe you were innocent if you had a dog."

He clicked off.

"Damn," she said aloud. She went back to the kitchen and put the phone down on the island.

Sue looked at her, waiting.

"It's started," she explained, more furious because of the tears threatening to spill from the corners of her eyes. "Some of my students canceled. It's the burglary. Strunk's accusations. Marcus said it will be all over town. My life here will be ruined." A tear rolled onto her cheek and she swiped it away. "Damn it." She looked up at Sue. "I'm just tired." She grabbed the towel from Sue's shoulder and wiped her eyes. She didn't want Sue to think she couldn't handle herself.

"Do you really think they canceled because of the burglary?"

Energy surged through her. "Let's see. A dog I trained let some crooks waltz right in and steal forty grand worth of jewelry." She noticed her hands had begun to shake, but she didn't care. "Would you hire me?"

Zero appeared next to her, nudging at her.

Sue smiled. "I already did."

"Yeah, well." Alyssa tossed the towel onto the counter and rubbed the dog's ears. "I need a few more folks like you to drop into town this week and hire me before I get fired."

Sue picked up the towel. "I'm afraid there's just one of me."

Alyssa thought that was a damned shame. There Sue stood, tall and solid and barefoot in her kitchen, chocolate hair and even darker chocolate eyes, with a towel in one hand and a newly washed coffee mug in another. A swimmer's shoulders, forearm muscles that rippled each time she wiped the mug. A lot more appealing than the rest of the world right now.

Alyssa's skin vibrated, suddenly sensitive. *She's actually fabulous*, Alyssa thought.

"So, do you have time for this client tonight?" Sue asked. Her voice sounded different. Softer. "Proceeding as normal and all that? Maybe seven?"

Alyssa's day flew by. A call to the phone company got her a promise that a repair team would be there right away, which translated into nearly two days, thanks to the weekend. She left Sue at the cottage and went to the office not knowing what to expect, but every-thing seemed normal. No angry mobs greeted her. Just Hendrix and a scowling Marcus.

"Strunk called," said Marcus. "Wanted me to remind you to see a doctor about that hand."

"It's Saturday."

"Do what he says, Alyssa. I don't want him coming around here."

Everyone else showed up for puppy class, even Delia, so it went smoothly after all. Brian Sybesma worked Nestor as he usually did on Saturdays. Delia chattered nonstop about the burglary and Alyssa thought she saw some suspicious glances directed her way, but no one said anything.

After class she settled in the office to order supplies for her July puppy class because she refused to believe she wouldn't have a job. Then she pulled out a phone book and began to list all the possible places she could leave business cards and brochures for DOGS. For the first time she thought about hair salons. She bet people com-plained about their misbehaving dogs while having their hair dyed. She'd begun to add them to the list when Marcus and Hendrix returned from lunch.

"Strunk called again while you were in class," Marcus said. "I don't want the police around. Doesn't look good."

"Hey, at least he isn't just stopping by."

"But he might if you're here. Go home."

"I'm working on a marketing plan, Marcus," she said, pointing toward her monitor. "It would be easier if I could do it here on the computer."

Marcus grunted and sat at his desk. "Fine. But if he shows, you both go."

Strunk did not show so Alyssa worked for a few hours in peace. Soon she had a list of nearly sixty salons, barbershops, gunshops, fishing tackle stores, boat supply places and holistic health centers to visit—all within an hour's drive.

Around 3:30 she left the office and stopped at Melanie's where

71

she found her friend still in pajamas having an afternoon snack. "You sick?"

"Hey, I had the day off. Sorry about missing class, but if you have to get dressed, it isn't a day off."

"Well, Strunk didn't take the day off." She told Melanie about his checks on her. "Why is he so set on me?"

"Strunk bullies everyone," Melanie said. "He hopes you'll confess in a dramatic collapse and improve his chances for promotion."

"I feel like collapsing." Alyssa fell onto the empty couch. "Where's Nestor?"

Melanie sat down next to her. "Jeff has him at the park. I believe the phrase he used was 'chick magnet.' The puppy's good for his social life." She turned sideways and poked Alyssa. "So, how's your social life?"

Alyssa started to tell Melanie about puppy class but Melanie stopped her.

"You *know* that's not what I mean."

"God, Mel, it's a disaster. I'm actually attracted to her." She told her about the touch, the omelet, the moment of lust that had stopped her in her tracks and her sense that Sue felt the same.

"It doesn't sound like a disaster to me," Melanie said, a wide grin shining over her steaming coffee cup.

"What do you mean? It's awful." Alyssa jumped up and paced in front of the couch.

Melanie took a bite of her bagel covered with peanut butter. "What're you afraid of?"

"Nothing." Alyssa's shins touched an end table, so she did another about-face and paced some more.

"Well, you've been a nervous wreck since she showed up."

Alyssa stopped. "Melanie, give me some support here. I'm upset because one of my guard dogs' houses got robbed and the cop in charge of the investigation is accusing me. There's no evidence pointing to anyone else and I'm losing clients."

"There really isn't any evidence from the scene yet other than that footprint. No strange fingerprints or fibers have turned up. We don't even know if they're able to pick a lock, since they just opened the door at Delia's."

"But you do know they got past a good dog." The whole thing seemed worse the more she thought about it.

"Of course, it's early yet. I can get you an update tomorrow." Melanie stared hard at Alyssa. "When it isn't my day off." She wiped her mouth. "You get your phone fixed today?"

Alyssa put her hands on her hips. "Are you changing the subject?"

"Sure. Look, you can't do anything about the burglary, so why worry?"

"Do all mothers of teenage boys talk like you?"

"Only the sane ones." Melanie smiled. "Not many moms eat peanut butter bagels either. You gotta know how to stay calm. Sit down."

Alyssa sat and pointed to the last quarter bagel on her plate. "You want that?"

Melanie stuck the plate out to her. "Should I drive out to your place tomorrow, look around? You might have a sick animal on the loose if it's chewing on phone lines. That happens."

Alyssa bit into her bagel and almost choked. *Sick animal is right.* Then she thought of the door. Melanie would ask too many questions. "No, Mel, that's okay. Sue's checking on it today."

"She's still at your *house?*"

"So what?" Alyssa tried to sound cool.

"And you say you're developing a thing for her?"

"Not a 'thing.'" Her tongue wrestled the peanut butter on the roof of her mouth. She didn't want Mel to jump to conclusions. "Lust. Pure and simple. That's all."

"And she lusted after you too. You said so." Mel's eyes glittered with delight.

It sounded silly now. "Maybe not. I might have read it wrong."

"Oh, bull. No one reads the lust connection wrong. You're just chickening out." Mel grinned again. "I think you should screw the hunt for clients and go home, where you should screw—"

"For God's sake, Melanie!" It all sounded so, well, it sounded

73

pretty good. "You're not helping. I have too much else to deal with. Namely, half the town thinks I'm involved in that burglary."

"Suit yourself. But I find a little sex clears my mind and helps me think better." She sipped her coffee. "Are you seeing her tonight?"

Alyssa nodded. "We have a lesson at seven."

"So what're you going to do?"

"Well, we should start working on Zero's control tonight."

Melanie stared at her, then swatted her. "I mean with Sue! The lust! Remember?"

Alyssa remembered. "I'm going to pretend it didn't happen."

"Loosen up, Alyssa!" Melanie shook her shoulder gently. "You need to have some fun. You've been way too tense. I say you should kiss her at least. Then decide from there."

"Melanie, it isn't that easy." She leaned forward, elbows on knees.

"It sure is. Just pucker up and go for it." Melanie looked at her as if she were a scientific specimen. "How long has it been since you've had sex?"

"Jeez, Mel! I thought you'd take my side."

"Relax," Melanie said, motioning for her to sit. "Sue's okay. She really is a Web designer. Even though it is my day off, I talked to her former partner on the force. He couldn't say enough good about her. Or enough bad about her ex." She rested her head back against the couch. "She sounds like a good one."

Alyssa nodded. "Maybe."

"Open yourself up to it, Alyssa," Melanie said. "You don't want to miss your chance."

This was too much for Alyssa. She didn't want to think about this now so she stood. "Thanks, Mel. I gotta go. Tell Jeff and Brian I said hi."

Still, she drove home wondering about Sue. She hadn't lied after all. She didn't seem the type to work for Covington. So why had she attached herself to Alyssa?

She thought again of the electric moment that morning. She knew Sue had felt it too. Sue was good-looking, as Melanie delighted in pointing out. And she was devoted to Delia, so not a total loser. Maybe she'd misjudged Sue because the phone calls had unnerved her so. She thought of Sue sitting stubbornly in that damned chair last night and chuckled. *Idiot.*

Of course, she'd done it too. *That made us a pair of idiots.* What a sight they must have been.

The thought chilled her to the bone. What if the caller had been watching? The lights had been on. He'd know something was up between her and Sue.

Because something was happening, she couldn't deny that. And she didn't think Sue would either. A bond was forming between them.

Then Alyssa thought of Vinnie, dead in the sunshine.

Chapter Eight

Shortly after 7:00 that evening, Sue stood near the Point Betsie lighthouse, watching the bronze sunlight dance on the rippled water of Lake Michigan, wondering how she had gotten herself into this.

"Hey, Sue." Alyssa's voice came from behind her, a few yards up the beach. "Let me play with Zero a minute to get his motivation up, then we'll be ready."

Sue didn't feel ready. She admired the view, the sun still hanging high in a pale blue sky. It wouldn't set for another two hours or more. It had a nice straight course to run every day. That's why she'd come to Radley, to find her own course.

She could have spent this evening in her kayak, slicing through the sun's shimmers on blue water. The rhythm of the paddle, the pull across her shoulders and back, the patterns of her movement on the water all cleared Sue's head. She'd kayaked in the Detroit River and canals of Belle Isle after Mary Ellen left, and always finished feeling like she had a handle on things.

"Come on, Zero," Alyssa said. "Let's go burn off some energy."

Sue watched her run barefoot along the water, the dog bounding by her side. She didn't know if even a good paddle would help her get a handle on how she felt about Alyssa Norland and what she should do about it.

She had spent too much of the day thinking about Alyssa. It had taken the morning and early afternoon to replace the broken doors and frames. She had put in a few hours at home for her newest client, a local cherry orchard association. Luckily, they didn't want anything too fancy, so she could easily meet the deadline for a basic layout. After that, she'd checked on Delia and found her delighting in the fame of having been robbed. On her way back to Alyssa's, Sue bought steaks, then made a Caesar salad and opened a bottle of Shiraz.

She loved watching Alyssa eat the dinner she made. Just like she loved the sight of Alyssa running Zero on the beach.

It hadn't been a fluke. The energy she'd felt when Alyssa gave her *that look* this morning had driven her all day long while she pounded on nails then on her keyboard.

"Hey, quit daydreaming." Alyssa stood beside her, her breath coming hard from the run. "Pay attention and learn something."

"Okay. What do you want me to do?"

"Heel him a minute, just to warm up," Alyssa said. "Then we'll work on the jumping."

As Sue worked Zero through figure eights, Alyssa applauded.

"Okay! Let me show you how to correct the jumping." She stood ten feet or so in front of them. "The key is to give him something constructive to do to keep him out of trouble."

"Like people."

Alyssa put her hands on her hips and shifted her weight to one hip. "I suppose."

This was the Alyssa Norland she'd watched working with her students, fiery and smart. So different from the middle of the night when she was afraid.

"Okay, hang on to the leash," Alyssa said. "I'll walk away and come back, and when he starts to get excited, tell him to sit."

She jogged about thirty yards up the beach, then turned and walked toward Sue and Zero. Alyssa's feet blended into the sand and her hair gleamed in the sun.

"Now, Sue. He's pulling on you. Tell him to sit," she said, still twenty feet away.

Pay attention. Sue ordered Zero to sit, and the dog did, quivering.

"What a sweet boy," Alyssa cooed, stepping closer. "Aren't you handsome?"

Sue felt her own urge to leap toward Alyssa.

"Is it fair to tease him like that?" Sue asked, certain that, from her perspective, it wasn't.

"Sure. If a stranger tempts him with a dog treat, you want him to listen to you. And he's doing well."

Alyssa bent and smiled, but the dog could stand it no longer. He jumped toward her and got caught at the end of the leash.

"No, Zero," Sue scolded. "Sit." The dog sat and she praised him.

"We'll try again." Alyssa backed up a few steps. "Let's just talk a minute and give him a chance to succeed."

"How'd you learn to do this?" Sue asked.

She put her hands on her hips again. "Still checking on me?"

"No, no." Sue smiled. "You just seem to always know what to do with a dog. I was curious, that's all."

Alyssa rubbed her arms against the cool breeze. "I always got along with dogs. I went to college, did the whole business major thing, but the corporate world didn't work out for me. So I went to dog school and learned to train."

"So you do obedience and guard dogs. Any other kinds of training?"

"Some tracking with one or two local law enforcement people. Melanie hooked me up with them. She wants to get into search and rescue, so I'll help her there."

Sue nodded. Alyssa's hair looked so soft in the breeze. "I can't imagine there's a huge market for guard dogs around here," Sue said.

"A lot of wealthy people from out of state spend their summers here. Most of my clients are obedience, and some do personal protection."

Sue glanced at Zero, who was still sitting. "Good dog." Zero wagged his tail. "What's personal protection training?"

Alyssa folded her arms. "Instead of training a dog to guard an area, you train the dog to guard a person—specifically, the person who gives the command."

"Like attack training?"

"No. It's much safer, actually. In attack training, a command sends the dog a distance to put a bite on someone. You know, like police dogs?"

Sue nodded. How could talking about attack dogs be so incredibly sexy?

"In personal protection, you train the dog to do two things. First, on command the dog will growl and bark at anyone near you, but he stays within six feet of you. If more than one person approaches, the dog will circle you. He doesn't leave you for a bite." Alyssa's hand moved through the air in demonstration. She held her head high and exuded the grace of self-confidence. "Second, if anyone comes closer than six feet, then the dog bites without additional command."

"Not many dogs are trained in that, are they?" Sue had never heard of it.

"No," she said, "but they should be. It's an intimidating display that scares off most attackers." She leaned forward as if imparting a special secret. "It can be signaled with a cue so small that no one else sees it, and so any potential attacker thinks the dog is vicious and out of control."

Sue leaned closer as well. "How's that work?"

"Imagine you're with your dog. Someone approaches who looks fine to you, but suddenly, they pull out a gun. They tell you to hold on to your dog, then turn over your wallet. You move your hand slowly as if you're going to grab the collar." She bent to the side to illustrate. "And instead you touch two fingers behind the ears and press. The dog explodes barking. Or, if the person is already within six feet, the dog bites." She straightened. "Kind of cool, huh?"

Alyssa's smile dazzled Sue. "That must be a heck of a surprise."

"It scared me when I first saw it, and I knew it was coming."

"Can you train a dog to do that?"

"Sure," Alyssa said. "I've done two around here. The records are confidential, though. People don't want anyone to know their dog has that training. I don't even put it in the files. I just list it as advanced obedience. Which it is, really." She pointed to Zero, who hadn't moved from his sit. "He could do it someday. He just needs discipline." She looked back to Sue. "You interested?"

Am I ever, Sue thought. "Maybe."

Alyssa pointed to Zero. "Hang on to him. I'm coming closer."

She took a few giant steps toward them. "Such a good boy, Zero."

Zero didn't move.

"See, he's doing better," Alyssa said. "I'll just stand here a minute to test him." She looked around as if searching for something to say. "So, this morning you talked about Web design as a job full of freedom. You can go anywhere there's a cable hookup."

"Yep." Sue smiled. *Wow*. She had really listened to her.

Alyssa swept a windblown tangle of hair from her eyes. "That sounds good. But too much freedom can be dangerous for a dog," she said and took another step toward them.

Zero didn't move.

"Dogs aren't people," Sue said.

"No, but people can get lost and lonely too, if they have too much freedom. Or too little."

Sue struggled to keep up. They'd gone from dogs to loneliness in a matter of seconds. "Well, people get lost and lonely even in a committed relationship, if it's the wrong one."

Alyssa turned toward the water. "Do you miss being partnered?"

Why did she care? "Not to my first partner, no." Sue couldn't take her eyes off of Alyssa's body, shadowed by the warm light above her. "I thought we wanted the same things. Turned out we didn't."

Alyssa's hair flowed in the breeze in rhythm with the slapping shore. On the water, the reflected yellow stretched into the sky as if exchanging energy with the sun.

Sue had never seen a woman look so beautiful.

"What do you want now?" Alyssa asked, her voice soft.

"I-uh—" Sue hesitated. "I'm not sure."

"How will you know if it's right, then? That it won't end in misery?"

Sue didn't have a clue. But she didn't want to say that to her.

"I guess when you find the right person," she said, "you take the risk. If it works out it would be worth it, right?" A connection like she'd felt with Alyssa this morning. And all day, when she wasn't even there. And right now.

Could it be she'd found her course?

By 8:30 the sun's light had begun to redden everything Alyssa could see. "Zero's been really good. Release him with lots of praise."

Sue knelt to hug Zero, then reached up to clasp Alyssa's hand. Alyssa felt her heart swell.

"Thanks," Sue said. "We came a long way tonight, don't you think?"

"Yes." Alyssa tried to ignore the touch and to think only about how well Sue had praised and loved her dog.

Sue turned Alyssa's hand over and traced her thumb across the bandage. "How's this?"

"Good." She meant both the wound and the touch. "It didn't hurt to handle the leash at all."

Sue looked into her eyes, then raised Alyssa's palm to her lips and kissed it gently. "To help it heal, my mother always said."

Alyssa felt the touch of Sue's lips travel directly to her heart, which suddenly felt even more full. It had been so long since someone had taken care of her.

Sue rose almost effortlessly, dropped Alyssa's hand and looked out across the water. A few puffs of cloud had bunched along the horizon, their edges turning pink as the sun lowered.

Alyssa wanted to move to Sue, to kiss her and feel her touch like that shaft of sun.

"So," Sue said, "do you think the risk would be worth it?"

It's happening! Alyssa took a deep breath. "What risk?"

Sue didn't move, but Alyssa could feel the energy coming off her in waves. "You know what I mean," Sue said. "I haven't misread this."

"No." Alyssa didn't move either.

"No, it isn't worth the risk? Or no, I haven't misread this?" Sue stared at the water.

Before Alyssa figured out what to say, Sue placed a palm where Alyssa's shoulder curved into her neck. Alyssa could feel the rhythm beating there, hard. Then she felt Sue's hands slide around her, and Sue lowered her lips to Alyssa.

Alyssa welcomed her, tasted her. Desire cascaded through her body. *Uh-oh.* Was she ready for this, now?

Alyssa felt Sue's lips leave hers, moving across her jaw. Sue's breath rushed near her ear, twisting her passion even tighter. She turned her head to find Sue's lips again, and her quiet moan delighted Alyssa.

I could have her in bed tonight if I wanted to, Alyssa thought. And she wanted to. *We would touch and make love. I could relax.*

Alyssa pulled away from the kiss. "Sue." She felt warm and strong against her, but Alyssa knew she couldn't give in. Not until this other mess was cleaned up.

"What?"

"You didn't misread this."

Sue smiled. "Nope. At least our instincts agree about something. And the risk will be worth it."

Sue bent toward her again, but Alyssa stepped back out of the embrace. The breeze that blew where they had touched felt cold against her skin.

"I have too much to sort out yet." She watched Sue thrust her hands into her pockets. "Okay?"

"You don't think I'm going to make love with you, then plant evidence in your house, do you?"

Make love. It sounded magnificent when she said it. Alyssa swallowed. "No." She willed herself to stay still. "Do you still think I had anything to do with the theft?"

Sue stared at her. "Did you? Anything at all? Even under force?"

"No." Alyssa's voice came out firm, for which she was grateful.

"Okay," Sue said. "I believe you. Though now I really don't know what's going on."

"What do you mean?" Alyssa dug her toes into the warm sand.

"Somebody's still after you. Is that just a coincidence?"

"I guess so. I can't put it together myself."

"You don't know who it is?"

"No." That wasn't a lie. Not completely.

"Oh." Sue looked skeptical.

"We'd better get back," said Alyssa. They walked together from the beach down the soft, sandy road. "Listen, Sue. Thanks for everything today. Like the new doors."

"Hey, I helped break them."

"Well, I appreciate it. I'm sure Delia will be glad to have you back on her property tonight."

"Alyssa, I'm staying here tonight."

Alyssa stopped so Sue did too. "Did I invite you to stay another night?"

"Not technically, no, but—"

"But nothing." Who did she think she was? Cook her a few meals, kiss her and just assume she could spend the night?

"It makes sense," Sue said. "Until we know about this stalker." She paused. "You take the bed. I'll sleep on the couch."

Alyssa began to walk again and Sue followed. "Don't give me orders. I'm not Zero. And I've got things under control in my own home."

"What if he comes back?"

"I'll handle it," she said.

"With a coffee table and a leash?"

"It worked on you. And now I've had practice."

"Look, Alyssa. I've got my camping stuff in the car, you know, from my aborted trip. What if I just crawl into a sleeping bag on your living room floor?"

Alyssa stared.

"Pitch a tent in your yard?"

"Are you nuts?"

Sue didn't laugh. "You don't have a phone. How will you get help?"

Alyssa had already thought about this. "You told Strunk you'd give me your cell phone."

Sue exhaled in frustration. "Don't you see how much easier this would be if I stayed?"

"Don't you see how much riskier it would be if you stayed?" They turned from the road into her driveway. Alyssa stooped to put on her sandals against the gravel. When she stood, Sue pulled her close.

"If you won't take a risk with me, don't take any risks with him." Sue's fingers felt cool as they stroked the hair back from Alyssa's face. "Let me stay on the couch."

"Another order. That's why you're leaving," she said.

Sue let her go. "It's your house." They stepped onto the porch.

"They said my phone will be fixed first thing Monday morning. I can just give your cell back at the office then. I have a kids' camp at eleven, so I'll be there by nine-thirty." Alyssa dug in her jeans pocket for the new house key and used it. The door swung open. She listened. *All quiet.*

"Promise me you'll call if anything unusual happens. I'll borrow Delia's cell so you can reach me wherever. Okay?"

"Okay." They entered the cottage and switched on some lights.

"Are you sure?" Zero trotted ahead and jumped up on the couch. "We enjoyed the luxurious accommodations."

Alyssa was sure that if Sue stayed, she'd never spend the night alone on the couch.

"I'm sure, Sue. Thanks. I can get along just fine."

Sue nodded, then handed her the cell phone. Without another touch, and with a terse good night, she and Zero left.

Alyssa watched her car disappear around the dunes, suddenly unsure if it had been wise to resist her own desire and fears. Because now she was all alone and the looming night could conceal anybody.

Just after 10:30 that night, Sue pushed open the heavy green door and stepped up into the Twelve Point Tavern for the first time. She sidestepped two bearded pool players, then nodded to the four men and two women crowded around the circular bar before she claimed the last open stool.

"What can I get you?" asked the bartender, a skinny man with bony cheeks and a bouncing Adam's apple.

Sue ordered a draught, then looked around. A television flashed scenes from car races in one corner, just above a jukebox that blinked in silent rhythm. Strings of clear lights hung from the black acoustic tile ceiling, providing the only other light.

Behind her an open doorway led into the nearly empty dining room where, Delia had told her, families ate pizza and her friends had their monthly night out. They'd been here last night during the burglary.

That was part of what drew her here. Maybe she could find out something more.

So did her concern for Alyssa. She couldn't stop thinking about her. Sue shouldn't have ordered her around. No wonder she'd kicked her out.

She'd been tempted to drive to Alyssa's, check things out. But she could be asleep. Sue didn't want to scare her or look like she didn't trust her. She had paced in the apartment, cursing Alyssa's insistence on doing this alone.

"A buck," the server said, clunking the beer onto the counter. He took Sue's five and returned with change. "You living out at Delia and Carolyn's place?"

Sue knew news traveled fast in a small town, like it did in neighborhoods in Detroit. She sensed the others listening for her reply. "Yep."

"Used to live here in the summer, huh?" said the woman across the bar.

Sue didn't recognize her. "It's been nearly twenty years."

"Now you're back." The bartender's face remained immobile when he spoke, except for his Adam's apple. His thin eyebrows, the ledge of his cheekbones, the meager line of his lips—all stayed horizontal, even when he spoke. His gaze held just as straight. The effect made Sue uncomfortable.

"Paul says there was a burglary out there last night," pronounced the woman. She had heavy black hair and wore a sweatshirt proclaiming "Property of Radley Ravens."

Local high school, Sue thought.

"Bad situation, I heard," Paul, the bartender, continued. He had one of those voices that made it impossible to tell if he was twenty-five or forty-five. Sue guessed closer to forty.

"At least no one got hurt," Sue said, sipping the beer.

"Including the robbers!" huffed the Ravens backer. "Carolyn paid big money for that dog, and it didn't even get a bite." The woman swigged a mouthful from her mug. "I told her, waste of good money."

The man next to her, who looked about sixty, wore a black sweatshirt and camouflage hat. "No woman'd train a hunting dog of mine."

"You don't do so great at training your own, Gibbs," accused the younger blond man who sat next to Sue. He turned to Sue and pointed to Gibbs. "His retrievers maul the ducks."

"No one's broke into my place, though, have they?" Gibbs said. Sue could tell he'd been here long enough to consume more than a few beers. "And I don't have some fancy-trained guard dog."

The Radley Ravens fan nudged him. "Delia and Carolyn don't keep a loaded gun in every room like you."

Paul turned, and for the first time, Sue saw his face shift with a small smile. "And you don't have anything worth stealing, Mr. Gibbs."

"That's the truth." Gibbs raised his glass and drained it in affirmation. He immediately received another.

"I don't know, though," Paul began after a few seconds of silence, "as I'd have one of Alyssa Norland's dogs protecting my house if I had something to steal."

Sue's heart jumped, alert at Alyssa's name.

"You know," said the young man next to Sue, "I'm wondering too." He shook his head. "My wife wants a dog for guarding, and for company too. Doesn't want an alarm system."

"She can't think a dog's safe," said Paul.

"Get her a gun, Jimmy," encouraged Gibbs.

The young man shook his head. "No guns. Not with the kids."

"Well, teach 'em to shoot. That's the trouble with the world today," spouted Gibbs, "nobody knows how to use a gun."

That's hardly the problem, thought Sue.

"Well, I sure wouldn't get one of those dogs," insisted Paul. "At least, not from her."

Sue felt her muscles tighten. "Why?"

Paul turned an expressionless face to her. "Because someone got in despite that dog somehow. Who else would know how to do it?"

"You mean she broke in and got past her own guard dog?" asked the woman next to Gibbs.

"It makes sense," said Paul, wiping a glass.

"See, if they'd had a gun, someone could have taken her down," Gibbs declared.

"They weren't home, Gibbs," the woman reminded him.

"In fact, Delia was here at the time of the burglary," Sue said.

Jimmy turned to Sue, one eyebrow raised. "What do you mean?"

Sue felt the others look at her. "Nothing." She emptied her glass. "I'll take another."

"I heard the cops think Alyssa did it," said Jimmy, glancing at Sue, "because the robbers didn't hurt the dogs, you know?"

"Boy, that'll put a dent in old Marcus's shine, won't it?" Gibbs laughed then finished his glass.

Paul served him another and said steadily, "Well, Mr. Dixon could fire her."

"On what grounds?" Sue asked, her fingertips flattening against her beer glass as her grip tightened.

The others all turned to her.

"Thieving," said Gibbs, kindly, as if talking to someone a little slow. "Stealin' your landlady's stuff."

"Or helping somebody do it," offered Jimmy.

"Maybe just for being bad at her job," said Paul, his dark eyes glazed. "Who else do you think might have done it, Missus Hunter?"

Sue was not surprised that they already knew her name. "Ms. And so far, the evidence that I've heard doesn't point to anyone."

"You're kidding, right?" asked the Ravens woman.

"No. You're all talking about circumstances. Not evidence." Sue flexed her fingers around the glass, pumping out her anger. "I just think we shouldn't decide she's guilty without any evidence."

Paul stepped closer to Sue, lifted her half-full glass, and wiped the counter dry. "You think she's innocent?"

Sue weighed her words carefully. "I don't think there's evidence that she's guilty. Too many unanswered questions. How would even she get past the dog? Who knew the house was empty or where the jewelry was kept?"

"Those," Paul said, replacing Sue's glass, "are a lot of questions."

"They need to be asked," Sue said, looking at the others.

"We should be fair," said Jimmy.

"Fair!" shouted Gibbs, loud enough that the two men playing pool turned. "Ask Carolyn and Delia if losin' all them jewels was fair."

"Carolyn's out of town," nudged his neighbor.

"And where the hell were you," Gibbs asked Sue, "when Delia was gettin' robbed?"

"Home asleep. Just me and my dog," Sue replied.

"See?" exclaimed Gibbs, with a dramatic wave of his hands. "Dogs are no good for protection. Gotta have a gun."

Sue watched the people around the bar sink into their own thoughts. Alyssa was going to have a tough time finding new clients if the rest of the folks in town had already tried and convicted her like this bunch. She thought again of Alyssa's fear and desperation last night, and of her energetic power during their kiss. She could help her defeat whatever frightened her. She could free all that energy. *And maybe she'll turn it toward me*, Sue thought.

That was definitely worth the risk.

Chapter Nine

Saturday night passed quietly for Alyssa. She didn't even have trouble falling asleep, she'd been so exhausted from the previous two days. She slept until nearly 11:00 then puttered around her kitchen fixing coffee. She wished Sue were there to cook breakfast for her again.

Around 11:30 Sue's cell phone rang. Seeing Delia's number on the caller i.d., Alyssa answered.

"Why the hell haven't you called me yet?"

Alyssa recognized Sue's voice. "Because I just got up."

"Oh." Silence. "Well, then, I guess it's a good thing I didn't call at six-thirty, which is when I started worrying about you."

Alyssa sipped her coffee. "Everything was perfectly quiet. My doors and windows are all still unbroken."

"Good."

Another pause and Alyssa resisted filling it.

"Well," said Sue, "I guess I'll go."

"I do have lots of work to do," said Alyssa.

"On Sunday?"

"In the summer, this whole part of the state hops on Sunday afternoons. I've got most of the day so I'm going to hit the far reaches and see if I can round up some clients." She needed a day to focus on this. And a day away from Sue.

"Well, okay."

Alyssa could hear the discomfort in Sue's voice. "Look. I've got your cell phone. I promised I'd call if anything happened, right?"

"Right."

"So, trust me. If I don't call I'll see you tomorrow at the office."

Alyssa hung up and leaned against the counter while her mind settled. She wasn't sure she liked Sue's checking up on her. On the other hand, she wasn't sure she didn't like it either. She definitely needed a day to herself.

She showered and dressed and at 12:30 headed out of the house. First stop, the Braeburns'. If anyone had a pulse on the summer community, it was Samantha Braeburn.

The Braeburns' summer place was an impressive three-story brick home towering behind an echoing pillared porch. No chairs or swings or plants. Just empty stone. A wrought-iron lamp as big as a tree trunk hung from the patterned ceiling high above her head. *If that thing fell*, she thought as she looked upward, *it would split me in two.*

She rang the doorbell and glanced at the colorful, manicured gardens. They'd built this place in the middle of acres of woods on a high bluff overlooking Lake Michigan. A manufactured cobblestone path led from the porch through a flawless lawn to the circular drive. The perfect turf ended in the thick scrubby woods that grew on the backside of the dune.

She heard steps and took a deep breath.

Samantha Braeburn opened the carved wooden door and blinked mascaraed eyes at Alyssa. Then she smiled, her bright red lipstick

91

outlining white teeth. "I know you." Her voice floated outward from the house.

"I'm Alyssa Norland, the dog trainer working with Adam and Buck." She extended her hand.

Samantha grasped Alyssa's fingertips with her own heavily ringed ones and gave a quick squeeze. "Of course. The lesbian."

Alyssa kept her gaze steady. Was her sexuality an issue?

"Calvin has already left for Evanston. He has to work this week. He'll be back here on Friday." Samantha blinked again and held her hand up to examine her rings. She made no move to invite Alyssa in.

Alyssa forged ahead. "That's okay. I was in the area and thought I'd stop by and see how Adam was doing with yesterday's lesson."

The woman acted as if she'd never seen her own jewels before. She couldn't take her eyes off them. "Adam," she said without looking up, "is in the media room cleaning the carpet." She brought a hand to her face and pinched the bridge of her nose. "That dog had an accident. I told him to get it clean. I told his father to call the fencing people and get a kennel built. Dogs belong outdoors." Samantha looked up and smiled, then returned her gaze to her large-stoned rings. "Would you like to come in?"

Alyssa wanted to burst out of her skin and retreat. But she said, "I'd like that," and smiled. "Let me run to my car first. I have some special carpet cleaner that might help."

Samantha's eyebrows arched, and she twisted her hand so that the sun caught her rings at a new angle. "Yes, you would. Fine."

Alyssa grabbed her bag of cleaning supplies from the back of the Jeep and rejoined Samantha who waited in the doorway.

"Adam will be glad to see you," Samantha said. "I'm afraid I'm peevish about my carpet." She led Alyssa into a marble-floored foyer. "When that dog is outside permanently things will be fine."

Alyssa doubted it. She followed Samantha through a formal living room with a hardwood floor and an ivory Oriental rug, down a hall carpeted in white Berber. *God spare all children and puppies from growing up in houses with white carpets.*

Samantha led her into a room dominated by a widescreen TV.

Dwarfed by the nearby speakers, Adam crouched in the middle of the room with a bowl of water and a roll of paper towels.

"I'm almost done, Mom." His worried face relaxed into a delighted smile when he looked up. "Miss Norland!" He instantly looked sober again and glanced at his mother. "Buck was bad."

"I see he had an accident," Alyssa said, kneeling beside him. The brown stain on the carpet was quite small. "We'll get this fixed in no time."

The enzyme stain remover did the trick and in a few minutes the carpet looked like new.

"See, Mom," Adam said. "It's gone!"

Samantha squatted down in her tight red skirt and ran her ringed hand over the damp spot. "Indeed. Did you thank your friend?"

Adam blinked at Alyssa. "Thank you, Miss Norland."

Alyssa winked at him. "You're welcome. And I'll leave this cleaner with your mom in case it happens again."

Samantha stood and Alyssa did too. "Adam," his mother began, "please run upstairs and play a computer game."

Adam looked like he'd rather stay here and do whatever the grownups were going to do, but he nodded. "Okay."

"See you Wednesday evening, Adam," Alyssa said as he ran from the room. "You have a terrific son, Samantha."

"Yes." Samantha walked to a dark oak cabinet and swung open the doors, exposing a dazzling array of bottles and crystal. "You know, Miss Norland, I have a few homosexual friends back in Evanston. Most are partnered."

Alyssa smiled. *What's the point?*

"Would you like a drink?"

Considering that she planned to spend the day talking to people, Alyssa did not. "Just some juice?"

Samantha shrugged and bent down. A mini refrigerator hid behind the cabinet's lower door. "Tomato?"

Alyssa dreaded drinking red juice on this white carpet, but she felt sure Samantha would read no as rude. "Sure, thanks."

While Samantha poured, Alyssa studied the room. Home theater system, leather-bound books, brass lamps with leaded glass shades. All very beautiful and all very cold.

"You have a beautiful home here," she said as she accepted the tumbler from Samantha.

"Yes." Samantha poured herself a tumbler of vodka then added a splash of tonic and some lime. "It keeps me busy." She pointed to the spot on the carpet. "Cleaning, you know. And keeping up with Adam."

Alyssa didn't see how either of those things kept Samantha busy at all. She wasn't sure what did. Though her face looked hard, Samantha couldn't have been much older than forty. What did she do with her time? "Have you thought about having Buck trained as a guard dog for your home?" She sipped her juice.

Samantha's eyes opened wide, an expression accentuated by her makeup. "Of course. That's why we got him. I'd never have a dog in the house otherwise." She screwed up her face. "The dirt!" She sipped her drink, then raised it, studying the crystal in comparison with her rings. "But it makes Adam happy. And keeps him busy when he isn't off playing with the other children on the beach."

"I'm glad Buck is working out for your family," Alyssa said. "You'll want him to grow up well-mannered, like your son."

Samantha smiled. "Of course."

"I'd like to suggest, then, that you will have more success if you don't keep Buck in an outdoor kennel."

The other woman looked puzzled. "But if he's outside, he can't make mischief in the house."

Alyssa nodded. "True. But he can't learn any manners if you keep him isolated. A little patience, love and the right tools"—she patted the bottle of cleaning fluid—"and you'll get the dog you want. And still have a beautiful home."

"I have found that patience often leads to bigger problems," Samantha said, her face serious as she drained her glass. "Still," she continued, pouring herself another cocktail, "I can see what you mean about isolation." Her thumb twisted her wedding ring and the diamond next to it. "Isolation is no good."

I'm not going there, Alyssa thought. *Just stay focused on helping the dog.*

"I'll be glad to help with Buck in any way, Samantha. I can give Adam private lessons if you like."

Samantha smiled. She could be beautiful, Alyssa thought, if she weren't so sad.

"You're a nice person, Alyssa. Adam talks a lot about you."

"Thanks. I'm a good trainer too. In fact, I'm hoping you would think it appropriate to recommend me to some of your friends."

"My friends?" She looked confused.

"Yes. Your friends, neighbors. Anyone who, like you, is interested in the security of their home. Dogs bring love and loyalty into a home. And they don't quit working during an electrical storm like many security systems." She pulled several business cards from her pocket. "I'm looking to expand my client list and word-of-mouth is the best way."

Samantha took the cards. "You might try the Blue Seahorse. I'm there most afternoons." She actually smiled. "With Calvin gone and Adam playing, it's good for me to get out. A lot of the wives do it." She fingered the cards. "Marcus Dixon has been in there once or twice, charming the ladies. Maybe you'd step on his toes if you came?"

"We work together," Alyssa said, "for the business. We don't stake out separate client lists. He put me in charge of increasing business, so I'm sure he wouldn't mind. It's a great idea. Thanks."

Samantha nodded, her eyebrows lowered in thought. "I have a charity event this evening. I'll mention you there if I can. Everyone will be talking about the robbery, you know. How silly it was for Delia to keep that jewelry in a house." She paused. "I'm going unescorted."

Alyssa thought of several replies but just nodded.

"Cal wanted to keep Adam from your class yesterday but I wouldn't hear of it." Samantha fingered the cards again. "Not yet."

"Thanks for your support." Alyssa shifted her weight to head for the door but Samantha stepped in front of her.

"I've been wanting to ask you something." She blinked. "Adam tells me you don't have a dog. That seems very strange. I'd rather not have one, but I do. You love them but haven't got one. Why?"

That caught Alyssa off guard. "My dog died." Why did Samantha care?

"Yes, but there are others. You preach that dogs bring love and loyalty into a home. So why haven't you done that for yourself?"

"I—"

"And you're single," Samantha interrupted. "All alone in the world. Are you really that strong? Or is it just easier since you're gay?" She reached for the vodka bottle again.

Oh, for God's sake, Alyssa thought. Not the gay-people-don't-commit song again. She swallowed the last of her tomato juice.

"Or could it be that, gay or not, you don't really believe in love and loyalty? Like me?" She poured herself another drink.

"No. I believe in those things." She did, she was sure of it. She wasn't like Samantha Braeburn at all.

"All right. But there are plenty of gay people in the area and you're open about it, so surely you aren't going to tell me you simply haven't had time to date."

Actually, Alyssa had thought exactly that.

Samantha's thin lips stretched into a weak smile. "I tell you what. I believe in Adam. He has more love and loyalty than either of us." She raised her glass in salute. "I'll be happy to recommend you to my friends, for his sake. After all, we are kindred spirits." She finished her drink with two swallows. "Now let me show you out."

The rest of Sunday flew by as Alyssa drove up to Leelanau and spoke to people in the shops and restaurants. They hadn't heard about the burglary and many were willing to spread the word about DOGS to their customers if Alyssa would do the same for them. She returned home that evening with a bag full of business cards and brochures and a pound of dark Sumatran decaf from her favorite coffee roasters.

The night passed quietly except for a few enticing dreams. The next morning the phone repair folks showed up at 8:00 so Alyssa headed to the office. She thought she could write up a report on her weekend activities for Marcus before she had to leave for the Golden Eagle Day Camp.

A little while later, Alyssa looked up from the notes on her desk as she heard a car pull into the DOGS parking lot. She saw Zero's head hanging out of the side window of Sue's wagon, pointed nose-first into the wind, looking for all the world like a misplaced hood ornament.

She glanced at her watch as she rose: 9:26. She smiled. Right on time.

Alyssa moved through the old cottage into the kitchen area, where coffee brewed and where Sue would enter through the back door. She was glad she'd had another uninterrupted night's sleep. She felt a whole lot better than she did the last time she saw Sue.

Alyssa poured two fresh cups of coffee and felt the warmth rise from the mugs. She remembered the dreams that laced through her sleep, of Sue lying warm against her. She could still feel Sue's imagined fingers exploring her body, and fresh desire curled through her.

She swallowed with anticipation as she heard Sue's steps on the stairs. *Keep cool. Just smile to welcome her.*

The back door swung open and she raised the cups as Zero and Sue entered.

Zero saw her and leapt, pulling the leash from Sue's hands.

"No!" Sue shouted, too late.

Zero landed his front feet high on Alyssa's shoulders. She tipped back against the countertop, and her hand shoved a mug into the steel sink. She heard it crack as she brought her knee up. As Zero leaned into her, her knee hit his chest and he fell back with a look of surprise.

Sue surveyed the situation. "So much for Saturday night's training."

Alyssa looked at the dog, then at his owner. "Being with you is always so action-packed."

Sue cocked her head. "Actually, I'm steady Eddy. I thought all this commotion was your doing."

Alyssa turned to the sink where one DOGS mug lay split. "Not me. My life was calm until you showed up."

Sue came up close behind her. "Do you prefer a dull existence?"

"Not dull, no." Alyssa rinsed the sink, then reached above for a new mug. Sue's long hands pressed past Alyssa's hips, stopping at her belly.

Alyssa set the mugs in the sink. She should stop this now. But she didn't move.

"I didn't think so." Sue pulled closer, leaning against Alyssa's back. "I haven't stopped thinking about you." Her breath skirted the skin on Alyssa's neck. "How much you taught me on the beach. The idea of you all alone in the dark for two nights. I hated it."

"I was fine," Alyssa said. Heat spiraled from her spine into her legs. *Weak-kneed. Like some damn ingénue.*

Sue sighed. "I'm sure you were." Her lips brushed behind Alyssa's ear. "No nasty visitors?"

"No." Alyssa shivered against the touch.

"So you didn't wish I was there?"

"No," she lied. *Only all night.* She'd managed not to think about Sue much all day, but as she dozed in bed she thought of Sue's broad shoulders and long legs and how they would feel next to her. And then the dreams. She'd woken up full of a desire she couldn't shake, and now Sue wasn't helping.

"Well, I wanted to be with you."

Alyssa took a deep breath. "Would you like a cup of coffee?"

"I can think of something else I'd rather taste." Sue kissed the back of her neck.

Alyssa turned around, laughing. "Sue, what has gotten into you so early this morning?"

Sue looked serious. "The need to get into you."

Sweet Jesus. Yearning blossomed in Alyssa's center. "The coffee will get cold," she said.

Sue reached over and took the mugs from her, then placed them on the countertop. "You were beautiful on the beach."

Alyssa touched Sue's chest just below her neck, felt the muscle there rise and fall with her breath. Desire swirled in Sue's eyes as her hands trailed up Alyssa's shirt.

"You were part of the landscape, glowing and powerful," Sue continued as her thumbs lifted the weight of Alyssa's breasts. "I've never seen a woman like that."

Powerful. No one had ever said such a thing to Alyssa in her life. She felt powerful too, with Sue's hands moving slowly upward. She tingled under the circling pressure and leaned into Sue.

"Kiss me," Sue said.

"Don't order me—"

Sue pressed her lips against hers and Alyssa felt the surge of knowing that she had never wanted anyone this much in her life.

"Maybe that wasn't an order, but more of a request," Alyssa murmured.

"Uh-huh," Sue replied without moving away.

"I guess I could honor a request." Alyssa's lips parted and she tasted the sweet corners of Sue's mouth. Then Sue kissed her harder.

"Yes," Alyssa whispered. The longing surprised her, coming from someplace deep, beyond her thinking.

Sue's hand dropped, then returned under Alyssa's shirt, fingers soft against her back. She pressed her hips into Alyssa's gently, and suddenly Alyssa felt Sue everywhere, and needed her even closer.

In fact, she needed Sue naked. *Now.*

Alyssa felt cool air over her breast as Sue pulled her bra down. Sue rolled one nipple between her fingers and Alyssa's knees really did go weak.

Alyssa's brain struggled to think through the white heat. *Floor? Table? Desk? Where?*

Behind the pounding of her heart, she heard the sound of tires on gravel.

"Shit!" she said, pushing Sue away and hitching her bra back into place.

A car door slammed and her cloud of passion cleared almost instantly. "It's Marcus." Zero jumped up, ears forward to listen to the stranger approaching.

"What time are you done tonight?" Sue asked, her face full of desire.

"Six or six thirty." Alyssa shoved a cup of coffee into Sue's hands.

"I'll work hard. Get done early and come by." She smiled. "I'll bring salmon filets."

Alyssa's head swirled. If she came, they would never make it through dinner before they wound up in bed. That could be bad.

Or very, very good.

She heard footsteps on the back stairs, and grabbed a cup of her own. If it weren't for Marcus, she'd be naked on a table by now.

"Can we talk about it later?" Alyssa asked.

Marcus entered carrying a briefcase and a bundle of leather leashes. Hendrix bounded in and greeted Zero then Alyssa.

Marcus's pale blue eyes darted around the kitchen. "Ah, Ms. Hunter. Glad to see you." He bent to pat Zero. "Your dog?"

"All mine."

Marcus nodded to Alyssa. "Did you sleep well?" He crossed through the kitchen's double doors into their shared office area.

"Yes." Alyssa rubbed the soft yellow fur behind Hendrix's ears and tried to catch Sue's eye to tell her to leave.

"Good," her boss said from the other room, then reentered the kitchen without his bag. "It was probably the last time for a while." He stood with his arms folded, obviously prepared to announce something that had not pleased him.

"Why?" Alyssa asked.

He blinked across his long nose at her, glanced at Sue, then back to her. "The Braeburns were robbed last night."

Chapter Ten

Alyssa closed her eyes against the sudden rush of blood to her ears. "Oh, no."

"When?" asked Sue.

"They think around midnight. Adam was at a friend's house, and Samantha was at some charity function in Glen Arbor."

"What was taken?" asked Sue.

"Cal's grandmother's crystal, a painting, whatever of Samantha's jewelry she didn't have on or in the safe. Cal said it was the first time he was glad his wife wears so much of the stuff at once."

Alyssa remembered how Samantha had stared at her own rings. "The puppy?"

"Fine, I gather. Cal wasn't focused on that when he called me at three this morning, livid, on his way back from Illinois."

"Why'd he call you?" Sue asked.

Marcus stared at her. "Because Alyssa works for me. And she was at the house yesterday afternoon. He thinks I should fire her." He slid his gaze toward Alyssa, checking her reaction.

She wouldn't blame him if he did.

"Fire her? Why?"

"Because she's the only connection."

Alyssa felt the weight of his statement. He was right.

"That's ridiculous," Sue interjected, stepping closer to Alyssa. "They don't even have a guard dog like Delia. How'd they get into the house? Was it professional?"

"Samantha swears she set the alarm, but it never went off. Calvin said something about a broken window in the French doors." Marcus shook his head at Alyssa. "You were *there* yesterday. For God's sake, Alyssa, what were you doing there?"

"Networking for new clients!" She pointed to him. "At your request."

"Hey!" Marcus's voice sounded squeezed and sharp. "I never sent you to the Braeburns."

"Whoa, whoa." Sue held a hand between them. "Relax. This isn't helping anyone."

Marcus sighed. "It's just that you're training their pup. And you're close to Adam. Calvin claims the boy would have told you anything, including where his mother kept her stuff. And he says she served you a drink, so you saw the crystal."

"I don't know anything about the Braeburns' valuables. Did anyone even ask Adam if we ever talked about jewelry? Or a painting?" The room had grown hot.

"I tried to defend you," Marcus said, "but it was damned hard when Calvin pointed out you'd been through the house."

"Hardly through the house," Alyssa said, crossing her arms. "Samantha couldn't get a stain out of the carpet, so I offered to show her."

"Invited yourself in to case the joint, Calvin claims."

"Did he say that to the police?" Sue asked.

Marcus pursed his lips tight. "I imagine. He said it to me. I didn't point out that Samantha's condition certainly made it all uncertain."

"Condition?" Sue turned to Alyssa but Marcus answered before she could.

"Samantha Braeburn is an expensive drunk," Marcus said. The whole town knows it. She drinks at the Blue Seahorse most afternoons and starts earlier at home, I hear."

"Then she can't be trusted when she says she set the alarm," Sue said.

"I know she had started drinking before noon yesterday," Alyssa confirmed, "because when I saw her she was already tipsy."

"Well"—Marcus raised his arms in a gesture of hopelessness—"just remember to tell that to Strunk."

Alyssa tried to swallow but her tongue stuck to the inside of her lower lip. "Is he coming here?"

Marcus looked at the ceiling in exasperation. "I hope not. You have camp in an hour and I have three clients and a vendor. Cops don't make a good impression."

Alyssa stepped toward him. "Marcus, I am so sorry."

"Alyssa, it's not your fault," came Sue's voice, low, behind her.

She turned to her. "I know. But the business." She turned back to Marcus. "I don't know what I can do."

"Me either, hon." He smacked his hands together and rubbed them against each other. "You could leave town until things get quiet, but that wouldn't look good."

"No, it wouldn't," Sue said.

"Of course, people talked enough after the burglary at Delia's," Marcus continued, "but with Calvin storming around town accusing you . . ." His voice trailed off.

Alyssa's head thrummed. Both Strunk and Calvin Braeburn accusing her?

"Aren't you overreacting?" Sue asked. Alyssa felt Sue's hand firm against the center of her back.

Marcus drew himself up. "No, I don't think so." He smiled, his lips stretched across his teeth. "You're new here, Ms. Hunter, and haven't learned how things work. Bad news moves through this town faster than a thunderstorm off the lake."

"He's right," Alyssa admitted. "I deal with a lot of sensitive information about people's lives and property. A solid reputation is crucial."

"Then you have to talk to the police," Sue said. "Both of you. Tell them about the situation at the Braeburns' and why you were there." Her finger tapped against Alyssa's spine. "Tell them everything that's been going on."

Alyssa knew Sue meant the cut phone line and the note at her house.

"Yes," Marcus said. "Talk to the police. Just try not to do it here, okay?" He walked toward the swinging doors. "Police start digging around and all kinds of stuff comes up that's best forgotten." He left the kitchen.

"Only if you have garbage to hide," Sue said after him. She stepped around Alyssa, shaking her head. "You've got to talk to the police," she whispered. "This is nuts."

Alyssa wondered what expression Sue's soft brown eyes would hold if she knew Alyssa had broken into the labs at Covington Enterprises and stolen a dog. That she'd been arrested for theft? Would she, or any potential client, understand that the charges against her had been dropped? Or would they remember only that she'd worked for a company that stole dogs, that she herself had stolen someone else's?

She couldn't risk it.

"Alyssa?" Sue waited for her reply.

"I gotta get over to the camp. Hey, Hendrix, let's go." She headed to her desk for her training bag.

"We'll talk later," Marcus said as she walked by his desk.

So much for increasing my client load, she thought, and without even glancing at Sue, she strode through the kitchen and out the door. When she reached her car, Alyssa reached down, unclipped Sue's cell phone from her waistband and held it out. "Thanks for letting me use it." She forced a smile. "Don't worry about me today, okay? You need to get on with what you came here for. Work. Or play. Water

104

and woods, remember? It's a beautiful day. Work the dog. Go kayaking. Enjoy yourself."

Sue didn't move. "I do have a lot of work to do. In fact, I packed my laptop in case I decided to keep my eye on you."

"Not necessary."

"You sure?"

"Yes." She felt like she had too many eyes on her as it was.

"Okay. Promise you'll call me tonight," she said. "So I know your phone's working."

That seems fair, Alyssa thought, *a kind of truce*. "I will. And we'll set up a time to work Zero again."

"Deal." Sue took the phone and clipped it to her belt. Zero, sensing something was about to happen, stood beside his owner. "Except for one part. I *will* be worrying about you."

Alyssa watched Sue walk around her car.

What an ass. She has to have the last word.

Of course, she thought, Sue's last word had been "you." Meaning her. That made her feel warm, even though she wasn't sure she wanted Sue thinking about her.

She saw Sue's shoulders stiffen with frustration as she unlocked the car door and let Zero in. And she had to admit she'd never seen a pair of jeans look better.

She climbed into the Jeep and found her sunglasses on the dash. Not a bad day for a session at camp. The sun shone white under a sky filled with high, light clouds.

Who was she kidding? The day sucked. And it wasn't even noon. The Braeburns were robbed. She hadn't had time to absorb it. She was glad Adam hadn't been home last night. And Buck would be some comfort to him.

She started the car and headed out the drive. She should drive over there. Surely Calvin would listen to her if she explained about the carpet and about needing new clients.

She braked at the end of the drive. *Today is not the best day to talk to him about that.*

She'd talk to Sue tonight. She'd been a cop, so maybe she'd come up with a plan, if she spent the afternoon thinking about her.

She thought of Sue's touch then shook her head. That feeling was amazing! Somehow it made all the rest of this horror bearable.

She pushed on the gas pedal and the car leapt ahead. She had a few hours free after camp. Maybe she'd spend some of it thinking about Sue too.

Alyssa and Hendrix met the director of the Glen Arbor animal shelter at Golden Eagle Summer Camp. He brought three dogs and after she did an obedience demonstration with Marcus's dog, she taught the kids the basics of grooming and safety around unfamiliar dogs.

Then she stopped to see Dr. Lindsey, the vet, who told her he'd be happy to recommend her to his clients and to other vets. He also told her that Teddy had not been drugged or injured in any way that he could discover, and he had already reported that to Deputy Strunk who had called early that morning.

She had known Deputy Strunk would gather no moss.

Then she stopped at her physician's office. His nurse told her that Strunk had called four times wanting a report on her hand. The doctor was only too happy to get the deputy off his back so he saw her immediately. He proclaimed her hand uninfected and in no way a dog bite.

Unsure what to expect, Alyssa returned to the office shortly after 4:00. She sighed her relief when she saw only Marcus's van in the lot. God, how she hated this. She had loved her job and looked forward to coming every day. All of this had taken her joy away.

Hendrix bounded across the yard and up the steps where he stood waiting to be let in, golden tail wagging. Marcus was probably right. She did need a dog of her own. Someone to keep her company. To sleep with at night.

She thought again of Sue and how abruptly she'd left her this morning. The kiss. Those touches. And then the news about the Braeburns. It had just been too much.

As she opened the office door, she wondered if Sue still planned to bring that salmon for dinner. Should she call her or leave well enough alone?

"Alyssa!" The door swung shut behind her as Marcus hurried into the kitchen from the office. "I need to talk to you." He gestured back toward the office.

Alyssa followed him through the swinging doors to his desk and sat in the client chair. "Hendrix was great at camp."

"Great. Right." He sat, his fingers tapping against the desk. "Alyssa, I don't know how to start. I did what I had to do," he whispered, looking around as if he didn't want to be overheard. "My first concern has to be the business, you know that."

Alyssa struggled to keep her voice natural. "What happened?"

He flattened his palms on the desk. "Just remember, you are not the business, Alyssa. It belongs to me."

Alyssa felt fear and rage prick up her spine. "Sounds like you're ready to sacrifice me. What happened?"

He did not look away. "Cal Braeburn's threatening to sue me for employing you. I heard from his attorney today. I have to do what's best for my business, Alyssa. You know that, so don't argue."

"Supporting me and my innocence would be best for business, Marcus. I didn't do anything wrong."

He sighed and rubbed his hands together. "Alyssa, think realistically. You weren't bringing in enough before and this is sure to cost you clients." He tugged again at his waistline. "I want you to consider resigning."

Alyssa felt everything in her body stop. "What?"

"Don't be dramatic. You heard me. It'll be best for the business. And for you." His eyes narrowed. "Better than if I fire you."

"Fire me! Are you firing me?"

He shook his head. "No. Not yet. Cal's a pain in the ass and I won't give him the satisfaction. At least not today."

107

She looked at Marcus, seeing him as if for the first time. His gray hair swept back from his face neatly. He had alert eyes in a rounded face. She'd watched him work. He was a terrific dog trainer and a smart businessman. He could be a hard-driving boss, but he'd given her a great opportunity and he ran a tight ship. She appreciated that.

"Look. I know you have to put your business first. I also know my work could help your business."

He remained silent.

"So I'm not going to resign. That would look like an admission of guilt. I'm going to go on just as I always have. I'm innocent. People will respond to that when the real criminals are found."

Marcus sighed. "Alyssa, people have long memories. Innocent or not, your connection to this—to any crime—will cost clients. We can't afford that."

Alyssa pulled her hair from her face. If he knew about Chicago he'd surely fire her. "I am not involved."

He laughed. "Oh, yes, you are, honey. You're smack in the middle of it, and the sooner you realize it, the sooner you can do something about it."

"My reputation is stronger than this." She hoped it was true.

"You think so?" He shrugged. "Okay. I guess you'll prove it by getting those new clients. Plus making up for any existing clients we lose."

"No problem." Her gaze shifted to her hands. She had no idea how she could pull this off.

"I don't know how you're going to do it with this hanging over your head."

"It's not hanging over my head. I'm innocent." She pulled her neck to the right to stretch it. "You sound like you want me to fail."

"Hey," said Marcus, pointing at her. "Don't accuse me of that. No other trainer would have you with something like this. As if the dog's failure wasn't enough, potential involvement in a burglary? Come on, Alyssa. If I weren't on your side, I'd fire you now."

She believed him. "Well, thanks for not firing me."

"Public image is everything. Get the clients, if you can." He rose, indicating the conversation had ended. "Now I have a client coming at four-thirty. It would be best if you went home."

Sue's kayak whispered through the calm lake water, trailing bright ripples. Sweat rolled over her torso as she pulled her paddle through the water, puffing with each rhythmic stroke. As she glided toward the beach, she focused on the resistance of water against wood.

Sort of like Alyssa's resistance against her.

She'd left the DOGS office worried but couldn't figure out where to go. She didn't want to talk to Strunk. She'd talked to Delia briefly. Sue's report of the conversation with Braeburn upset Delia, and she worked her anxiety out by fussing over the fingerprint dust left throughout her house. She announced it the perfect day for a cleaning marathon and suggested Sue call Melanie Sybesma for more information about the investigation. Then she began to attack her house with cloth and dusting spray.

Melanie hadn't been home, which didn't surprise Sue. She hadn't yet returned Sue's calls.

She thought she might hear more if she went into town, so she took her laptop into the Twelve Point around 1:00. A woman tended bar this afternoon and once the lunch group thinned, Sue found herself one of only three patrons. She didn't recognize the others and they never spoke, not even to the bartender, who just automatically provided new drinks. She didn't find out a thing but she got a lot of work done for the cherry growers.

Shortly after 4:00 she returned home and met Delia in the driveway with a bucket of sinister-looking cleaning supplies.

"I finished my own place," Delia said, trying in vain to contain her fly-away hair inside a kerchief, "and I hosed out the garage. So don't pull in just yet, it's still wet. I thought now I'd start on your place."

Sue protested that she hadn't hired Delia to clean, but Delia insisted. "I'm on a roll, honey. Don't get in my way." Sue decided that was good advice and to go for a long workout.

A nice, calm afternoon. Just what she wanted.

Right.

Sweat trickled into her eyes and stung. She hadn't been calm because she couldn't forget Alyssa's response to her touch. Not for one minute, all day. She could feel Alyssa beneath her fingers even now.

Sue spun the kayak away from the beach and pulled harder on her strokes.

She'd better burn off a little more energy, in case she saw Alyssa later tonight. Otherwise, she feared what she might do.

Oh, what we might do.

Sue wanted Alyssa's fear to go away so they could do those things. And this time Sue could help. This wasn't like her mother's fear.

Sue paddled the boat around again and this time stroked hard all the way to the beach.

The kayak's nose shushed onto the sand, and Sue slid up and out of the boat. The cool lake water splashed against her calves as she pulled the kayak across the beach and flipped it upside down under the high wooden staircase that ran up the dune to Delia's house.

She grabbed her empty water bottle and began to climb the 100-plus steps to the top. She hoped Delia had finished in the apartment by now so she could shower and see about dinner.

As Sue climbed she thought about Alyssa. That morning she'd wanted to make love to her and knew she had wanted it too.

But when they did make love, she wanted no fear in Alyssa's eyes. Just desire.

Sue stepped onto the broad deck at the top of the stairs and turned west for a last view of the lake.

I could date her without getting involved in this case, she thought. Why not just let the cops handle it?

The sunlight sparkled on the water below, dancing a bright code. And she could read it clearly.

Because I am a cop. And because I'm falling in love with her.

The thought didn't scare her. She felt better, actually. Like some of that sunlight was in her.

That thought scared her. Next she'd be writing poetry.

Maybe after she cleaned up she'd call Alyssa and see if she should still come by with those salmon steaks. She could check the weather-stripping around the new front door.

Anything to be with her again.

Sue hurried along the boardwalk which circled the main house. She smelled something burning a second before she saw black smoke feathering upward from an open window of her apartment.

"Delia!"

Sue dropped her gear and ran across the yard. Flames licked at the inside of the window frame. "Delia! Zero!"

She took the steps up to her apartment two at a time, praying aloud her hope that they weren't in that hell.

Chapter Eleven

A cedar Adirondack chair on the landing had tipped over, blocking the front door. Sue yanked it out of the way, then laid her hand against the door that led into the galley kitchen, checking for heat. She didn't want to flood the fire with fresh oxygen.

But the door felt cool, so she pushed it inward and ducked as a wave of thick black smoke billowed out.

"Delia! Zero!" She yanked her T-shirt up over her nose and mouth and, crouching, crawled into the kitchen. The muddied glow of the flames ahead in the dining room grew with the new air. The heat slapped against the bare skin of her forehead, arms and shins. "Zero, come!" She didn't know how far she could go into the apartment before the smoke would force her back.

She heard weak coughing from somewhere ahead. "Delia!" Sue crawled a few more feet, the heat growing. Her eyes burned and watered, and she paused to let a fit of her own coughing subside. *Make this count*, she told herself. *Not much time.*

She reached up and tested the door on the right, which led into the main bathroom. Not too hot. Slowly she swung it open. Delia lay slumped against the edge of the tub with Zero next to her, his head across her thigh. He wagged his tail once when he saw his owner.

Sue stood, bending low. "Delia, let's go."

Delia coughed again and her head lolled.

Sue grabbed her under the arms and dragged her backward. Coughs tore through her lungs at the effort and she stumbled.

"Zero, come." She choked, backing away.

Sue pulled Delia onto the porch where she sucked in clean air. She hefted Delia's tiny body over her shoulder and carried her down the stairs, then lowered her to the lawn. Delia shuddered with coughs.

Good. She was breathing.

Sue looked around, but Zero hadn't followed. She ran back up the steps to the apartment, where smoke curled thick and black over the top of the doorjamb. Sue flew forward onto her belly, eyes closed against the poison air. She felt her way against the wall with a shoulder, until she found the bathroom doorway.

Blinking her eyes rapidly, she spotted the dog lying on his side. "Come on, boy," she urged, reaching forward to grab the dog's front legs. She inched backwards on elbows and knees, pulling Zero to the porch. Then she carried the dog down the stairs and laid him next to Delia.

Delia opened her eyes. "Don't . . . phone . . . Teddy." Delia coughed until she gagged, then closed her eyes again.

"I'll get help," Sue said, throat burning. But she already heard a siren in the distance.

Behind her, a window shattered and flames spiraled out of the apartment. As Sue felt Zero's chest for a heartbeat, the sky darkened with new smoke.

Delia choked and gasped for air and Sue rested her other hand against Delia's wrist. Pulse rapid, but steady.

She remembered the night when she was ten, when her mother first slipped into a coma from her cancer. Sue had knelt beside her in the circle of light from the bedside lamp, begging her to live. Mom had rallied and come home for those last few weeks. *Please*, Sue thought now, watching her friends struggle, *please hang on*.

Just after 7:30 p.m., Alyssa burst through the double doors into the emergency room waiting area where Sue sat alone in an orange vinyl chair.

"Melanie called me." Alyssa wanted to weep from joy. Sue was okay.

Alyssa sat in a blue chair next to Sue and smelled smoke. Black smudges crossed her face and neck. Raw spots glared from her bare knees where blood had caked over golfball-sized scrapes.

Alyssa rested a hand on Sue's thigh. "How's Delia?"

"I haven't heard."

Sue sounded sick with fear. Alyssa leaned closer, wiped a smudge from the corner of Sue's eye. "She's just got to be fine."

"People die, Alyssa. Even in hospitals."

"Well, not tonight they don't." She squeezed Sue's hand and held it. "You love her a great deal, don't you?"

Sue looked at her, eyes glittering. "Yes. She loved my mom and dad."

"How did they know each other? You said you summered here as a kid."

Sue sighed. "My mother knew Delia and Carolyn when she was young, when they still lived near Detroit. When they moved here, we visited every summer. We were like family."

"You *are* family. Family is who you love," Alyssa said. "Delia is my family too." She squeezed Sue's hand. "So how come no one else around Radley seems to know you?"

"Until this summer, I hadn't been back in twenty-four years. Since I was ten." Sue gazed down the hall again. "My mother died that year."

Alyssa's eyes closed slowly. *Oh, no*. It was too horrible to imagine.

A child, not much older than Adam, without a mother. Her heart ached. "I'm sorry," she whispered.

"I hate hospitals," Sue whispered in return.

Alyssa held Sue's hand in silence while nurses and gurneys whirled by them. This hospital served all the little towns along the lakeshore, and though small, had a strong reputation.

Delia will be fine, she told herself.

"So how was your day?" Sue's light tone steered the conversation in a new direction.

Alyssa followed her lead. "Fine. I managed to avoid Strunk all day. I expect he'll be around to see me soon, though."

"He was at Delia's when we left." Sue shifted in the chair. "Strutting around giving orders to the firemen, who ignored him." She chuckled. "He's sort of an ass. Like me giving orders to you. And you ignoring me."

Alyssa tightened her hand on Sue's. "I wish I could ignore you."

"I wish I could stop ordering you around. But I can't."

Alyssa needed a new subject. "How's Zero?"

Sue looked into the distance. "A paramedic revived him with some oxygen. He seems okay, just a little weak. He's out in the car."

"We'll take him to the vet tomorrow if you want, when things settle down," Alyssa said. She had to stay positive. "Melanie says you're a hero—you got them out."

Sue still stared. "The flames were in the dining room by the deck sliders. I have some candles. Maybe Delia lit one while she was cleaning."

"But why didn't she leave? I mean, she'd have heard the flames, or smelled the smoke, right? Zero must have noticed. Why didn't she get out?"

"A chair had tipped against the door."

A chill crept up Alyssa's neck. "The door was blocked?"

Sue shrugged. "I don't know how it got there."

Someone tipped it over, Alyssa thought. It would be just like Covington to send someone to attack her friend. "Thank heavens you were there," she said. The fluorescent lights reflected off the hospital's spotless linoleum floor, shadowing every line in Sue's face. "You sure you're okay?"

"I look a lot worse than I feel," Sue said.

Alyssa looked down at Sue's sport sandals, nylon shorts and filthy shirt. "Good. Because you look awful."

Sue smiled but did not laugh. "I'll feel better when I know what's going on." The corners of her eyes drooped with worry. "I'll feel better when I go in to see her and she gives me hell for doing something as foolish as saving her from that fire," she said.

Alyssa couldn't help smiling too. That was the sort of thing Delia would say. "How long has it been since you've spoken to someone here? Should I go find a doctor or a nurse?"

As if in response to her question, a doctor with short salt-and-pepper hair entered the room. "Susan Hunter?"

Sue rose and Alyssa followed.

"I'm Dr. Hoffman," he said, shaking their hands. "Delia Watkins insisted I come to find you." He looked a little annoyed. "She is a fussy patient and there's no denying her."

Alyssa felt her shoulders and chest relax with relief. "If Delia's fussing, then she's okay."

Sue touched her hand briefly.

Dr. Hoffman nodded. "Well, she inhaled a lot of smoke." He explained the details of her blood tests and chest scans. "She's physically and emotionally strong, and should recover fully." He went on, "Because of her age I'll keep her here for a few days just to make sure she progresses as we expect."

"Fine," Sue said.

"It looks like you need some care yourself," Dr. Hoffman said, squinting into Sue's swollen eyes. "You look fairly irritated. Did they see you downstairs?"

Sue nodded. "Released me and told me to go home."

"Good advice." He smiled. "But if you could do me a favor first, I'd be grateful."

Sue and Alyssa glanced at each other.

"Ms. Watkins is insisting, loudly, that she be permitted to speak to you. I've explained that visitors are restricted to immediate family, but she has not stopped her demands, even with sedation. I think the best way to calm her down, short of anesthesia, is for you to go speak to her." He grinned. "It's irregular, but it will be better for her health."

"Of course we'll go," Alyssa said.

"Just Ms. Hunter, I'm afraid, ma'am," the doctor said. "That's who she asked for."

Alyssa tried not to feel disappointed.

Sue turned to her. "She doesn't know you're here. That's all. I'll tell her."

"Okay. I'll wait here."

Sue went through the doors with the doctor and Alyssa sat in the orange chair Sue had occupied, feeling the warmth left over from her body. She wanted that warmth next to her. When she'd heard about the fire, she'd been terrified that something had happened to her, that she'd lost Sue before—

Before what?

"Damn," she whispered to herself as she hunkered down into the chair to wait.

In hospitals, Sue always felt ten years old: small, mystified and helpless. The smell of hospital sheets, the squeak and clack of shoes on the linoleum hallways, the blinking green and amber lights glowing on racks of computerized monitors—all nightmare images from the final weeks of her mother's illness. As she walked into Delia's room, her throat tightened. The years had made little difference.

"Ms. Watkins," Dr. Hoffman said, "you are supposed to keep that oxygen mask in place."

"It hurts . . . nose," Delia said. Her voice hitched and she coughed, then looked at the doctor with defiance. Not the fear of

117

approaching darkness that Sue had seen in her mother's eyes, but the light of obstinate life. Relief relaxed her.

"Let her be, Doctor Hoffman." Sue approached the bed. "If she's oxygen-deprived, she won't be able to harass you or the nurses." Sue pulled her face into mock seriousness, and Delia swatted her feebly with an I.V.-attached arm.

The doctor nodded, smiling. "Good point. Better for her recovery in the long run." He tapped his watch. "Two minutes, no more. Then rest." He left the room.

Sue enfolded Delia's thin hand in her own, careful to avoid the needle. She could feel the older woman's bones outlined beneath her flesh.

"You look like you've been through the wars," Delia whispered. With a glance at the door, she placed the oxygen mask over her nose and drew a few deep breaths. "You're a mess," she said with more strength.

"If somebody had bathed me and put me to bed, I'd look as good as you," Sue said.

"How's Zero?"

"Better than you, I think." Sue patted her hand. "He's in the car, resting."

"Teddy," she said. "I put Teddy on guard at the house when I went to the apartment, Sue. Practicing, you know. He's still there. You'll have to get in to get Tango. If the police want in—" She paused for a deep breath. "Don't let them shoot Teddy. Not even with a tranquilizer. He almost died when he was neutered. The anesthetic." Her throat caught over a cough. "Promise me," she managed between spasms. "Get Alyssa to help."

"She's here, Delia, in the waiting room. We'll take care of everything. Now, quit putting up a fuss and use the oxygen like the doctor said."

"Doctors are full of nonsense!" Her emotion brought more abrasive coughs from deep in her chest, and she winced against the pain.

"Use the oxygen," Sue urged.

Delia nodded. "In a minute. How's the building? Your apartment?"

"The apartment's gone. The ground floor isn't as damaged, though, and all the cars looked okay. Smoke and water everywhere, of course."

"All your things!" Delia squeezed Sue's hand. "But don't you worry. Insurance will cover it. In the meantime, buy what you need. I'll write you a check as soon as I get home."

"Thanks, Delia, but I won't need that."

"Of course you will. Have you even thought about what you lost?"

"No." She'd only been thinking about what—or whom—she hadn't lost.

"Well, you will. You'll sleep in the house. And take care of Tango and Teddy." She paused for a breath. "Get my keys from the nurse." She swallowed. "What started it, Sue?"

Sue shook her head. "I don't know. I haven't spoken to the investigators yet. What did you see?"

"Smoke." She reached for a glass of water, and Sue handed it to her, guiding the straw to her mouth. The wrinkles around her eyes creased deeply, her appreciation evident. "I was dusting the bedroom. Zero barked toward the living room windows, but I figured it was a squirrel or such. Didn't bother to look. Then I smelled smoke. By the time I got into the living room, the curtains were burning, and the couch." She paused for a few deep breaths and looked at her. "I never knew smoke filled a room so fast. Even with a window open."

"Fire is scary stuff," Sue said, squeezing Delia's hand again while she coughed.

"I tried to get out but the door was jammed." Her free hand drew up to her chest protectively. "I can tell you, that gave me a start."

Most people would have panicked, Sue thought.

"But I dialed nine-one-one. Then I tried to get out the bathroom window, you know, because it's over the stairs." Violent coughs seized her and she replaced the mask, breathing deeply from it. This time she left it in place. "But I kept coughing and falling down."

"You were very brave, Delia." Sue leaned forward and kissed her forehead. "I'm glad you're still here to infuriate the hospital staff."

Delia closed her eyes, drifting toward sleep. "Me too." Her eyes opened again. "Wait. Sue, promise me. No one should call Carolyn. She'll panic and fly home early. Don't call Carolyn." Her eyes fluttered closed again.

"Don't worry about that now. We can talk more in the morning." Sue wanted to soothe her to sleep.

Delia dragged her eyes open once more. "The dogs. Take care of the dogs."

Sue held her hand, knowing she would sleep soon. "Don't worry."

"Sue," Delia murmured, her eyes still closed, "sorry . . . too many hospitals . . . you . . . kid," and she drifted to sleep.

Sue watched her face relax and comforted herself with the sight of the rhythmic rise and fall of Delia's chest. At least Delia wasn't going to leave her yet. So she better get on with the cleanup. First, Teddy. She'd think about her own stuff later.

Sue released her sleeping friend's hand and went to find Alyssa.

Chapter Twelve

Alyssa parked her car behind Sue's in the corner of Delia's driveway farthest away from the blackened garage. Melanie was securing an end of yellow crime scene tape around a lamppost. The sun hung near the horizon, casting elongated purple shadows across the property.

Alyssa climbed out of her car and the smell of wet ash assaulted her. "Whew!" She shook her head to clear the sticky scent.

"It'll be in your hair for days," Melanie said, approaching. "How's Delia?"

"Good," Alyssa said.

Melanie pointed to Sue, who was talking to Zero through the window of her car. "And how's she?"

"Okay, now that she talked to Delia. Delia sent us out here to take care of the dogs."

"Good. Teddy goes wild anytime anyone approaches the house," said Melanie. "I don't know how any thief got past him."

Alyssa nodded. "Good. Was Strunk here to notice the well-trained guard dog, by any chance?"

Melanie laughed. "Yeah, briefly."

"I take it, then, that our favorite deputy has left for the evening?" Sue asked as she joined them.

Melanie shook her head. " 'Fraid not. Cal Braeburn called the Sheriff over at the county seat, demanding action on his burglary, so Strunk's under pressure to make an arrest. He had to go tend to that. But he'll be back. He wants to talk to you yet tonight."

"So you got stuck here," Alyssa said.

"Guess so. I can't wait to get home and take a shower."

Sue waved a thumb toward the burned-out building. "Why the crime tape?"

"The fire guys suspect arson from the burn patterns. That's why Strunk wants to talk to you."

"Arson?" Alyssa asked.

"Flammable fluid, one of them said," Melanie explained.

"I thought I smelled gasoline," Sue said. "But I wasn't sure with all that smoke."

Alyssa studied the small building, amazed that someone had done this on purpose. The brick outside the first floor looked vandalized on one side, as if buckets of black paint had been poured on the walls from above. Outside the second floor apartment, the white vinyl siding had buckled above the balcony deck. Black streaked upward from the window frames, where smoke had billowed.

Sue must have followed her gaze. "That's the living room," she offered, her voice strangely vacant. "Delia said the fire started there."

Alyssa studied her and wished she knew more about the signs of shock. "Should we leave this until later? Maybe go to my place until—"

"No," said Sue. "I have to see."

Melanie pointed to a strange collection of objects in the lawn. "The guys hauled some stuff out, to douse it good. They took some samples too."

Together the three of them walked up to the stinking array. The smell of wet ash hung heavy in the air. Alyssa thought she could taste it in her throat.

Caked with dried black fire retardant, Delia's truck stood in the middle of the front lawn. Next to it was a sofa charred to the springs on one end. Shreds of melted plastic and fabric clung to what looked like a curtain rod propped against a soaked recliner and a pile of half-burned books.

"My pictures." Sue knelt beside the remains of a large collage frame.

"Sue," said Alyssa. "I'm so sorry."

Sue nodded, picking at the edges of a broken piece of glass.

"I'm not sure about the computer," Melanie said. "The hard drive might be okay. It just got smoky. Tom Graham carried the CPU down instead of pitching it out the window." She pointed to the computer box which stood apart from the mess.

Sue glanced at the computer, then stood. "Okay, then I won't panic about that now." She forced a smile. "And hey, at least my Palm and my laptop are in the car."

"And the car's okay. Why weren't any of them in the garage?" Melanie asked.

"Delia was cleaning," said Sue. "Thank heavens."

"She'll be glad to know her truck survived," said Melanie.

As Alyssa circled the truck, something crunched beneath her feet. "Ew! What is this?"

Sue looked down. "Hunks of my area rug, I think. Synthetics melt."

"What a mess!" Behind her, Alyssa could hear Teddy barking inside the house. A pitch of panic threaded through his warnings.

"Let's take care of the dogs," said Sue.

"I suppose we should," agreed Alyssa. "Teddy's had a lot to contend with tonight. And Tango's in there too."

Melanie looked at Alyssa squarely. "I don't carry a tranquilizer gun. Want me to call county animal control?"

Alyssa shook her head.

123

"Delia doesn't want the dog tranquilized," Sue said. "Something about how he reacted badly to anesthetic."

"Then how will you—" Melanie stopped, then folded her arms. "Oh, Alyssa, I don't like this."

Alyssa didn't like it much either. She pulled her hair back and tightened her ponytail.

"Let me get the tranq gun," Melanie said. "It'll go fine and Delia will never know."

"What if it doesn't?" Alyssa asked.

"No," Sue said. "I promised."

"Easy promise for you to make." The anger in Melanie's voice caught Alyssa off guard. "You aren't going in there with that dog."

Alyssa moved to the back of her Jeep and opened the hatch. "Mel, you took one of Teddy's bites and survived."

"Yeah, with a sleeve."

Alyssa pulled a bite sleeve from her car. "I've got one." She laid it on the ground. "In fact, I've got two."

"You carry this stuff in your car?" asked Sue.

"I'm a dog trainer. Of course." She handed the second sleeve to Melanie. "It'll be fine."

"But you were there to call the dog off after the bite. Who's gonna do that for you?"

Alyssa rolled her eyes, hoping to exude more confidence than she felt. "That's the point, Mel."

"Don't screw with me, Alyssa." Melanie pointed to Sue. "You might fool Sue here, but I know that dog could tear you up. Kill you, even." Melanie turned to Sue. "Did she happen to tell you that?"

"No." Sue turned to look at her, eyes narrowed.

Alyssa exhaled and leaned against her car. "Sue, do you want to break your promise? As Melanie says, Delia might never know if we used a tranq." She glanced at Melanie. "Or, Teddy might react to the drugs and die. Or he could die if the dosage is wrong. Not exactly risk-free."

Sue held up her hands. "I don't think this is my decision to make."

Chicken, Alyssa thought.

"Actually, it's mine," Melanie said. "I'm the officer in charge of the scene right now. I could prohibit you from this."

Alyssa swallowed and put her hands on Melanie's shoulders, holding her at arm's length. "Come on, Mel. The house isn't even part of the crime scene."

Melanie stared at her. "Have you thought about it, Alyssa? You could get hurt, or hurt the dog."

"But I won't. I just have to figure out how to do it."

"Have you thought about what that would prove?" Melanie's hands wrapped around Alyssa's wrists with a tight grip. "It'll prove that you could have broken into the house!" She pushed Alyssa's hands free. "I don't like it at all."

Me either, Alyssa thought. "I'm not going to risk that dog's health, or Sue's promise to Delia, just to look innocent. I'm going to just go ahead as if no one suspected me of anything. Because I am innocent. Okay?"

"There is another way to look at it," Sue said, running her hands through her hair. "If Alyssa can prove how the real thieves might have done it, it could give Strunk a big pointer in the direction of the real criminals. Something to go on that might stop him from hounding Alyssa."

Melanie winced. "'Hounding.' Funny."

"That's me," Alyssa said, her gaze back on Melanie. "Friend to the police. Ever helpful. Junior crime-solver." She paused. "Come on, Mel. Let us do this."

Melanie took a moment to think it through then smiled. "It's pretty stupid." She hugged Alyssa and whispered, "And pretty brave."

"Great," Alyssa said. "You don't have to help. Go home."

"Are you nuts?" Melanie said, her eyes widening. "You need me as a witness."

"We're all set then," said Sue.

Alyssa looked from Melanie to Sue. "Well, there is one thing."

"What?" asked Melanie.

Alyssa glanced at the house, where Teddy's snarling head

appeared above a window sill when he jumped. "I really don't have any idea how to do this."

"Hey, if crooks can do it, so can we," Sue said, stepping forward.

Alyssa leaned into her car. "I brought some other equipment. We can walk through the possibilities."

"What do we have to work with?" Melanie asked.

Alyssa removed three leather leashes, a training collar, a narrow lasso of plastic-coated aircraft cable and a muzzle from her car. She dropped these onto the ground next to the two bite sleeves.

"First," she said to Sue, "let me show you how Teddy has been trained to attack."

She picked up a bite sleeve and handed it to Sue. "The dogs are trained on bite sleeves like this one. The hard plastic inside is reinforced so the bite can't penetrate. The outside is wrapped in cloth to give the dog a soft surface to grip, like flesh."

She watched as Sue inserted her arm into the sleeve. "There's a handle in there for you to grip."

Sue nodded.

"Dogs follow movement. So when taking a bite from a dog, you need to stand still, but wave your arm up and down." Sue moved the sleeve in a wide arc from hip to head.

"Not so much," said Alyssa, demonstrating. "Keep that sleeve between you and the dog."

Sue minimized her movements but kept the sleeve rocking. "Like this?"

"Good," Alyssa said. "The dog will go for the sleeve, not your leg." She crouched, her fingers touching the ground. "Melanie, watch and see if you can think of anything. If I'm a dog the size of Teddy, then I hit like this."

Mimicking a dog in slow motion, Alyssa pulled her fingers from the ground and lunged at Sue's chest. Her hands hit Sue's abdomen, and she stopped just short of biting the sleeve.

Alyssa stood, trailing her fingers down Sue's shirt. She smiled at

126

Sue, then looked at Melanie. "And that's Teddy's game. So what do you guys think?"

"If he's biting the sleeve, can you just drag him out of the house?" Melanie asked. "We could shut him outside after we get in."

"Then we'd have a guard dog running around the property," Alyssa said. "What would we do then?"

"Not a good solution," Melanie said.

"What about forcing him into a small room, like a bathroom?" Sue asked. "If he's latched onto the sleeve, could we push him to a specific spot in the house?"

"That's better," said Melanie.

"It might work," Alyssa said. "But he'd still be on guard. We could get into the house, but we couldn't take care of him." She rubbed her temples, thinking out loud. "We want to get control of him and get his working collar off. Then he'll settle. I think."

Sue brought the sleeve up. "If he bites my sleeve, can you approach behind him and get the collar off?"

Alyssa shook her head. "No. As soon as he felt a touch, he'd release your sleeve and go for me."

"Hey," Melanie said. "What happens if someone with a guard dog needs emergency help, like an ambulance?"

"I heard about that once when I was on the force," Sue said. "A guy had a heart attack in a house with a guard dog. Called nine-one-one, then passed out. When the paramedics got there, they had a cop shoot it. To save the human life."

Melanie winced. "Okay, that is not an option."

Alyssa's brain stirred the possibilities. "There has to be a combination that works. Teddy's trying to get hold of us, so how can we get hold of him?"

Sue put down the sleeve, then picked up the lasso. "What's this?"

"A snare," Alyssa said. "Super-strong aircraft cable, coated in plastic so it doesn't cut. Good for catching dogs, sort of like in a rodeo. I don't know if it will work on one who is attacking. Hard to lasso something moving toward you." *Maybe if two of us went in with sleeves*, she thought.

Sue turned it over, slipped it over her right wrist, then on her bicep. "Strong stuff." She slid it off her right arm and onto her left. "Moves smoothly."

Sue's action gave Alyssa an idea. "Hey, try something with me."

"Okay."

Alyssa looped the snare over her right arm and pulled it up to rest on her shoulder, then put the bite sleeve on. "Go slow now," she said, "and pretend you're the dog like I did."

Sue crouched, then moved toward Alyssa. Her hands met the muscles of Alyssa's abdomen, and she rested her chin against the sleeve, as if biting. With a free hand, Alyssa slid the lasso down over the bite sleeve and around Sue's neck. She then pulled upward, illustrating how that would tighten the snare.

"Hey!" Melanie sounded impressed.

Sue stood up, pulling the snare from around her neck. "Wow. That might work."

The pieces began to snap into place in Alyssa's head. "If I can get the snare around him, then I can control him with it."

"How do you keep him from biting you?" asked Melanie.

Alyssa remembered a technique she had learned in dog school. "I back up and start to spin in a circle, just fast enough so that the centrifugal force keeps him at the end of the line away from me. If he's aggressive, I move faster, and he'll get so dizzy it will knock the fight out of him. Then I'll start to give him obedience commands. He should be disoriented enough to try to obey."

Sue and Melanie looked at her as if she were crazy.

"I know it doesn't sound very good," she explained quickly, "but it works. It's not comfortable for the dog, but it won't injure him and it'll give us the chance we need."

"Won't injure him?" asked Melanie. "It sounds like you're going to hang him. That thing works like a noose."

"Well, it does. But the spin is short and smooth and slow. There isn't very much force against his neck. He won't like it but it won't hurt him. And once he's disoriented, we can get that working collar off."

"Have you ever done this before?" Melanie asked.

Alyssa lifted her shoulders. "Once, in dog school. With an aggressive Dalmatian whose life we were trying to save through rehabilitation."

"Once." Melanie did not sound enthusiastic.

"Melanie," said Alyssa, scolding.

"Sounds good." Sue rubbed her hands. "Tell us what we've got to do."

They took several minutes to iron out the details. Alyssa and Melanie thought Sue should stay with the cars in case something went wrong and she needed to call for help. But she wouldn't hear of it. Sue insisted on going in behind Alyssa.

"I'm close behind Sue then," said Melanie.

"No," said Alyssa. "You stay by the cars in case he gets loose. You'll be safe in a car and can call animal control."

"Wrong," said Melanie, her hands on her hips. "If you insist on trying this, you'll need a witness more than anything. I'm standing right where I can see." She tapped her foot on the ground. "So don't screw up. I wouldn't be able to sleep for a long time if I had to shoot Teddy to save your life."

They agreed that Alyssa, wearing a sleeve and snare, would enter after Sue unlocked the door with her keys. Then Sue would stay behind Alyssa, wearing the second sleeve in case she needed to follow and help.

While Alyssa redid her ponytail, she watched Sue fit her hand into the sleeve, gripping and regripping the handle.

"I know it seems like that lightweight plastic won't hold up against a Rottweiler's jaws," Alyssa said. "But it will."

"If you say so." Sue banged her fist on the sleeve and nodded as if satisfied.

Melanie put her arm around Sue's shoulders. "Look. If that dog comes after you, more than anything else, don't run. He'll go for a leg. Face him and keep that thing moving. And away from your boobs."

"Melanie!" Alyssa said, shocked.

Melanie laughed. "Just a little humor to lighten the moment."

"Thanks." Sue winked at Alyssa.

"I guess she's right." Alyssa picked up her sleeve. "Stay loose and alert. Frankly, Teddy's a deadly weapon right now."

She looked at Sue, who stood in soot-ridden rowing clothes waiting for her. The muscles in her arms and legs seemed coiled in readiness. *She'll be fine.*

"Let's go," Alyssa said, and the others nodded.

As they walked onto the porch, Teddy's barking grew frenetic. Sue propped the storm door open with her body and Alyssa moved in front of her, close.

She felt Sue's lips against the top of her head but did not turn. "Be careful," Alyssa said.

Sue reached around her, turned the key in the lock and opened the door less than an inch.

Teddy's low snarl curled toward them from somewhere on the other side.

Alyssa's heartbeat pulsed through her body, preparing her mind and muscles. She knew a full bite from Teddy had enough pressure per square inch to crush the bones in an unprotected arm or to tear leg muscle from bone.

"Hang on," she replied, shifting the snare around her shoulder, double-checking her grip inside the sleeve.

Sue nudged her with a sleeved arm. "You sure you don't want me to go first?"

"That would be silly, wouldn't it?" Alyssa turned back, but her spark of annoyance fizzled when she saw the concern on Sue's face. "I've been trained for this."

"Just thought I'd offer."

Alyssa placed her hand on the doorknob. "Stay out until I call for you."

Balancing all her weight on her toes, Alyssa raised the heavy sleeve in front of her and shoved the door open wide.

Chapter Thirteen

Teddy's growl remained steady. Alyssa took broad short steps, keeping her weight distributed evenly to reduce her chances of falling when the dog hit.

She had enough time to spot Teddy about ten feet into the shadowed foyer and to her right before he launched. Without thinking, she swung the sleeve in front of the dog and shifted one foot back. The Rottweiler's teeth flashed as he soared toward her, his lips drawn back before the bite.

Alyssa had taken bites a hundred times during her own training, but the sight of a giant dog exploding toward her, his wet mouth stretched to expose rows of sharp white teeth, still blasted terror through her.

Then the dog clamped down on the sleeve, dangled onto his back feet and shook her arm as if his life depended on it. *Good dog*, she thought, and her fear vaporized. This is what she had trained him to do.

Wrestling the sleeve to keep Teddy's attention, Alyssa moved her right hand to her left shoulder to slip the snare lower. *Slowly*, she reminded herself. If Teddy's attention got distracted by the movement of her unprotected arm, he might release the sleeve and attack her on that side.

Her sleeved arm began to ache from the dog's assault when, with one last furious shake to occupy him, she flicked the snare over his head.

Feeling something brush past his ears, Teddy dropped the sleeve and leaned back, ready to attack again. Alyssa watched his eyes and realized he focused now on her neck instead of the sleeve. As he leapt toward her, she brought the sleeve in front of her face, and turned to meet the dog with her hip and shoulder. The impact toppled her off balance, and she stumbled to her knees as the dog landed square on the floor.

Get up, Alyssa thought, her ears pounding. *Get the sleeve up before he springs again.*

Behind her, Alyssa heard Sue step into the foyer. "Hey, Teddy." Teddy's eyes shifted toward Sue. Alyssa threw off her bite sleeve, then grabbed the end of the snare just as Teddy hurled himself toward Sue.

The snare twanged and bit into Alyssa's hands as Teddy hit the end of it in midair. "Teddy, calm down," she said, keeping her voice flat and low.

The dog refocused on her, snarling, his hackles up. As he leaned back to prepare for another attack, Alyssa began to rotate, keeping him sidestepping at the end of the leash.

"No." She kept circling slowly, until she could tell from his eyes that he had become dizzy. She stood still. "Teddy, heel." He didn't move. "No!" she commanded, then took a step, but he still didn't follow.

When he growled again, Alyssa began to circle again, watching him carefully. He didn't move to attack, so she kept the pace slow.

She noticed Sue standing still in a shadow, smart enough not to interfere or distract the dog. *Come on, Teddy*, she pleaded silently.

"Heel." She corrected Teddy again and saw his confusion grow. She could tell he was considering whether to attack again and prepared to spin if she needed to. Then the dog shifted into heel position and sat. "Good boy, Teddy!" Alyssa said in her high, celebration voice, and the Rottweiler's stubby tail wagged once.

Within a few minutes the dog had given up on guarding, and patting his head, Alyssa removed his guard collar. Her heart had returned to its normal pace.

"All clear here?" Melanie peered around the doorway.

"Yeah," said Alyssa without taking her eyes from Teddy.

"You okay?" Sue asked.

Alyssa smiled at her. "Nobody got hurt." She ran her hand over the smooth short hairs on Teddy's square skull. "He's confused. But other than that, I'd say I'm terrific."

Sue grinned. "Yes, you are."

"Then I'm going home," said Melanie. "I've got to write this up and I'd like to at least lay eyes on my son and husband sometime tonight."

"Hey, Mel," said Alyssa, touching the cop's sleeve, "thanks."

Melanie nodded.

"I'll walk out with you," Sue said. "I have a question about the fire investigation." They left.

Alyssa knelt with Teddy, stroking him to soothe both herself and him. "We've had a heck of a week, huh, boy?" She hated to confuse him about his job, but she'd had no better choice. "Let's go find Tango."

Teddy trotted after her into the kitchen where the puppy sat wide-eyed in his crate. "Lots of commotion tonight, huh, little guy?"

The puppy stood and wagged so hard his butt hit the sides of his crate.

"I bet everyone needs to go potty," Alyssa said then led them through the kitchen door into the fenced area on the north side of the house.

The moon hung heavy and low, its dusty light curved like a fat letter C in the darkening sky. Below, the lake licked against the shore in tiny waves. Alyssa rubbed her left shoulder where it had already started to stiffen from exertion, and felt proud. *I got in without hurting the dog.*

Yes!

She pumped her fist in a private victory celebration. She really *was* good at this. Marcus shouldn't be giving her crap about clients. He shouldn't even think about firing her. When these burglaries got solved, she'd be right back in the swing of things.

She picked up a soft red ball, threw it for the dogs and thought about solving the burglaries. *The thieves could have done it this way*, she thought. Her work with Teddy tonight left him subdued but unharmed. No marks and no chemicals. She petted him again as he brought her the ball.

Anyone with a bite sleeve and something like the lasso could have gotten in as easily as she had.

She envisoned the gleam in Strunk's eye when he heard what she'd done, and her exhilaration soured. *I should enjoy the end of this sunset*, she thought, *because after Strunk hears about this, he'll have me jailed.*

"Screw Strunk," she said aloud. She'd worry about that in the morning.

"Everything okay out here?" Sue and Zero walked into the yard.

"Sure." *I might be going to jail tomorrow, but tonight I kicked ass. What's not okay?*

Sue's arm slid around Alyssa's waist and the weight felt nice, even if Sue did smell like an old campfire.

"I'm glad she has the good sense not to arrest me for proving I can break into a house despite one of my own guard dogs," Alyssa said. "I guess that's what friends are for."

"That was one of the most amazing things I've ever seen," Sue said.

"Thanks. Except, in a way, I handed the cops everything they

134

need against me." A breeze meandered up the dune from the lake, whirling across her skin. She shivered.

"Nonsense." Sue pulled her close and Alyssa felt her warmth. "I'd say you just proved your innocence. No one smart enough to pull off these burglaries would reveal themselves like you did."

"Oh, I don't know." Her eyes burned at the charred smell that hung on Sue. "If I were a smart attorney, I'd say I staged the whole thing tonight to make you think exactly that, and thus cover up my guilt." She chuckled. "I guess I'm glad I'm not a smart attorney."

"You'd never survive in court," Sue said. "Remember, your face gives you away. Besides, Melanie can give better testimony in court than either of us and she told me she'd swear on her life you didn't know if that trick tonight would work."

"I didn't. But I had to take the risk."

Sue pulled her closer. "Will you stay tonight? I—" She hunched her shoulders. "I don't know how to begin to take care of all . . ." She looked down. "Of three dogs."

Alyssa suddenly remembered the pile of burned things in the yard, the overwhelming job that lay ahead of Sue. "God, Sue. With Delia and the dog and all, I haven't really thought about the mess you're in. What about your work?"

Sue shook her head. "Like I said, the laptop with the most recent stuff and the Palm with my client list were in my car. I back up most of my Web stuff on my provider's server. So I might have lost a little work in there, but not much." She still stared at her feet. "Losing the desktop equipment sucks. It's a lot of money."

"But there's insurance, right? You, and probably Delia. You'll get it replaced, right?"

Sue shrugged. "Guess so." She looked up. "Yes. You're right. That can all be replaced."

Alyssa saw a thin smile play across Sue's lips.

"It'll be a pain, but heck, I'll look on the bright side." Her voice rose with exaggerated excitement. "I get to buy all new equipment. Delia said she'd cover me until the insurance got worked out. I'll try to look forward to the shopping."

135

Alyssa bumped her playfully. "Are you making fun of me?"

"No." Sue's tone dropped again. "I'm trying to make myself believe it. I don't want to feel quite this lost."

"I know." She did know. And sometimes the best thing was just to have someone stand with you, in silence, until you felt not lost anymore. In her own dark days, Alyssa had wished for that and had no one. She felt glad to be here now.

"Really," Sue said after a few minutes had passed, "it's just the pictures. My mom and dad. I can't replace them."

Alyssa wasn't sure if Sue meant her parents or her pictures. "I'm sorry."

"I have other pictures. In storage. But those were my favorite. A collage of camping pictures. We camped a lot when I was a kid." She chuckled lightly. "I always felt most safe in a tent. Isn't that bizarre?"

"I don't know." Growing up, Alyssa had camped a few times with family friends. She'd loved the darkness and the field of stars overhead at night. "I felt a lot safer as a kid in general."

"Yeah." Sue tugged on her shirt. "I'm gross."

"Smelly but safe," Alyssa said. "I'm glad." She stepped away from Sue. "How about you take a shower? I'll feed the dogs and toss those things in the wash. Do you want me to run home and find you some clothes?"

"No, stay. Please." Sue rubbed a palm against the dirt on her bare arms. "Your clothes will be just as small as Delia's. I'll wrap up in a robe or something and go shopping tomorrow."

"Well, I'll stay for a while. But then I'm going home. I'll help you out tomorrow morning, first thing."

While Sue showered, Alyssa brought the dogs in, fed them, then settled them in for the evening. She had just finished spreading an old lawn blanket for Zero in the kitchen when Sue walked in, pulling a Cherry Republic T-shirt down over too-small navy sweats.

"Delia probably uses this T-shirt as a sleepshirt," Sue said.

Alyssa grinned. "Those sweats look like capris on you."

Sue looked down at herself. "Yeah, it's a little goofy. But it'll get me through the night."

Alyssa noted with interest the slope of the pants just beneath Sue's belly button. She stretched her neck away from her sore shoulder.

"Hey, thanks for talking with me," Sue said, resting one hand on the refrigerator handle. "I feel a lot better now. The shower helped. I do know how lucky I am."

"Yeah, me too."

"You want a beer?"

"Thanks." One beer. Then she'd head home.

Sue gave Alyssa a beer, then placed a hand in the small of her back. "Let's get out of the kitchen. It's more relaxing in there."

Alyssa followed Sue into the camp room, watching her broad shoulders swing in time with curved hips, hearing her bare feet pat against the tile floor. And now she smelled clean, like the beach.

I could stay. Marcus had made it pretty clear he didn't want her just hanging around the office. She had planned on eating breakfast at the diner, to talk up her training services, but she'd have plenty of time in the morning to go home and change clothes.

At least she owned a change of clothes.

"Sue, do you even have any shoes other than those sandals?"

Sue stood in the center of the darkened room and lifted her beer bottle. "Here's to looking on the bright side. I get all new shoes."

They clinked bottles and Alyssa sipped. "Terrific."

"The beer?" Sue asked.

"And you."

She could tell by the way Sue's eyes darkened that she shouldn't have said that. Not in that tone of voice, and not standing in a dark room overlooking the moonlit lake.

"You know," Alyssa stammered. "I mean, you're terrific for not worrying about the material stuff."

"Uh-huh," Sue said.

Alyssa let Sue take the bottle from her hand but kept talking. "Melanie said something about arson. Why do you think—"

"Shhh." Sue had placed their bottles on a nearby end table and returned to stand in front of her. She did not touch her, but Alyssa could still feel her energy. "I'm looking on the bright side, remember?"

"I remember." Alyssa also remembered how Sue had tasted that morning. It made her mouth water.

"We deserve it, don't you think?" Sue asked, moving closer.

Sue still didn't touch her and it was driving her insane! "Yes, we deserve it," she said. *Touch me.*

Sue didn't move except to bite her lower lip, which made Alyssa want to kiss it.

"We make a pretty good team," Sue said.

How could Sue stand there, barely an inch away, arms just hanging at her sides? Didn't she want to touch her? Then Alyssa noticed her own arms hanging at her sides like useless lead weights.

Screw it. She could be in jail tomorrow. *Enjoy the night.*

She raised one hand to Sue's face. "Yes, we make a pretty good team." She touched Sue's full lower lip with one finger. "And yes, I want you too."

In an instant, Sue pulled Alyssa to her, and Alyssa twisted her fingers into Sue's damp hair.

"I just hope I don't live to regret this," Alyssa said.

"Me too," Sue whispered.

Before she could reply, Sue's lips covered hers.

Alyssa wanted to talk, to say anything, but she couldn't get her breath.

And she couldn't get her breath because she couldn't stop kissing Sue.

Oh, yes, she thought, leaning her hips into Sue's.

Then the doorbell rang.

Chapter Fourteen

At the sound of the doorbell, all three dogs leapt to their feet and barked in a frenzy of excitement and protectiveness. Teddy and Zero skidded on the tile floor into the foyer.

"Shit," Sue said, her lips still against Alyssa's.

Alyssa tried to pull back, but Sue held her in place. "We should get that," Alyssa said.

"Yep." Sue kissed her again, lightly. "But whoever it is, once we get rid of them, we're starting again right here. Okay?" Her eyes swirled with promise.

Alyssa nodded, heat still glowing within. "Oh, yeah."

As Sue went to the door, Alyssa called the two big dogs back into the kitchen and settled them into silence. Tango stood in his crate, watching with wide gold eyes.

"Deputy Strunk?"

Alyssa sighed when she heard Sue admit the cop, whose voice boomed from the foyer.

"Glad to see you in one piece, Ms. Hunter. I was here earlier to oversee the scene but thought I'd better drop by to chat. I hope you aren't busy."

"I am busy, as a matter of fact," Sue said as they entered the kitchen.

Strunk stared at Alyssa. "I'm surprised to find you here, Ms. Norland."

She smiled. "Would you like a beer, Deputy Strunk?" She stepped toward the refrigerator.

"No, thanks."

Alyssa looked at Sue and Strunk. "Maybe I should go."

"Yes, maybe," Strunk said.

"Absolutely not," Sue said at the same time. She stepped to the kitchen table, pulled out two chairs and looked at Alyssa. She met Sue's eyes, which flashed with determination, and sat down with a sigh. When Sue indicated that Strunk should sit, he did, then so did Sue.

The cop looked at Alyssa like he wished she would evaporate, but she met his gaze steadily. When he spoke, he addressed Sue. "I'm afraid I have some bad news. The fire that destroyed your apartment, Ms. Hunter, resulted from an act of arson." He sat back as if he had dropped a bomb and anticipated its explosion with glee.

Sue didn't give him the satisfaction. "I've heard." Alyssa wanted to kiss her.

Strunk unleashed another one. "We're working on the premise that the fire is linked to the burglaries."

"How so?" Sue leaned back in her chair. "The M.O.s don't match."

Strunk glanced at Alyssa, then again at Sue. "I know you're new in town, Ms. Hunter." He tapped his finger on the table. "And that you're a, uh, unmarried woman. And Ms. Norland—"

"What about her?" Sue asked, a distinct edge in her voice.

Strunk's eyes narrowed. "Ms. Norland is connected in some way with each of these events. In fact, she's the only constant among events that, as you have pointed out, otherwise have clear differences."

Alyssa started to protest, but Sue touched her hand and Alyssa let her take the lead.

Sue leaned forward onto her elbows. "I think you're wrong. For instance, I'm connected with the burglaries and the fire. I live here and I observed the Braeburns at class the other evening."

"Well, ma'am, I don't—"

"Delia Watkins is connected with all three events as well," Sue continued.

"No one thinks she staged her own injuries in order to—"

Sue interrupted him. "In fact, your colleague Officer Sybesma is connected to all three through the dog class, isn't she?"

Strunk had quit trying to speak.

"If you actually investigated these crimes," Sue said, "I wonder how many other people in Radley have 'connections' to these events? How about you? If we tried, could we link you to all of them?"

Alyssa thought Strunk would burst. Instead, he pointed a finger toward her. "Ms. Norland has proven she could get past the dog." He smiled meanly. "Of course, I've already heard how you broke into this house."

He is so predictable, Alyssa thought.

"We did not break in," Sue said. "We had permission and a key."

"And a guard dog to overcome." Strunk turned to face Alyssa. "Tell me, if you were a professional dog trainer and you overpowered guard dogs a few times, wouldn't it just keep getting easier?"

Alyssa had let Sue handle Strunk so far, but she'd had enough. "I *am* a professional dog trainer. I would never do anything to compromise a dog's training, except to save the dog. That's what we did tonight."

"How convenient that the victim herself asked you to do it." He leered at her. "I will, of course, have to interview Ms. Watkins again, to have that part of the story verified."

"Stay away from her," Sue said, her voice tight. "She needs rest."

Strunk's gaze slid toward Sue then returned to Alyssa. "I think someone who thought she was clever might decide to set a fire, to draw attention away from her other crimes." He bent his tall body over the table, leaning toward her. "I think someone might then show up as a heroine, helping the victims with their dogs." He paused. "Comforting them in all sorts of ways."

His implication struck Alyssa like a slap.

"Trying," Strunk continued, "to deflect suspicion away from herself."

His suggestion seemed so ridiculous, she laughed. "Are you accusing me of setting the apartment on fire? Of almost burning Delia and Zero to death? You're insane." She struggled to get her mind around it.

Strunk turned toward Sue. "It was arson, ma'am. A chair blocked the doorway." Strunk rested a hand on the table. "You were the target of that assault, Ms. Hunter, not Delia Watkins. It was your apartment, after all. Your car was parked in the driveway. Everything appeared as if you were at home."

"I had nothing to do with this," Alyssa began, but Sue squeezed her hand. *Okay*, she thought. *Your turn.*

She saw Strunk's gaze settle on their hands. Then he used his thumb to point at Alyssa without looking at her, keeping his eyes on Sue. "Arson, aimed at you, and this woman is associated with it. I'd advise you to consider whether you can find your pleasure somewhere else."

Sue released her hand and stood. "Good luck with your work, Deputy Strunk."

Strunk looked up at Sue, shook his head slowly and rose. He stepped away from the table, his hand resting on his gun. "She's pretty, Ms. Hunter, I know. Great body. You people let sex destroy your common sense. No wonder you have so much trouble getting any respect."

"You bastard," Alyssa said, not quite believing she had heard him right.

Strunk ignored her. "Don't forget to think, Ms. Hunter. Or I'll be scrubbing your blood off the floor someday soon."

Sue hadn't moved, except for a muscle in her jaw which had risen to a knot. "Leave. Now."

Strunk shook his head. "Whatever you want." They listened to his boots echoing in the foyer.

When the door slammed behind him, Alyssa let out a long breath. "What a jerk!"

Sue held out a hand to help her up. "Worse than a jerk. Just forget about him."

She stared. "Forget about him? Now he thinks I tried to kill you! How can I forget that?"

Sue came around the table to her. "Please, don't let him ruin our night." Sue's hands felt warm against Alyssa's shoulders. "Please, Alyssa. Don't give him that control."

Alyssa stood. "He's not even looking for the real criminals."

Sue took her hand and they walked back to the dark camp room.

"I should just do it myself," Alyssa said.

"Wait a minute there, tiger." Sue stopped and turned toward her. "He's a jerk, but he's a cop. These guys we're dealing with are dangerous. You don't need to take them on."

"Teddy's dangerous, but I figured that out," Alyssa said. Her mind locked on this new idea, a possible way out of this mess. "I can do it, Sue. It might take me a while, but I bet I can figure out a way to get these guys."

She felt Sue's fingers brush against her temples. "You are so sexy when you're determined," Sue said.

Alyssa focused on Sue, searching for any hint of sarcasm, but found none.

"Oh, I'm serious," Sue said. "You're determined and powerful and beautiful." She kissed Alyssa's forehead. "I've wanted you since I watched you teach that class last week." She kissed her jaw. "I can't believe it's only been five days." She kissed her ear. "Five days of wanting you." Her tongue felt warm and wet and Alyssa shuddered.

"I'm doing it, Sue. I'm going after them," Alyssa said. She just couldn't focus on it right now, because Sue had begun to do amazing things to her ear and neck. But she'd work on it tomorrow.

"Um-hmm." Sue's lips moved down into the hollow of her shoulder, igniting a flush of white heat.

This is need, Alyssa thought as she pressed toward Sue. Then, gently, smiling, Sue lifted Alyssa's shirt and bra and bent, mouth to her breast. Alyssa stopped thinking.

She sank slowly, pulling Sue with her, until they knelt on the floor. Sue's ribs felt smooth, her back broad and warm. When Sue began tugging on the buttons of Alyssa's jeans, she suddenly felt claustrophobic, bound by her clothes. She had to get out of them, and had to get Sue out of hers.

"Hold on," Sue said, smiling. She pulled a chenille throw from the couch and spread it on the floor. "Unless you want to find the bedroom."

In answer, Alyssa grabbed the waistband of Sue's sweats and tugged. Sue smiled.

Without clothes, Sue's body felt hot against hers, skin pressing skin in all the right places. Alyssa felt wet tugs as Sue kissed her breasts, a scratchy palm circling beneath her belly button, her knee bony against her thigh. She felt Sue's ribs expand with heavy breaths.

Every touch surprised her.

Sue's lips brushed the soft spot beneath Alyssa's breastbone. "Tell me what you like."

"That feels pretty good," Alyssa breathed.

Sue kissed her again in the same spot. "I mean, what you like *especially*."

"You." What did she mean, Alyssa wondered. Desire had sharpened her senses until she felt positively ravenous. "God, Sue. Please."

Sue slid her hand down Alyssa's body, over her curves. Then suddenly, she slipped inside her.

Alyssa gasped and tucked her hips forward. She moaned beneath Sue's touch and her stomach jerked with pleasure.

"I want to feel you everywhere," Alyssa whispered.

Sue's mouth closed over her breast again.

Every spark of energy in Alyssa's body centered around Sue's hand and mouth. She felt Sue's massage not just in and out, but around and over, pressing and releasing and sliding.

She had no idea her body could feel like this. She wanted to tell Sue she liked *this* especially, but she could barely breathe.

The tension within her coiled tighter, curling streamers into her legs and arms. She tried to slow her lungs. *Make it last*, she thought.

Then Sue slowed.

Stopped.

She removed her hand and kissed Alyssa gently on the stomach.

Then she shifted her weight and raised herself over Alyssa. Her hair curled over her brow and she grinned.

On her knees, she slid her legs forward against Alyssa's, pushing Alyssa's knees into the air.

"Oh, yes," Alyssa said, feeling herself opening.

Sue's hand slid into her again, so slowly. Sue leaned forward, her own pelvis pressed against her hand.

And then nothing else came slow or gentle.

Alyssa twisted to meet Sue and the coils within her sprang loose. She tasted Sue's ear, neck, shoulder, pulling herself up against her hand as it circled again and again.

Alyssa slid her hand down between their bodies, sticky now with effort, and found Sue's warm center. As she felt her way, Sue rolled her eyes, then closed them. "God, yes. Stay right there."

She felt slick and swollen and Alyssa couldn't believe it felt this good to make love.

After several breathless minutes, Sue said, "I can't wait," her voice lighter than usual. She buried her head in Alyssa's shoulders and pulled her hips up, giving Alyssa more room to move. Alyssa felt Sue's chest moving against her own, until her breath came in shallow gulps. "I'm there."

With a long slow gasp, Sue's body relaxed and began to shudder, strong movements that radiated outward from her center. Her arms and legs twitched in rhythm and her hips pressed against Alyssa's in a counter beat.

"It's good," Sue whispered once.

Alyssa smiled against Sue's forehead.

Sue's dance lasted longer than Alyssa would have predicted, then she settled with a sigh. "Don't leave me," she whispered. "Not yet."

"No."

Sue rested a minute, then raised her head, kissing Alyssa lightly on the nose. "Hey, thanks."

Alyssa smiled, and Sue kissed her again harder. With renewed force, Sue kissed her way down Alyssa's neck and breastbone, until her tongue rolled Alyssa's nipple. Then Sue's hand again, between her legs, sliding. She thrust her hips gently, then harder. Alyssa rode the edge for a long time then felt herself plunge.

Her neck stiffened as the heat swamped her, and her fingers grasped Sue's hair. She stopped breathing to let Sue's rhythm move through her uninterrupted.

It lasted long enough that she thought she might pass out. Then the flood eased and she breathed again, her head fuzzy with warmth, her body soft under the weight of Sue's.

Neither of them moved, except to catch their breath. She loved the way Sue's head rose on her chest each time she inhaled.

"Like I said before," Sue murmured, her lips still against Alyssa's breast, "you are amazing."

"I can't talk yet." Her head still felt fuzzy.

Sue raised her head and Alyssa wondered at the melting darkness of the brown in her eyes. Sue grinned. "Took your breath away, huh?"

Alyssa smiled and closed her eyes slowly.

"Well, I guess now we know what you like, especially," Sue said, and rested her head against Alyssa again.

Alyssa felt Sue's breath regular and soft against her shoulder, then drew her own deep breath, lifting her chest beneath the weight of Sue's arm. She exhaled and snuggled into the soft sheets of the guest bedroom. They had moved here from the floor, and made love again, before Sue fell asleep.

Sue lay on her side facing Alyssa. Her curls brushed against her eyebrows and over the pillow.

The night felt quiet. For the first time in days, perhaps even in years, Alyssa felt peace. *Enjoy it now*. Tomorrow, she was going after the bastards who had almost killed Delia, no matter what Sue said.

She smelled Sue's skin against her own, closed her eyes to better concentrate on the warmth and fell into a deep sleep.

Chapter Fifteen

When Sue woke up, she saw cloudless blue sky outside the guest room windows and the bed empty beside her. The sunshine she liked. The empty bed she didn't.

She hoped Alyssa hadn't been seized with a bout of independence and sneaked home without waking her. If she did, she'd have to go after her.

An exclamation came from somewhere beyond the bedroom door. She was still here. Sue pulled on the sweatpants and T-shirt and headed out to help with the dogs.

The ceramic tile floor felt cold beneath her feet as she entered the kitchen, where Alyssa stood slicing bagels. She wore a white cotton robe she'd found and the auburn of her hair glowed against it. Curved shadows drifted across her exposed cleavage.

"When it comes to leering, you're as bad as the dogs," Alyssa said, motioning downward with the knife.

Beside her, three very interested pairs of canine eyes watched each movement of her hand as she worked with the food.

"Except it's not the bagel I want to get my mouth on," Sue said.

"I'm ignoring that," Alyssa said without looking up. Still, a pink blush rose in her cheeks. "Just because we had sex once doesn't mean we're going to have it all the time. I've got to concentrate today."

Her seriousness didn't deter Sue. "We had sex more than once." She moved close behind her.

"Do you want a bagel?"

Using her chin to pull back Alyssa's hair, Sue nuzzled in and kissed her neck. "You're not a bagel."

"Do you want peanut butter?" Alyssa asked, raising half a bagel to Sue.

Sue slipped her arms around Alyssa's waist and fingered the knot holding the robe closed. "Not on my bagel. But it might be interesting on something else." She slid her hand inside the robe and pressed a palm against Alyssa's smooth belly. She longed to go lower, but she held back, then kissed her neck again.

Sue felt Alyssa's involuntary shudder of pleasure. God, she loved this. And she loved knowing Alyssa did too, no matter what she said.

"Sue. This all seems so normal, you know? A sunny Tuesday morning, breakfast, dogs, another person to eat with."

"Mmm," Sue said. Alyssa's hair smelled of lavender and passion. "Don't forget the afterglow of great sex." She pulled Alyssa closer, loving the softness of Alyssa's skin beneath her hand. "Why not? Just for a little while longer. Then we'll deal with whatever you want." She kissed Alyssa's ear.

"I don't know."

She sounded really worried this time, so Sue leaned her head against Alyssa's. "Say the word, seriously, and I'll stop. I don't want to, but I will if you want me to."

Alyssa put the knife and bagel down and turned to face Sue. Her fingers felt cool when they slipped around Sue's waistband, and Sue breathed deeply. She wanted to be attractive for Alyssa. She wanted Alyssa to know she could be counted on.

She also wanted to make love to her, and if Alyssa didn't decide in half a second, Sue would have to decide for them and go take a cold shower.

Alyssa's fingers left Sue's sweats and tugged open the knot to her own robe. She pulled Sue's hands from around her waist and placed them on her breasts. "I guess another hour couldn't hurt." She smiled and the corners of her eyes turned upward. "I've heard good sex clears your head."

Her breasts rested in Sue's hands, already alert at the touch. Just the look on her face turned Sue on. She liked knowing she could do the same for her.

Sue bent to kiss her. "An hour, huh? Okay, lady, let's see what we can do with an hour."

It was almost noon when Alyssa joined Sue on the camp room couch with a cup of coffee. She was *not* going to think about the incredible sex she'd had with Sue. She'd just sit with Sue for a minute, and be on her way. She'd already blown her plan for breakfast at the diner. Instead, she'd decided to go to the office. She was still an employee at DOGS and, damn it, she had every right to go there to work. She needed the computer to finish that flyer on temperament testing she'd promised the breeder in Interlochen. If she finished that, she could find some quiet time to think about how she could nail these crooks.

Then she felt Sue's arm around her shoulders. *Okay*, she thought, *maybe I'll sit here for two minutes.*

"Socks," Sue said. "Dog food and dish and treats. Some groceries for us." She sipped her coffee. "I suppose I should write down the stuff I need. I'll never remember it all."

Messy curls lopped over Sue's forehead. She looked mighty relaxed for someone coping with a fire. Alyssa would never be that calm.

Although, she thought, *Strunk could show up any minute to haul me to jail, and here I sit*. She smiled into her cup. *That's what good sex'll do for you.*

"Hey." Sue leaned toward her and they kissed.

She tasted like coffee and cream and herself.

"Do you want to come shopping with me?" Sue asked when they parted. "Or should I go when you're at work?"

"You'd better do dog and Delia duty first, don't forget." Alyssa tried to make herself look stern. "Delia will want a full report on the dogs, so unless you want her busting out of the hospital, you'd better stop by and see her. Your clothes are clean."

"True. Okay, shopping after. You'll come?"

"Give me a few hours at the office and I'll come," said Alyssa. If she concentrated she could finish that flyer and they could drop it off in Interlochen on the way to the Traverse City mall. "I need to get some vertical blinds for my slider anyhow."

Sue turned, pulling her arm from Alyssa. "You know, Alyssa, Strunk's a bully. Not all cops are like that."

She sounded serious. Those chocolate eyes, so sweet and warm. Alyssa saw herself there and liked what she saw.

"You want to be a cop again, don't you?" and as she said it she knew it was true.

"Yes." Sue's eyes flared with energy. "But not in Detroit. I want to be out of the city. Could you—" She stopped.

"Could I what?" Why was she holding her breath?

Sue offered a half-smile. "Nothing."

Alyssa rested a hand on Sue's thigh. "Do it, Sue. You need to help people. I've seen it. And I know what it's like to be in a job, in a city, just for the money. You need to go where your passion is."

She thought a shadow of desire passed over Sue's face, and her body tingled in response.

"What was your job?" Sue asked.

Alyssa looked down. "Public relations. In Chicago." She studied the coffee remaining in her mug.

"You don't want to talk about it," Sue said, resetting her body sideways on the couch so she could see Alyssa. "Now there's two things you don't want to talk about. That note I found on your porch and your job in Chicago. Related?"

She's too curious, Alyssa thought, *and she can do more than a casual check. Better give her something.*

"Okay. I had some trouble there." Her mind raced. How much could she tell to keep Sue satisfied?

Sue tensed. "Keep going."

"A man there threatened me." Alyssa hurried ahead so Sue couldn't ask questions. "I don't know who it was." Technically, she didn't.

Sue set her cup down and leaned closer. "Did he leave notes?"

"No. Just phone threats." If she left it there it would be a lie. She couldn't do it. "And someone shot my dog."

Sue exploded. "Shot your dog? Someone shot at you? Jesus, Alyssa!" She pushed up from the couch and crossed the room.

Alyssa held up her hands. "It was over a year ago, Sue. In another state." She hadn't expected Sue to react so vehemently.

Sue took a deep breath and shoved her hands into her pockets. "Then what?"

"It frightened me, and I didn't trust the cops. The woman—" She forced it out. "The woman who shot Vinnie wore a cop's uniform. That's how she got so close. So I left. And I quit P.R." She smiled. "Became a dog trainer, and I'm infinitely happier. Which is why you should do what you want to do."

"Happier until this week, right?"

Damn. Sue wasn't going to let this go.

Sue knelt in front of Alyssa, her arms in Alyssa's lap. "Is that why you attacked me the other night? Because you thought I was that woman? Or the man? Have you been getting phone calls again?"

She'll know if I lie. "Yes. On Wednesday at work, and Friday night at home. He said he knew about Vinnie. And I could tell from what he said that he could see me. He was near the house. But nothing since then. Honest."

Sue stared at her, blinking. She looked angry and Alyssa felt herself growing hot.

"Why didn't you tell me?" Sue asked.

"Because of the burglaries and the fire. And you." Why was Sue looking at her like that? "Well, I just didn't know how to tell you." Sue's stare pissed her off. "Stop looking at me like that."

Sue kept her voice steady, but Alyssa could tell she struggled for control. "I cannot believe you didn't tell this to Strunk the other night."

"Why? He wasn't listening to me!" Alyssa's heart began to pound.

"Then why didn't you tell me?"

"Because it's my business. I shouldn't have told you now. You're gonna get angry and I hate that."

"Whoa, whoa." Sue's hand surrounded hers. "Back up. I'm not angry with you. I'm angry *for* you. I want to protect you. I want to kill the creeps doing this to you. So sue me."

Sue's emotion hooked something deep within Alyssa, dragged up the memory of Covington's anger, and before she knew it, she began to cry. "Why do people do that?"

Sue's arms, warm and strong, encircled her and her cheek pressed against Alyssa's head. "Do what?"

"Get angry and then want to hurt somebody." Alyssa sucked a ragged breath and willed herself not to sob.

"I wouldn't really hurt anyone, Alyssa. It's just—" Sue held her tighter. "No one should have to live in fear of their world falling apart. No one."

Alyssa nodded, swallowing.

"I've been there. It hurts," Sue said.

Her mom.

"I can't stand it," Sue continued. "That's why I became a cop."

Alyssa wiped her eyes. *Get a grip.* Sue's anger was not like

Covington's. They were not the same. In fact, she couldn't imagine two people more different.

"It's who I am, Alyssa. I can't change it."

She knew. "Yes." She sighed, wanting to soothe them both. "I don't know that it's the same people. It could be anyone who knew what happened."

Sue pulled back. "What do you mean? Did this make news or something?"

She'd said too much. She didn't want to get into all that had happened with Covington Enterprises. And she didn't want Sue searching the Internet. Changing her first name wouldn't be enough to fool her if she did a serious search.

Alyssa shook her head. "No, no. The cops, some neighbors." Sue didn't look like she was buying it. "You know," Alyssa said, hoping to change the subject, "I never closed that whole episode, which is why I want to close this one. I want the thieves and the arsonist caught. I'm going after them. Somehow."

From the kitchen, Tango yelped in his crate.

"I'll put them out," Sue said. "And then we're talking about this."

"Nothing to talk about," Alyssa said after her. "Unless you want to help." Sue took the dogs out into the yard.

Alyssa couldn't sit any longer. She got up and wandered across the room, grabbing the chenille throw from the floor where they had left it last night. She'd almost told Sue everything. What would she think?

She should tell Sue. Because she liked her. A lot.

Of course, whoever was watching her had figured that out, and had lit that fire just to hurt someone she loved. She bunched the blanket to her face, trying to block out the truth. She could smell herself and Sue on the fabric.

I have to keep Sue safe.

Outside she watched the dune grass wave across the top of the bluff. In the distance, the lake waves crested and broke all the way to the horizon.

A long way.

She could run. She'd done it before and escaped for almost a year.

But then she'd been alone. Now she had Sue, who wouldn't stay out of it, Alyssa knew.

But could she drag Sue into this twisted game even deeper?

She heard Sue reenter the kitchen. "Hey, Alyssa!" She stood in the doorway. "Tango and I need to blow off some steam. Have you seen that rope toy he runs around with?"

"Sure, it's right here." Alyssa threw the blanket on the couch. At least Tango could enjoy himself. She grabbed the rope toy and held it up for Sue to see. "You know, I've done it with a hundred dogs. Switched games. I can do it here." She slapped the toy against her palm. "I have to stop playing this bastard's game and figure out a way to get him to play mine."

"The people behind that note, your phone calls, these burglaries, the fire," Sue said, her face tense, "are not the same as a collie pup. Not even an attacking Rottweiler."

"I'm doing it," she said, tossing Sue the toy. "But I'll have a better chance if you help me." She put her hands on her hips. "You have to decide. Are you in, or are you out?"

Sue passed the toy from one hand to the other. "I don't like it, but I'm in."

155

Chapter Sixteen

That evening, after nine, Alyssa watched Sue's Subaru pull into her driveway. She unlocked the door, then went to the kitchen and scooped decaf into the coffee maker. She added an extra scoop because Sue liked it strong. The day had started so well and gone downhill, fast. She hoped she could still rescue it this evening.

She'd finished the flyer and delivered it to the breeder along with two dozen business cards. Then they'd gone to Traverse City to shop. Alyssa had marveled at the speed with which Sue chose the jeans, shirts and shoes she wanted. Sue moved just as fast when ordering new computer equipment. Alyssa had never enjoyed shopping much herself, but even she couldn't make decisions that fast.

"You gotta know what you want and go for it," Sue said when Alyssa remarked on her speed.

She'd done that last night, when she wanted Sue. For the first time in a long time, she'd gone after what she wanted, and it had felt so good.

Then they'd gone separate ways—Sue back to Delia's to care for the dogs and Alyssa to the Twelve Point to pick up a pizza for dinner. When she walked in, all conversation stopped. Everyone's eyes had turned to her. Some held suspicion, others questions, still others fear.

Alyssa clicked the coffee basket closed and turned the appliance on. *Damn Rodney Covington.* He was ruining her. He had almost killed Delia. And he had gone after Sue. How could she fight him?

The front door opened and closed, and Alyssa felt herself relaxing because Sue was here safe. "Safe," she said aloud.

"Did you say something?" Sue asked, as she and Zero entered the kitchen. Sue looked warm and touchable in a soft, dark purple linen shirt.

"No," Alyssa said. "Hey, boy." She rubbed Zero's ears.

Sue slid a hand across her shoulders and rubbed her back. "Well, doctor," she joked as if to a third person, "I found her in the kitchen muttering to herself. You want to talk about it?"

"How's Delia?" Alyssa asked.

"A lot better. I ran by the hospital and found her pattering around in her pajamas and moccasins. But I got her settled. They'll probably release her tomorrow." Sue kissed her temple lightly. "So, back to my question. You want to talk about it?"

Alyssa spread her hands flat on the cool blue countertop. "Sue, what would you say if I told you I'm going to leave Radley?"

"I'd say, 'Of all the things I might have thought about you, I did not think you were a quitter.'" She paused. "Then what would you say?"

Alyssa turned to her. "This isn't a game. Delia nearly died in a fire meant for you."

"We don't know—"

Alyssa would not be stopped. "Because of me."

"It's not because of you, Alyssa. It's because of the people after you."

Alyssa drew her hands to her head as if trying to hold it together against the rush of emotions there. "Oh, Sue, I don't know."

"Hey." Sue rubbed her back again and it felt so good. "I thought

157

you were hatching some grand plan to prove your innocence. Is leaving part of that?"

"My innocence. I don't have any power over that anymore. I can't change what people think of me. And I haven't figured out how to turn it all around yet."

"We'll figure it out together."

"I'm not sure I want you involved in this. What if there's another fire?" She rested her forehead against her chest. "The whole town knows we're hooked up by now."

"You think so?"

"Of course they do." Sue hadn't lived in a small town before, so she couldn't understand.

"No, I mean, do you think we're hooked up?"

She tilted her head back and looked at Sue. Those silly curls and dark, dark eyes. The cheekbones. The desire and kindness and anger she'd seen on Sue's face. The heart she felt beating right now as they held each other. Sue was her best reason to leave Radley, and her best reason to stay.

" 'Cause I think we are, and if we aren't, you should set me straight right now," Sue said.

"We are," Alyssa said. Sue felt so solid and strong. "Of course, it won't help you build a new life here."

"Doesn't matter."

Alyssa saw the passion she now recognized flicker in Sue's face, suffused with tension and intensity and energy, unstoppable.

"Because I want—" Sue paused and lowered her head unbearably close, so close Alyssa could feel Sue's breath on her lips. "You." Sue inched forward, her lips brushing against Alyssa's. "You've done this to me, Alyssa."

Alyssa pulled her hands from Sue's, reached up and tugged her hair to draw her closer. *Yes*, she thought as their tongues touched, *I caused this heat in you.*

Sue made her feel like she could conquer anything. Her hands left Sue's curls, dropped to the gentle curve of her waist, and drove upward against the skin of her belly. Sue moaned.

Yes. My touch. Moan again. She fingered Sue's nipples and Sue gasped.

Alyssa smiled.

She pulled Sue's T-shirt up, exposing her breasts. Alyssa's tongue traced the outlines of Sue's ribs and she laughed at Sue's gasps and sighs. She tasted salty and smelled of newly bought clothes.

Alyssa wanted Sue out of control with pleasure because of what she did to her.

The fly of Sue's new jeans remained rigid under her fingers. She knelt down, pulling and twisting it, her knuckles rubbing against Sue's stomach. She could feel the fine hairs just below.

"Oh, God, Alyssa." Sue moaned.

Finally the button slid through its hole. Alyssa unzipped the fly and pulled jeans and panties down to Sue's ankle. Sue pulled one leg free.

"Sue." Alyssa blew a soft breath over Sue's thighs, pleased when she heard Sue inhale sharply. Opening Sue gently, Alyssa tasted her, slipping her tongue across her warm, sensitive flesh. She could feel Sue's heartbeat there.

Let's see what I can do for you.

She held Sue's thighs, taut with lust, like a marble statue come to life. She could feel Sue's excitement peaking in the sway of her hips and it fueled her own. Sue's knees bent and she leaned back hard against the counter, crying out and shaking from pleasure.

I did this, Alyssa thought as Sue shuddered and gasped.

Suddenly Sue pushed Alyssa away, stepping from her jeans in one fluid movement. She pulled Alyssa to her feet, her chest rising and falling with the strength of her desire, the rest of her body quivering.

"Wait," Alyssa said. "I wanted you to—"

"No—you," Sue said. Her mouth covered Alyssa's with hot kisses as she peeled Alyssa's clothes off. In a matter of seconds, Sue slipped a leg between Alyssa's and lifted until Alyssa's butt rested against the counter. Alyssa wrapped her legs around Sue's waist, pulling her closer with her heels.

"Now," Alyssa said. "Deep."

Sue slid her fingers into her, then leaned forward, filling Alyssa as she held her in place by the hips. Then she began to move her hands inside and out.

"Wait," Alyssa said, her fingers tracing up Sue's shirt to pull her hair. She pulled her knees up around Sue's ribs.

"Alyssa," Sue said, her face nuzzled in Alysssa's shoulder.

Alyssa knew what they each wanted, and arched to tip her hips forward. "Kiss me there."

She felt Sue's mouth nip her breast, her belly, then lower, pulling against her proud flesh. Alyssa's body seemed to stretch out of itself, floating and expanding, filling the room with vibrant energy. Then she threw herself back, her legs gripping Sue as slowly, outward from her center, her body relaxed before the current of release, the leading edge of a turbulent orgasm.

Sue leaned into the strength of her spasms until Alyssa shouted her pleasure so that it echoed against the room's big windows.

Then they stood, breathing together for many seconds.

"You . . . amazing . . ." Alyssa said between breaths. She'd never had anyone respond to her like this sexually.

"I'd like to do it again," Sue whispered, standing. "When you're ready."

Alyssa smiled.

"Oh, God, yes. Let's go to bed." Sue bit her collarbone.

In bed, they made love again, this time more slowly. Alyssa discovered that a playful bite on the earlobes made Sue crazy, information she enjoyed using several times.

After midnight, as they lay sleeping, the phone rang. Alyssa started from Sue's arms.

"Leave it," Sue mumbled, reaching to pull Alyssa back to bed.

"What if it's the hospital? Delia?"

"Okay," Sue grumbled, releasing her hand and burying her head in a pillow.

Alyssa grabbed the bedside phone on the third ring. "Hello?"

"You've had some trouble, haven't you, Miss Alyssa?"

Her heart lurched, and she reached behind her to touch Sue.

"Trouble follows bad girls. Girls who keep secrets. And you are a bad girl."

She hit Sue harder. "Who are you?" she asked.

Sue sat upright in bed, her eyebrows raised in a question. Alyssa nodded and Sue threw the covers back and stepped into her jeans.

"Someone who knows your troubles, Miss Deborah. Someone who could kiss you and make it all better." Her skin crawled as he laughed a high-pitched giggle.

"Keep him talking. I'll look around," Sue whispered, then left the bedroom.

"I'd be there tonight," the caller continued, "if . . . I suppose you think you can trust that woman? That Hunter?" His voice sounded like a metal blade being sharpened, growing more dangerous by the second.

"Yes." Alyssa drew the blanket closer.

"But you don't know who to trust!" His voice hurt her ear. "I will tell you," he said, suddenly quiet. "I know everything. So I'm the only one you can trust. I know it all."

Alyssa heard the front door click shut as Sue left.

"Will you help me then?" Alyssa asked.

"I'm the one who watches over you. I know all your secrets. That woman just makes it worse for you."

"Are you nearby somewhere?" she asked.

"No." He sighed audibly. "Now I'm far away. I'm tired of watching you with her. Worse than animals. Abomination, they say. It disgusts me."

Alyssa shivered. They had planned to put up the slider blind tonight but she'd wound up in bed instead. Had he watched them together in the kitchen? She sickened at the thought. She wanted to hang up, but she had to keep him talking while Sue looked around.

"I could treat you so much better than she does. I would give you what a woman is meant to receive."

"You said I can trust you," Alyssa interrupted, barely able to listen to any more.

"I'm the one who's interested in you," he said. "The others only

161

want revenge. Or money." He chirped another laugh. "Of course, I want money too. But I have so much more to offer."

How much information did this guy have? "How do I know I can trust you? I would trust you if I knew I could."

"If I could trust you," he said, his voice dripping sadness, "then I could help you." He began to hum a tune she recognized as a children's song. "But I know how disloyal you are, you see." He hummed again.

"You know everything about me," she said, trying to sound weak. "But I don't know you. Help me trust you."

His humming stopped. "Would you like me to tell you everything I know? Or just the parts about Mr. Covington and what he has planned for you now?"

Alyssa could barely hear the man's thin voice over the crackling of the phone.

"Or would you rather hear about how we got past the dog? Or watched the building burn?"

So it *was* all linked to Covington. "Tell me everything," she said.

He laughed again. "Ah, sweet girl. You trust me now, don't you? You want something I have?"

"Yes." She swallowed. How much would he tell her?

"Then ask again," he ordered, his voice clipped and stern, "like a polite girl."

Alyssa softened her voice. *Play along, keep him interested.* "Please, would you tell me more?"

The caller cackled. "I cannot resist your charms. I will tell you all, but only to you, and only in person. I must get something of what I want too, you see."

She shivered at the thought.

"Thirty minutes," he said, "at the end of McPherson's Road."

Too isolated, she thought. And she didn't know the area. "I can't," she said. "Why not the tavern? It's open another hour or so. I could buy you a beer."

His silence scared her. When he spoke, his voice was cold. "I want you alone, where I can touch you. Just a little. Like a man. Not like—"

"I can't get to McPherson's that fast." She mentally scanned the area for a place that she knew, where he might agree to go. "Cow Leg Road. I can get there." She'd done tracking exercises there with dogs. "There's a clearing near the second crook to the north."

"You must come to me alone," he said.

"I will. I'll be in my car."

"When you get there, get out of your car. Stand by it. Alone. I mean it." His voice was sharp with warning. "I'll watch. I'll know. Bring someone and I won't be gentle. That fire was nothing compared to what I could do."

"Okay," she breathed, and the connection clicked dead.

Maybe she could end it all tonight. The possibility energized her. She swept out of bed and pulled on jeans and a sweatshirt, her body bouncing with excitement. She headed for the foyer, intent on calling Sue when she opened the door.

"Just us," Sue said, patting Zero. "No sign outside. You dial star sixty-nine?"

Alyssa grimaced. "God, no. I never thought of it." She grabbed the phone and dialed.

"The number you have requested," intoned the mechanical voice, "is not available."

"Damn," Alyssa said, clicking off the phone.

Sue put her hand on Alyssa's shoulder and kissed her forehead. "You okay?"

She didn't feel like cuddling. She needed to move. "Terrific," she said, ducking away.

"Same guy?"

"Yes, but things changed this time. I got some information. He knows about the burglaries and the fire, and—" She left off Covington's name. "It's connected."

She didn't like that narrow look in Sue's eye, so she bent to get her shoes near the door.

"Anyone in town could pretend to have information on those things," Sue said. "Where are you going?"

"I arranged to meet him."

Sue said nothing, and when Alyssa glanced up, she saw Sue biting her cheek. She turned back to tying her shoes.

"The guy said he had information for me, and I got him to agree to meet me."

"Where?"

"You wouldn't know it." She stood and realized her car keys were still on her dresser. She tried to duck around Sue again, but Sue stopped her, blocking her against the wall with an arm on either side.

"I know all the main roads around here. I'm a fast learner."

"Hey, I'm the good guy here, remember? Let me go." Alyssa tried again to move, but Sue blocked her.

"Tell me there are houses, bright lights, plenty of people, that sort of thing. Even though it's after midnight."

What could she say? "No."

"Then what?"

"Woods."

Sue's brows plummeted, but she said nothing.

"I picked the spot," Alyssa said. "I know it. I've worked there with Melanie and other cops. With tracking dogs. Even in the dark. There's a road and a clearing. I won't leave the car." She lifted her chin. "I picked the spot. He agreed."

Sue dropped her arms. "It's ridiculous. You aren't going." She walked down the hall toward the bedroom.

"What do you mean I'm not going?" Alyssa followed. "You are not my keeper."

"Well, you need one. If you walk out of this house alone, I'm calling the police."

Alyssa grabbed her keys. "You don't know where I'm going."

"No, but Melanie does. You just told me so. How many places have you practiced tracking?"

She'd do it too, Alyssa knew. Call Melanie and tell everything. "What gives you the right to interfere?"

Sue closed her eyes, obviously controlling her anger, but Alyssa didn't care. She hadn't done anything to Sue.

"Answer me, Sue. You must have some weird ex-cop logic for this."

When Sue opened her eyes again, they were dark and bottomless. "If nothing else, I have an interest in protecting Delia." Her words were measured syllable by syllable. "I promised her. If this guy knows something about the burglaries, I have a better chance of finding out what he knows if I go with you than if you go out there alone. Pure self-interest. Okay?"

Alyssa grabbed her keys from the dresser. Was that all she cared about?

Sue sat on the bed. "Tell me what's going on, Alyssa. Why are you doing this?"

Alyssa sat down hard on the other side of the bed. "Because I'm tired of him yanking me around, forcing me to react every time he decides to play this game. I want to take control of this."

Sue nodded. "Okay." She didn't sound sure.

"It's the key to changing a dog's behavior," Alyssa said. "I suppose you think it sounds stupid, but—"

"No, I don't think it sounds stupid." Sue smoothed a wrinkled area of the blanket. "In fact, it makes more sense than anything else you've said."

"So what do I want him to do?" She watched Sue's hand moving back and forth. "Come to me, right? Reveal his identity, his information. He's been hidden up until now, but I want him out of hiding." Her plan gained momentum. "I need to reinforce it, give him some reward, so he'll do it now, and do it again."

"How?"

She winced. "This guy wants me scared. If he's involved with the burglaries, he wants to discredit me. And—" She swallowed. "He wants me. He said so." She tried to smile. "Ick."

Sue did not smile back. "Well put. Ick."

"So," Alyssa continued, "I'm giving him what he wants. Me."

Her statement dropped into silence. She waited, but Sue said nothing.

Alyssa stood. "Look, I have to go. I'm meeting him in a few minutes."

Sue stood. "I'm going with you."

"Sue." The truth was, she would like Sue there, but not if she wanted to take everything over. Alyssa knew what she was doing, and they had to be careful.

Sue chewed on her cheek. "I'm not kidding, Alyssa. Take me with you and I won't call the cops."

"We agreed I would come alone."

"And you'll stick to some agreement you made with this guy? You expect him to honor his agreement to you?"

"That's not it. He said he would hurt whoever else came." If he worked for Covington, he would do it, too. "I can't risk it if you're going to blunder around in this."

"Blunder?" Sue's eyes darkened, and Alyssa prepared for an explosion of anger. But when Sue spoke, her words came quiet and cold. "I can't risk your going alone, Alyssa. Period." She crossed her arms. "I won't allow it."

"You won't allow it?" All of Alyssa's nervous energy burst from her. "I don't remember giving you decision-making power in my life."

Sue shrugged. "I'm not a tyrant. But I'm not letting you go out there alone."

Alyssa blinked, unsure how to proceed. She believed Sue would follow her, or call the cops, no matter what. "You come, but I'm in charge. We agree on a plan, or I'm dumping you at the side of the road."

"Deal," she said.

"I'm not kidding," Alyssa said.

"I know," Sue responded as they walked through the house. "I promise to try to make myself useful if you promise not to be reckless. Believe it or not, Alyssa, I want to see this whole thing cleared up as much as you do."

You don't know the half of it, Alyssa thought.

Chapter Seventeen

The headlights of Alyssa's Jeep swept across the trees as she pulled from Cow Leg Road into the clearing. Her brake lights cast a red glow in her rear-view mirror as she stopped the car then turned the engine off. She left the lights shining and they threw the woods into a contrast so stark that it looked like a black and white photograph. She got out of the car and stood near it, making herself visible.

She'd dropped Sue off along the road about a half-mile back, on a trail that cut across to this clearing. She should be here by now, but Alyssa had heard nothing.

Of course, if Sue was good at her job, Alyssa wouldn't hear anything.

Her hands felt heavy and uncomfortable so she tugged at her ponytail, then forced her hands to hang at her sides. They twitched, so she clasped them in front of her and leaned against the driver's door.

The night woods thrummed with insects, punctuated by an occasional owl call. Behind that, silenced boomed. She felt alone, floating in a vast space.

Sue's here, she thought. *Somewhere here. Hang on.*

She looked at her watch. *Five minutes late. Where was that bastard?*

"I'm here." The high-pitched voice came from the dark ahead of her, just out of the triangle of her headlights. "Turn out the lights and we'll talk."

Make him think it's his game. "If I do that, you can't see me." Sue wouldn't be able to either.

"True." His voice was soft, barely louder than the insects. "Still," he said, "there is enough moon to see by. I can make do for tonight with your silhouette, and save details for later." His voice shifted, suddenly ordering her. "So turn out the lights."

Alyssa needed to keep him talking. She closed her eyes to help them adjust to the dark and opened the Jeep's door to switch off the lights. When she opened her eyes again, the moon cast a fuzzy light, muted by thin clouds and the leaves of the beech trees.

"What can you tell me about the burglaries and the fire?" she asked, facing the direction from which his voice had come.

"Come this way." He had moved to her left, into the darkness nearer the road. "I have answers."

Alyssa's head snapped around. She peered into the darkness but saw nothing. "Where are you?" she asked.

No reply.

But he stood there somewhere, she knew, waiting for her to walk up to him. He said he'd wanted to touch her.

She shuddered. Maybe she could wait him out. See if he spoke again. "How can I find you?" she said aloud.

Silence.

She ought to do what he wanted. Walk right over there. But her feet wouldn't move. She'd wait just a minute, give Sue a chance to maneuver in that direction. Then, if this guy tried to grab her, they could grab him instead. It could work.

168

After all, she'd come out here to offer herself as bait.

She swallowed and told herself she'd wait two minutes. If nothing happened, she'd walk over there.

Slowly, she began to count off the seconds in her head.

Until she'd settled in Detroit, Sue had walked many times in the night woods with no campfire or flashlight. Tonight, in the utter darkness, she felt her senses tighten once again, razor-sharp. She heard her breath leave her body and imagined it floating upward to be inhaled by the trees. She could feel the muscles of her eyes stretching, pulling at every thin wave of light in order to construct a picture of the area.

She had watched Alyssa get out of the car and talk to the man. Sue squatted, making a less obvious profile for anyone else to observe, and listened, keeping her eyes closed against the piercing light of the headlights. When Alyssa turned them off, she could see well.

Her eyes darted around the perimeter of blackness, memorizing the shapes in the surrounding woods. Her gaze swept around again, higher, in case the stalker used an old tree stand. Her eyes remembered, then scanned again, looking for change. Change meant movement, and movement would be the man.

When the man spoke again, Sue's head snapped around. He was on the move. Pine scent rose from her footfalls as Sue stepped across the soft needle-covered ground. *Stay put*, she ordered Alyssa silently. *Give me a chance to get there.*

Sue moved slowly, then paused to listen. Alyssa's warm engine clicked in the cool evening air. A whisper of wind brushed the soft leaves and needles against each other, and above her, a branch creaked. Alyssa shifted her position against the car, clearly nervous. Otherwise, Sue heard nothing.

Sue imagined Alyssa anxious for some sign that she was there, watching her as promised. But any sign to her could be seen or heard by the man, so she didn't dare risk it. Alyssa would just have to trust that Sue would protect her. *And I will.*

Suddenly, the compromise and self-deception of the last few years fell away. In the darkness, Sue understood with sudden clarity. *I am a cop.*

She would protect Alyssa or die trying.

The moon lost a half behind a cloud, then quickly reappeared. Alyssa stepped away from her car. Sue crouched slowly, willing her back. What had happened? Had she seen her, seen something else? Sue still heard nothing, saw nothing.

From the opposite side of the clearing came a large crack, deep enough to echo in the trees. Sue's head snapped up. Had the guy moved, or was there someone else? She looked at Alyssa who stood rigid, staring at the spot where the guy had been when he had spoken. She'd heard the noise behind her, Sue could tell, but she didn't turn.

Sue knew she had better get over there and find out who made that noise. What if the caller had brought someone else? Sue moved slowly, curling each foot from toe to heel onto the ground, feeling for sticks before she rolled her full weight into the step. She carried her body in a crouch, abdominal muscles tightened into a curl, supporting her upper body through the slow steps. She felt like she was swimming, the fluid darkness washing around her.

Then Sue stumbled over a branch and, reaching out, caught the rough trunk of a jack pine tree to hold herself upright. She almost cursed aloud but didn't want to make any more noise.

A shadow shifted ahead of her and she heard the whisper of cloth on cloth. *A person.* The sound moved about twenty feet ahead and to the right, away from the clearing. *I can get him, and maybe end this now.*

Sue followed, closing the gap between them. She had just begun to calculate the distance she needed for a good tackle in the dark when she heard Alyssa's Jeep start.

Something had happened. They had agreed Alyssa would stay in the clearing for thirty minutes if nothing happened, and meet back at the drop-off point. But it hadn't been thirty minutes, Sue knew. Something had happened.

He lured me away, Sue realized as adrenaline flashed through her. She couldn't protect Alyssa from here. She turned away from the shadow and began to run back toward Alyssa. *I left her there alone.*

Sue's muscles strained as she willed herself to move faster through the trees. *I left her. If anything happened—*

She saw the headlights snap on and turn back down the road, moving slowly. She'd never catch the Jeep on the road, but the trail cut straight, while the road curved. Maybe she could beat it back to the intersection.

She found the trail and ran, lungs sucking air, legs pushing, but not fast enough. She moved so much faster in the water, she thought. Why couldn't she just skim the forest, like she did the lake in her kayak?

The headlights reappeared just as Sue entered the road from the trail. She stood in the center of the two-track road, forcing herself upright though her body heaved in its attempts to get air. If the car didn't stop, she would stop it.

The Jeep sped closer, then with a dusty skid, lurched to a stop ten feet away.

Alyssa, colorless and haggard, stepped out from the driver's seat. "Where the hell were you?" Her eyes flashed.

Sue leaned against the hood of the car and struggled for breath. She wanted to hold Alyssaa but needed just a few more breaths.

"And how the hell could you make so much damned noise?" Alyssa said.

Sue checked her watch, still leaning. "That wasn't thirty minutes," she said, her breath slowing. "What happened?"

Alyssa seemed not to hear her. "If he knows you were here and comes after you . . . if he kills you, it's not my fault. Do you hear me? Not my fault!"

Sue heaved one last heavy breath and stood straight. "Why did you leave early?"

"I got the hell out of there after that noise in the woods." She shook with rage.

"I didn't make it," Sue said.

"Well, I didn't know. What if someone had gotten you, if you were fighting . . . ?" Her voice trailed away and she shook her head. "Damn it, Sue, I brought you out here to help, not make it worse."

"I never should have let you do this," Sue said.

"Screw you. You didn't 'let' me do anything. You don't have that kind of power over me. Get in the car, or I'm leaving you here, as promised." She slid in and slammed the door.

Sue walked around the Jeep and opened the door.

"You made the decision to come along," Alyssa said as soon as Sue had pulled the door shut. "In fact, you blackmailed me into agreeing, which was a low thing to do, now that I think about it."

Sue buckled in and the car jerked her back, spinning the tires on the dirt road. "Whoa, Alyssa! Take it easy."

"You coerced me." Alyssa gripped the steering wheel. "You made this decision, not me. I didn't want you out there. So don't blame me."

Her words stung. "I'm not blaming you for anything." The car continued to gain speed, bouncing on the rough road as it neared the junction with M-22, the main route. "But can you not kill me now?" Sue asked. "Or is that part of your plan?"

Alyssa slammed on the brakes, propelling them forward in their seats. Sue thought she saw tears brimming in Alyssa's eyes, but none fell. "What were you doing out there? Swinging from the branches? I had to pretend not to hear you, so I wouldn't give you away!"

Sue pulled her shoulders back. "Do you think I'm that big of an idiot? That I'd stake out the woods and make that kind of noise?"

"How the hell do I know?" Alyssa slammed her palm into the wheel. "How am I supposed to know?"

"You're supposed to trust, Alyssa." Heat boiled in Sue's chest. "After all this, you still don't trust me?"

"It's only been a week, Sue," Alyssa countered, her voice quieter.

"Yep." Sue felt frustration percolating in her. "An important week. Life-changing for me. I thought for you too, but I guess I was wrong." Her throat burned. "Get us out of here, please. I want to go back to Delia's."

Alyssa didn't move. "If you didn't make that noise, then someone else did. Who? What did you do?"

Sue's jaw tightened. She didn't have to explain herself, to prove her competence to Alyssa. Still, she'd tell her and show her what a bitch she'd been for overreacting. "I don't know. It might have been one or two. I followed the noise, saw a man, tall, ahead of me. I followed him, and almost had him too, until you started the car and I ran back to find out what had happened to you." She shook her head. "I could have had him." She looked at Alyssa and even in the darkness saw the flat wall behind her eyes. She hadn't seen that there before. "What now?"

"You left me." Alyssa turned away from her and began to drive.

Another round of frustration burst in Sue. "I was trying to catch the guy. That's what you wanted, right?" Alyssa drove in silence, without looking at Sue. "Besides," Sue said, "you just got done saying you didn't want me there. So what does it matter that I chased the bastard who's been tormenting you? You didn't need me anyhow."

Sue turned and fell back into the seat. How could Alyssa be mad when she'd risked her neck to chase this guy? Screw her. She could take it from here on her own.

"You're right," Alyssa said. "I don't need you. So there's no point in discussing it further."

They rode the rest of the way to her house in silence. As Alyssa parked, Sue told herself what a relief it would be to get back to a normal life. Just Zero, a few clients, the quiet click of the computer keys, the swish of oars in water.

Of course, thanks to the fire, she had no place to live or work. But at least she wouldn't have an uptight wacko yelling at her to praise her dog for obeying, or standing up to crooks armed only with her sense of justice.

Of course, she'd miss the turbulent desire in those green eyes.

Damn. In so short a time, how had she gotten to want Alyssa so much?

Sue looked at her, and realized with mild surprise that neither of them had moved since she parked the car.

"Sue." Alyssa stared straight out the windshield. "I know you're going. But one thing about dogs is—" She paused and glanced toward Sue, then smiled a little. "You sick of hearing me talk?"

"Go ahead."

"Well, with dogs, you never leave an interaction unfinished, you know? If the human is stupid enough to go away mad, well, the dog isn't. He just goes ahead and loves you. Does that make sense?"

"Yep."

"I like that about dogs." Alyssa shifted so she faced Sue. "I shouldn't have said all that back there. That noise, well, I got so frightened and . . . well, I'm sorry." She blew out the breath she'd held. "I should have trusted you." She shook her head. "No, that's not right. I do trust you, but I let my fear—"

Sue placed a hand on Alyssa's thigh. "It's okay. I thought I'd catch him for you. Be your hero, you know? And I didn't think. I let him lure me away and when I realized it, it scared me to death."

Alyssa furrowed her brows in what Sue thought was amusement. "You wanted to be my hero? Like rescuing me from the railroad tracks?"

Sue laughed. "I know better. You could rescue yourself. I just thought I could stop the train."

"I thought that if something happened to you—" She grabbed Sue's shirt and pulled her close.

Alyssa's kiss felt desperate and moist and good.

Then she shoved Sue hard back into the seat. "I love you and it pisses me off." She leapt out of the Jeep, slamming the door behind her.

Sue followed her onto the porch. "Why?"

"Why do I love you, or why does it piss me off?"

"I'm not stupid enough to ask the first," Sue said. "Why does it make you angry?"

174

"It messes things up and makes it all harder." Alyssa opened the door and Zero bolted out, happy to see his owner.

Sue petted the dog. "Hey, boy." She followed Alyssa into the house and watched her turn on all the lights.

"We have to hang the blinds for that slider tomorrow," Alyssa said.

Sue felt thankful that she'd already adjusted to Alyssa's conversational jumps, so moving from dogs to love to blinds in the space of thirty seconds didn't bother her. But she thought maybe they should get back to that love thing.

Alyssa headed her off. "Well, I guess we didn't do so well at turning the tables did we?" She plopped down on the couch, leaned her head back and closed her eyes. "I am so tired."

"Well, there's one thing we know." Sue felt some measure of relief. "He doesn't want to kill you. Or he could have done it." She didn't add that that was precisely why Alyssa shouldn't have gone out there in the first place.

"No. I never thought he did."

Sue knew Alyssa hadn't told her everything. She said she loved her, she'd agreed to work together on this, but she still kept some secret.

"Sue, do you think he was testing us, sort of the same way we were testing him? To find out if I'd come? If you would come?"

Sue's stomach tightened. "Possibly." She just wasn't equipped for this. She needed to call the police. No point in suggesting it, though, she knew. She could just call them herself, but then she could kiss Alyssa good-bye. And she wasn't ready to do that yet. "Do you want to go to bed?" she asked.

"I'm not in the mood," Alyssa responded. She acted like she was in another world.

"I meant to sleep. I need to sleep." That's probably why she couldn't figure out what they should do. She just needed sleep.

Alyssa opened her eyes. "You'll stay?"

"I'd like to." She lifted Alyssa's hand and kissed it gently.

Alyssa smiled and closed her eyes again. Within seconds Sue heard her breathing deepen, and she slept.

Chapter Eighteen

Alyssa spent much of Wednesday morning trying to keep her job instead of thinking about the fiasco in the woods. Marcus admitted to liking her ideas for getting new clients but continued to call her a hazard to the company. Delia phoned the office from the hospital and announced that two of the ladies in her tavern group had visited her and promised they'd use Alyssa if they ever got dogs. Marcus just shrugged then left the office for lunch. Minutes later, the phone rang.

"Dixon's Obedience and Guard Services," Alyssa said.

"What is going on with you and the woman?" Melanie said. "I haven't heard from you since Monday night."

"None of your business," Alyssa replied, glad to hear from her friend.

"Oh, yes!" Melanie laughed.

Alyssa got the mental image of Melanie dancing a jig.

"I won't ask about the sex," Melanie said, "but lordy, I want to ask about the sex."

"Let's just say, I can see clearly now."

"I knew it." Melanie sighed. "Well, you deserve something wonderful, what with all the other crap going on."

"Anything new I should know about?" Alyssa asked. *Like, has Strunk publicized my record yet?*

"Well, we checked the victims' phone records and found no similarities. They don't share many life patterns."

"What do you mean?"

"Oh, things like Delia hangs out at the Twelve Point, but Samantha goes to the Blue Seahorse. And of course, Sue just got here, so she hasn't been much of anywhere around here yet. They all shop at Harry's Stop-n-Go, but so do we all. They don't use the same insurance or hairdresser or housecleaners or landscape people. Just the same dog trainer."

Alyssa closed her eyes. "Strunk must love that."

"He's out of town somewhere, beating the lab boys for test results. It takes forever when we have to send everything out. The luck of living in a small town." She sighed dramatically. "At least nothing happened last night."

Alyssa thought again of the trip to the woods. No sense in telling any of that to Mel now. "Right."

They chatted another minute about Melanie's son and his summer job, then hung up. Seconds later, the phone rang again.

"Just me," came Sue's voice. "Phone was busy."

"It was Melanie."

"Good. You're still among the employed?"

She leaned across her desk. "Barely, but yes. No new clients today though."

"Hang in there." Sue sounded energized and upbeat. "I'm at Delia's, but I've got to hit a sports store to replace my workout gear. Can I meet you at home in a couple of hours? We can do the blinds."

She looked around at the empty office. She'd done so much paperwork to fill the hours without clients that her desktop was bare. It depressed her. "Sure. I'll meet you then."

"Okay. See you there."

She hung up and rose from the desk. Her gaze landed on the bulletin board filled with photos of her clients and their dogs. She hated to think she could lose all this. There had to be something she could do.

The phone rang again, and before she'd brought the receiver to her ear, she knew.

"You brought the woman, Miss Deborah."

She said nothing.

"So much for trust. I tested you. I made that noise, and you didn't look, didn't even flinch, because you thought it was her, didn't you? You thought you'd help her hide? But she came to me in the woods and let me lure her away."

Anger leapfrogged over her fear, and Alyssa burned in silence.

"I should have listened to Mr. Covington. He knows all about your sins and the punishment you need."

"I've had it with him." The words escaped Alyssa's mouth before she realized what she'd said. But as soon as she said them, she knew they held the answer. "Tell him that I'm coming after him. Just like I did before. Got it? You tell him. And I'm taking him out for good this time." She slammed the receiver down and stood staring at it. It didn't ring again.

Her hands shook and she felt lightheaded, so she sat. What had she done? She had no idea how she could play this out.

A little before 8:30 that evening, Sue knelt in the grass beside Delia's puppy Tango, trying to get him to stay in the down position with all the other puppies nearby. The scene in the training yard looked nothing like it had last Wednesday evening. Only Sue, Adam Braeburn and the teenager with a Chihuahua had shown up. Zero watched from the back of the Subaru.

"If you can take three or four steps away from your pup, do that," Alyssa said to the little group.

Sue couldn't even get Tango to stay put long enough to take one step. She'd never realized how easily distracted a puppy could be when he wanted to play.

"Try five seconds, then praise. Then try ten seconds." Alyssa stood above her. "Remember to praise the dogs when they're good."

Sue smiled and nodded. She watched her go over to Adam, appreciated the curve of her back as she showed the boy a better position for his feet.

"Wait a minute," Calvin Braeburn demanded. He and his wife approached from the sidelines where they'd stood watching the entire class with deep scowls. "We want to hear every word you say to our son."

Ouch.

As Alyssa worked with the boy, Samantha stationed herself with one elbow balanced on a hip, her hand upward and empty as if holding an imaginary martini. The real thing had probably been there not too long ago, Sue thought, watching the woman's upper body waver in small circles.

"If you roll him over onto one hip, he won't move," Alyssa said.

"Cool, Miss Norland. You're a really good dog trainer because you know all the tricks."

"Bah!" said Calvin.

Sue didn't think anyone said "bah," except in old movies.

Samantha opened her darkened eyes wide in surprise, then snorted with poorly suppressed laughter at her husband.

"She's got plenty of tricks, son," Calvin said.

Sue saw a long thin muscle in Alyssa's neck tighten. "Mr. Braeburn, I'd love to talk to you after class, but right now, I'd appreciate you not disrupting my work with the students."

Kick his butt, Alyssa. Sue loved it when Alyssa showed some spunk.

"I'd say class time is up now." Calvin pointed to his watch, which he'd checked at least a hundred times in the last hour. He turned to Alyssa. "And I have plenty to say to you."

Alyssa explained the homework for Saturday. "Your dog should be able to stay for one minute," Alyssa said.

"A whole minute," said the girl with the Chihuahua. "Cosette can't do anything for a whole minute!"

"She'll surprise you," said Alyssa.

Sue stood and stretched her back, pretending not to listen.

"Yeah," said Adam. "I saw this show on cable and dogs can do the coolest things!"

"Except guard houses effectively," said Calvin. "Or is that just your dogs, Miss Norland?"

"No, Dad," Adam insisted. "They can guard stuff and track bad guys, even through water. Like Officer Sybesma's dog will do." The boy looked around. "How come she isn't here?"

"Good question, Adam," said his father. "What do you think, Miss Norland? Shouldn't the police be here?"

This guy was a real pain. Sue took a few steps closer to Alyssa, pretending to adjust Tango's collar as she walked.

"She's working overtime," said Alyssa.

"Investigating you?" Calvin asked.

Okay. That's enough of that, Sue thought. "Hey, Adam. Won't it be cool to watch Nestor learn to pull a boat?"

"A big one?" Adam had met Sue at the start of class and marveled that she had a kayak.

"Good. It's Marcus," said Calvin. "I'd hoped to speak to him."

Sue saw Alyssa's boss and his dog headed toward them from the cottage.

"Everyone have a nice class?" Marcus asked.

"It was lovely," Samantha said.

"Samantha, get the boy and the dog to the car." Calvin spoke without even glancing in her direction.

Sue hoped Samantha didn't intend to drive anywhere.

"Let's go, Adam." His mother swept an arm around him. "You must have homework."

"School's out, Mom."

"Well, read a book or something."

"See you, Adam," Alyssa said.

Adam waved, and Sue winked. *Cute kid.* Someday, she'd treat her own kids better than the Braeburns did Adam.

"I want to thank you for coming today, Calvin," Marcus said, "given the events of the last week."

"I came because I could not figure out how to tell the boy that one of his new heroes, the dog trainer, is a thief and a liar."

Sue stepped forward. "That's a little out of line."

She saw Alyssa shoot her a look. *Just trying to help*, she thought, then shoved her hands in her pockets.

Calvin focused on Sue. "If your landlady hadn't nearly died in a fire, she'd be working that pup."

"How is Delia, by the way?" asked Marcus.

"Good. Thanks for asking," said Sue. "I brought her home earlier. She's just not up to a tango with Tango. Yet."

"She got lucky." Calvin licked his lips, then turned to Alyssa. "I don't know how many men—or women—you may have charmed, but not me. You're in this up to your ears and I know it."

"And your evidence is—" Alyssa let the question hang.

Very nice, thought Sue.

"I don't need evidence. I've got instinct about who's playing straight and who isn't. It's how I succeed in business."

Sue rocked on her feet.

"And something's fishy about the dog training." Calvin pointed at Alyssa. "And you, somehow." Then he pointed at Marcus. "You for keeping her on."

"Now hold on," said Marcus.

"You don't even have a guard dog," said Sue. "The situation is quite different from Delia's. The robberies may not be connected."

Everyone stared at her in silence for a few seconds.

"Or my house may be the next to burn," said Calvin. He pointed at Marcus. "It's your business, Dixon, but you're insane to let this woman ruin what you've started. The whole town knows she's in on this."

"Not really," said Sue. Braeburn turned to her, his face swelling with fury, but she cut him off before he could speak. "The real criminals know she's innocent. In fact, I imagine they're pretty interested in keeping everyone else's attention on Alyssa. Doesn't that make sense, Mr. Braeburn?"

He gaped.

Sue smiled as sweetly as she could. "Of course, you're spending a lot of energy pointing the finger at others, aren't you? Literally, in fact, which my mother taught me was quite rude." She shrugged. "I wonder what the whole town would think of the fact that your wife isn't even sure she turned on the alarm. You know, if someone mentioned it at the Twelve Point later this evening?"

Braeburn's face darkened to ripe plum. "You involve me in this," he said, his voice shaking, "and I'll sue you, I swear. I have a reputation." His inflated chest collapsed in exasperation and he turned back to Marcus. "Dixon, dump her before you lose the rest of your customers." He twisted toward Alyssa. "You'll be lucky if you have anyone left to teach on Saturday." He marched to his car.

"Uptight, isn't he?" Sue said as they watched the Braeburns drive away.

"Trying to tell me how to run my business," Marcus said.

"But he was right," said Alyssa. "Half my class was missing!"

Sue wished she could have rounded up all Alyssa's students and brought them in herself.

"That's a problem for you," Marcus said, "but I gave you until next Monday. I'm not going back on my word."

"Do you really think five more days is enough time?" Sue asked. She doubted Strunk would have the case wrapped up by then.

"I can't survive another week with people canceling and dropping out of classes," Marcus said. "It's all I can do. Anyway, Hendrix and I are heading over to the *Radley Record*. They want an interview and I'd prefer you stay out of the paper. If I take the dog, they'll jump on the photo op."

"Thanks, Marcus." Alyssa sounded relieved.

Marcus patted Alyssa's shoulder. "Hang in there, hon, it'll all be over soon."

After class Sue and Alyssa visited Delia. They agreed Delia shouldn't be alone her first night out of the hospital, so Alyssa went home alone.

Sue had installed the slider blinds that afternoon, right after Alyssa told her about the latest call. They only made her feel a little better. More than once she wished she could hide outside and watch what was going on.

The next morning she pulled in at the office just before 9:00 and found Sue waiting in the parking lot, her car parked next to Marcus's van.

"No news is good news, right?" Sue asked as she closed her car door.

"All quiet. You?" Alyssa opened the gate.

"Delia and the dogs slept all night. She was up and sassy at about seven." Sue followed her to the office. "I thought I'd stop by for a cup of coffee. I didn't realize your boss would be here. I need to talk to you."

"Okay. Come in and let's see what's up. He might be leaving soon."

Hendrix greeted them in the kitchen. As they walked into the office, Marcus waved a blue folder at Alyssa.

"This is the purchase order for Holloway's," Marcus said. "I was going to fax it later, but why don't you go? The drive to Traverse City will give you some time to yourself and keep the wolves away, at least for the day."

Holloway's Wholesale Animal Supplies stocked everything needed for keeping and training all kinds of pets and livestock. Alyssa loved walking the broad, high aisles, looking at all the latest gear and imagining ways she could improve her classes.

183

"I don't know," she said. "I don't want to leave you with all the work, Marcus. There's the lessons in Interlochen."

"Nonsense, honey." He patted her arm again. "You do those before. Or after. I'll cover the rest."

"Alyssa, I think you should talk to the police today," Sue said, "instead of leaving town."

"She isn't flying to Rio," Marcus snapped. Alyssa saw his eyebrows furrowed in annoyance. Then he smiled at Alyssa. "Take your time, have dinner. Work some more on new clients. If Strunk comes looking, I'll tell him he can find you at home later. Okay?"

"No, Alyssa." Sue stared at her hard. "I've been thinking and you really should go to the police."

Alyssa looked from Sue to Marcus. She knew they had her best interests at heart. But if Sue was going to start badgering her again about the cops then another road trip sounded good. "I'll go."

"Great!" Marcus patted her shoulder, then turned to Sue, all business. "Did you need a private session today, Ms. Hunter? I'd be glad to help you out."

"No," Sue said.

Her face looked dark and closed.

"Fine, then," Marcus said. "Shall I walk you to your car?" He took a step and gestured to Sue to move ahead, but Sue stood still.

"We have some paperwork to do," Alyssa improvised. She needed to talk to Sue alone.

"Oh?" Marcus's gaze shifted again from one to the other. "Then I'll go. Hendrix, heel." He nodded and led his dog to his van.

As soon as Marcus' car started, Sue turned to her. "Alyssa, I thought about it a lot last night. You need to tell the police about what happened in the woods."

"No." She tugged her hair back from her face. "I'm doing my job."

Sue placed her hands on Alyssa's hips, but Alyssa backed away. She didn't want to be touched now. It kept her from thinking clearly.

"I know," Sue said. "I'm trying to help."

"Thanks. But Marcus is helping too."

"His advice isn't very wise."

"Why? Because it isn't your idea?"

"Of course not." Sue slid her hands into her jeans pockets. "Because he doesn't know what's going on. Because calling the police makes sense."

It made no sense to Alyssa. "Sue, I'm not letting them win. That means I'm free to do my job, and that includes running errands for my boss. I refuse to act differently, because nothing is different. Don't you see?"

Sue shook her head, and Alyssa could see her frustration. "Look, Alyssa, we've got to think. What other possibilities are there? Who else could have done this?"

"Do you mean, besides me?" What was she implying?

"Yes, besides you." Sue pulled her hands out of her pockets and ran them through her curls. "Both houses, both dogs? The fire? Who else?"

Her face flushed with rage. "How would I know who else?"

"Well, think!" Sue paced a few steps across the office, then back. She stopped in front of Alyssa, staring at her hard. "Could it be Marcus?"

"What?" She couldn't believe her ears. "No! I've brought a lot of business to this firm. He has no reason to do this."

"Okay, who else then?"

Alyssa felt frustration squeeze the energy from her. "You're as bad as the police."

Sue stepped forward and took Alyssa's wrist. "Someone's setting you up, Alyssa. Threatening you. How does it all fit together?"

"I don't know!" she yelled, hoping volume would stop the questions. Tears threatened and she did not want to cry. "Please let me go."

Sue dropped her hand. "You can't tackle this on your own," she said, her voice sharp. "This guy's getting closer and you know it. Being so damned self-reliant won't help you."

Alyssa pointed a shaking finger at herself. "I've taken care of myself for a long time. I've had to."

She blinked against the burn in her eyes. "Now I've got to get to Traverse City."

Together they walked to their cars. Sue stood next to her wagon watching Alyssa get into the Jeep.

"At least let me come for dinner. We'll talk."

"You'll talk," said Alyssa.

"No, I promise." Sue leaned over the roof of her car. "I'll listen. Please."

Alyssa started the Jeep. Maybe it would work. "Okay. Five-thirty."

As she drove away, Alyssa admitted she didn't know how any of this would turn out. But she knew one thing for sure. She wanted to tell Sue everything.

Chapter Nineteen

Alyssa couldn't tell Sue everything when she first arrived that evening. Sue had been too excited to show off the new hiking boots, shirts and shorts she'd bought the previous day. She watched Sue's body bend and stretch and admired the lines of her butt. *Will I lose her when I tell her?*

It didn't seem right to ruin a good dinner by telling her, Alyssa reasoned as Sue cooked. And discussing it so soon after eating would give them indigestion.

"I bought you a present," Sue said after they'd washed the dishes. "A sleeping bag. So we can go camping. It's in the car. Want to see it?"

Alyssa said nothing while Sue demonstrated how the sleeping bag would zip together with hers. Sue nuzzled Alyssa's ear and sparks skittered down her spine. "I can't wait to christen them, so to speak."

Alyssa tilted her head so their mouths met.

"I need you so much," Sue said, and they walked back inside.

In the bedroom, Alyssa ran her fingers up Sue's back, tracing the lines of ribs and muscles there. She knew what they felt like arched. She needed that. At least one more time before she told her.

She slid her hands around Sue's ribs to caress her breasts through her bra. Sue moaned. *I'll tell her after*, Alyssa thought.

Through the fog of her desire, Alyssa heard a car in her driveway. She pulled away.

"Damn!" Sue said. "Strunk?"

"I thought he was out of town," Alyssa said. She looked out the window. A huge red truck skidded to a stop behind Sue's car.

"It's Delia!" Alyssa said. A black head bobbed in the seat beside Delia, but it didn't look like Teddy. She watched as Delia opened the truck door and a barrel-chested but leggy Doberman pinscher leapt down.

What the hell? She recognized Blade, the Vandenbrinks' dog.

Alyssa strode through the foyer and opened the front door just as Delia stepped onto the porch.

"Sorry to bother you, dear," said Delia. "It's a downright emergency."

Zero dashed past Alyssa, ignored the Doberman and leapt against Delia's shoulder, knocking her backward against a roof support.

"Zero, no!" Alyssa grabbed his collar and yanked him backward. He scrambled to keep his balance. "Sit!" Ears flattened outward with contrition, the dog sat, his head hanging. "Good dog." He wagged.

"Normally, I'd be better prepared for that." Delia chuckled as she regained her balance. "I'm afraid I'm still a little wobbly."

Sue crossed the porch to take Delia's arm. "You shouldn't even be out of the house yet."

She waved Sue off. "Nonsense. Here," she said, handing Sue the leather leash. "If you want to help, take Blade. My walking him is driving Tango crazy." She tipped her head toward her truck, where the collie pup stood on the seat, nose pressed to the window, eyes wide.

Alyssa ran her hand along the Doberman's back as Sue took him into the house. "Why do you have Blade?" She freed Zero from his sit and they followed Sue into the house.

Delia sat on the couch. "I feel like I've been out of it for three days. Tell me what I can do to help you, Alyssa dear." She smiled, her lips thin and prim. "I know the folks in this town can be nasty and I suspect you're feeling it. Then I'll tell you why I have Blade."

Blade sniffed around the room. Zero, still contrite, lay in the foyer, his head on his paws.

"I'll get the tea," Sue said, squeezing Alyssa's shoulder.

Alyssa sat in the armchair across from Delia and explained everything that had happened at class, how clients had canceled and about Marcus's pressure on her.

"I wish I could offer to beat that Marcus Dixon up," Delia said, accepting a steaming mug from Sue. "I could, however, go to the tavern and carry on about how ill that man Strunk has treated you. Might help some and it would give me pleasure."

Alyssa loved the idea, but Sue interjected. "No thanks, Delia. Don't draw attention to yourself until this is over."

Delia sighed. "I wish Carolyn were here. She's so good at figuring out complicated things with little parts. The thing that I can't quite get is why the Braeburns, when they didn't have a guard dog and the other two did? That little Buck doesn't count, not yet."

"The other two?" Sue asked.

Alyssa didn't look at Sue. Instead she looked at Blade, the most advanced dog she'd ever trained.

"Not the Vandenbrinks?" Alyssa asked.

Delia nodded. "Last night."

Damn. "But why haven't we heard about it?"

"No one knew," Delia explained. "Randall and Claire spent yesterday and most of today at the casino in Traverse. They came home just a few hours ago to find the lock broken. Jewelry, a gun, some coins. I don't know what all."

Alyssa moved from the chair to sit on the floor beside the

Doberman. His sleek short coat exposed every ripple of muscle and bone. She examined his neck, where a lasso might have caused an abrasion. "Did a vet look at him?" she asked.

"Randall said Strunk had blood drawn right away to test for drugging."

"So Strunk is back in town," Sue said. She stood by Alyssa looking down. "You see anything?"

"No, but a padded cable wouldn't leave a mark." She stroked the dog and looked at Delia. "How did you find out about this?"

"Randall's a raving lunatic, that's how. He might be ten years younger than me, but the man's an old coot if ever there was one."

"You trained Blade, I assume?" Sue asked.

"Yes. A single dog, guarding special areas in the house, like Teddy." Alyssa took Sue's hand as she stood up from the floor. "Thanks." She sat back down in the chair.

"So the idiot calls me at home when I'm trying to nap." Delia coughed into her fist. "Never even asks after my health. Doesn't give a fig for the garage. Just starts raving about wanting me to help him get you arrested, dear. Can you imagine?"

Alyssa could imagine.

Sue sat on the edge of her chair. "Does this guy have a lot of influence?"

"Some," Alyssa said. "He's wealthy and a year-round resident. A surgeon at the hospital in Traverse City."

"That's why I think it's time I stepped into the fray," Delia said. "If this war is going to be fought in the gossip trenches, it's best to send in the right troops. I'm connected, and I can take out that old fart, I guarantee." She harrumphed.

"I still don't understand how you got the dog," said Sue.

"Oh, well, Randall had made his speech to Strunk and he was meeting Marcus at the office, I guess to tell him to fire you and he wanted me to go along and support him. So I went." She smiled. "Not to support him, of course. I figured we needed someone on the inside, finding out what was going on. So I pretended I was concerned and went."

190

Alyssa couldn't help laughing. "Delia, you're brilliant!" The woman beamed. "But you should be resting!"

"Hogwash. I'll rest later. This is more important." She finished her tea. "Hits the spot." She handed the empty mug to Sue. "Thank you, dear."

Really, Alyssa thought, *I should adopt her*.

"So I went to your office, Alyssa," Delia said, "and there was Randall, screaming about liability and suing Marcus."

Alyssa pressed her palms into her forehead. "Poor Marcus."

"Randall said he wouldn't have any dog trained by you in his house. Called Blade a 'booby trap.' Said there was no telling when the dog might attack him. He was headed to the vet to have Blade put down! Can you imagine?"

Alyssa struggled to talk over the lump in her throat. "Kill the dog?"

"He was raving." Delia waved her hands to illustrate. "I told him to give me the dog, for heaven's sake. And he did. Right then and there. Wrote up a paper too, on Marcus's computer, that if Blade attacked anyone it was my responsibility, not his. And I wrote on it that the dog was mine and he could never have him back. And we signed it." She coughed again.

"Do you need something? Some water?" Sue asked.

Delia waved her off. "No." But she kept coughing.

"This is too much for you," Alyssa said. "You've been a terrific help." Alyssa stood, pulling Sue up beside her.

Delia's coughing ended and Alyssa saw her eyes watering. "I can't take him, darling," Delia said. "Not now. Teddy's still too trauma-tized and Tango's such a handful. I don't want to dump more on you, but—" She coughed again. Still, she tried to stand.

Sue helped her up.

"You saved his life, Delia," Alyssa said. "But it's my fault he almost died. I'll take Blade."

Sue kissed Delia on the cheek. "Don't worry about us, Delia," she said. "Whatever happens, we can deal with it."

You hope, Alyssa thought, but nodded with confidence.

"Before I head home," Delia said, grasping Sue's arm, "would you be a dear and take Tango for a little run? Just to see that he's gone potty and romped with Zero for a minute or two?"

Sue nodded. "Sure," she said, kissing Delia again. She called Zero and left.

As soon as the door closed, Delia sat down again and leaned forward on the couch. "So how are things going with the two of you, dear?"

Alyssa tried the obvious first. "Zero's training is—"

"No, no, I mean the romance." Her eyes flared wider as she said the word.

"Delia!" Still, Alyssa couldn't repress the grin.

"Oh, good!" Delia sat straighter. "I knew you were the perfect match. That's why I sent her to you."

Alyssa didn't know what to make of that. "I thought you sent her because Zero jumped."

Delia waved her hand again. "Well, yes, but really, who cares? I used it as an excuse to get Sue to meet you. I think she needs someone like you."

This got Alyssa's attention. "Really?" She sat back down in the chair. "Why?"

"You won't leave her. She's had so much loss in her life. She told you about her last partner? Giving up the force?"

"Yes."

"And her mother?" Delia's eyes looked sad. "Though that couldn't be helped."

"Yes." Sue hadn't told her much really, but she hadn't wanted to ask.

"So sad, of course. But Hugh lived up to his promise and quit the force to stay safer for the child." She must've read Alyssa's confusion. "Sue's mother wanted it that way. She worried Hugh would be killed and Sue would have no parent left." She paused. "Though she could have come to Carolyn and me. But, better that she had her father."

"I imagine."

"And you're the most loyal person I've ever met. Of course, you have nothing to do with these burglaries. You're too honest."

Alyssa felt a twist of guilt. She hadn't been so honest. After all, she hadn't told Delia or Sue everything.

"Delia," Alyssa said. "There's more." She inhaled deeply. "Once, I was arrested for theft. In Chicago. And—uh—I did it."

Delia's eyes widened. "You did? I've never known a thief before."

"I had a good reason. I—"

"I'm sure you did, dear." Delia smiled.

"Charges were dropped. It's a long story. But if word of that gets out, especially now, things will look so much worse for me. Even if the real thieves are caught. And what will Sue think?"

"You haven't told her?"

"No." She rubbed her sore neck and closed her eyes. "She's a cop."

"Why did you do it? Steal in Chicago?"

"To save some dogs. I stole one from a lab." As Alyssa waited for Delia's response her heart seemed to expand in her chest.

"Well," said Delia, "it makes perfect sense to me. I'd have done the same. Only I wouldn't have been clever enough to stay out of jail."

Alyssa opened her eyes.

Delia smiled again. "Tell Sue. She's the best chance you've got to straighten all this out once and for all." Delia stood slowly and winked. "And I'm betting she's not a bad lover."

"Oh!" Alyssa threw a pillow in Delia's direction, careful to miss her. She stood.

Delia gripped Alyssa's arm in firm fingers. "And you love her, I can tell. You wear it on your faces, both of you. You can't really love each other well until you share your true selves with each other."

Sue's footsteps fell on the porch.

"Am I right?" Delia asked.

Alyssa hugged her, feeling the woman's tiny frame in stark contrast to Sue's. "Yes, you're right. I'll try."

"Tango should be ready for a nap now," Sue said. "They ran great loops around the cars." She motioned with her thumb toward the front door. "He's back in the truck."

"Then I'm on my way." Delia patted Blade. "You be a good boy."

"I'll walk you out." Sue offered her an arm.

Alyssa listened to the sounds of Delia's departure. She could hear their voices but not their words. *Probably telling Sue what a perfect match we are.*

Are we?

Alyssa went into the kitchen to rinse the tea things. She looked at Blade lying on the floor next to Zero. "What're we gonna do with you, boy?" The dogs' pointed ears twitched like antennae.

She heard Delia's truck rumble away and Sue came back in. "What a woman. Promise me you'll be like that some day."

Alyssa promised. Sue gave her a hug. "Sorry about the Vandenbrinks, babe."

"Yeah." She pulled out of the hug. She didn't want to relax. If she did she might start sobbing and never stop.

"But at least Delia saved the dog." Sue touched her arm. "Look on the bright side, right?"

Alyssa forced a smile. "Yeah. I'll feel a lot safer with him snuggled up beside me tonight."

Sue stepped closer and hugged her again. "What about me?"

Alyssa turned away, wiping the counter again. "Do you think you should leave Delia?"

"She's fine. I'll stay here."

"Okay." Alyssa hung up the towel and looked around. Everything neat and tidy on the surface. But in reality, nothing was neat and tidy at all.

Sue's sleep ended at 6:32 a.m. when the phone rang. *The stalker?* She shot out of bed and was stepping into her jeans when Alyssa answered.

"It's Melanie," she said.

Sue slipped back into bed, watching as Alyssa talked.

"Yes," Alyssa said, "we heard about the Vandenbrinks." She listened. "No. Delia told us. I have Blade here." She glanced at Sue. "What is it, Mel? You sound tense."

Sue felt her stomach tighten as she watched Alyssa's face. Bad news on the other end of the line. "What?"

Alyssa signaled Sue to wait. "But what?" she said into the phone.

Sue could hardly stand it. "What?"

Alyssa turned away so she could hear better. "Well, let him come, the bastard. There's nothing to hide."

Shit, thought Sue. Strunk must've gotten a search warrant.

"Just do your job, Melanie. Find the bad guys. Then everyone can just leave me alone so I can do mine." Alyssa clicked the phone off, tossed it onto the bed, and flopped back against the pillow, her arm thrown across her eyes. "I hate this."

Sue touched her gently. "That sounded a little rough."

Alyssa rolled away from her and padded to the bathroom. "I'd do just about anything to stop it for good."

Sue agreed. She got up and cooked a pot of oatmeal while Alyssa showered.

"Sorry," said Alyssa when she entered the kitchen, her hair dangling in wet curls.

"It's Melanie you need to talk to, not me." Sue handed her a cup of coffee.

Alyssa asked for some time alone, so Sue took Zero for a long walk on the beach. When she returned to the cottage at about 8:15, she found Alyssa sitting on the couch with her head in her hands.

"Melanie?" Sue asked.

"No." Alyssa didn't raise her head. "We're fine. Marcus called. Told me not to come in anymore. He pretty much fired me." She looked up, her eyes filling with tears. Sue sat next to her. "Said I had until Monday to find new clients like he promised, but really, what's the point? I can't do it." Then she put her head on Sue's shoulder and cried.

Sue could hardly stand Alyssa's pain and her own inability to do anything about it.

After a minute, Alyssa calmed down. "Sorry. I must look like shit."

"No." Sue rubbed her back. "I've got an idea."

Alyssa sniffed and waited.

"Well, we both feel like crap because we can't do anything to help you. And you can't help your clients because they're being jerks. So, let's go spend the day helping Delia. She's got a mountain of stuff to do, still cleaning up after that fire. It'll keep our minds off it and the dogs can all run around together."

"What if Strunk wants me?"

"Trust me, love," Sue said. "If he wants you, he'll find you. At least if you spend the day with me and Delia you'll have an alibi in case anything else happens. What do you say?"

Alyssa smiled grimly. "It all sucks."

"Yes it does."

Alyssa nodded. "But your idea's a good one. And at least someone will feel better at the end of the day."

Alyssa enjoyed most of the day at Delia's, even managing to relax and laugh at the sight of fuzzy blond Tango running circles around three big dogs. They cleared a lot of paperwork, got carpenters in to finish enclosing the building and lined up several contractors to provide estimates on reconstruction. She'd even gotten in another lesson with Sue and Zero, who obeyed perfectly as long as he was on leash. She had never seen a dog so obstinate about jumping up on people when he was off leash. Then Delia insisted on cooking her famous chicken pot pie for dinner. Strunk never called.

When Sue asked if she could spend the night again, Alyssa agreed readily.

They arrived back at her cottage shortly after 7:00. Zero and Blade flopped to the floor by the couch and went right to sleep.

"They had a busy day," Sue said, looking out the slider toward the dunes.

Alyssa laughed. "Us too." She moved next to Sue and kissed her cheek. "What do you think the odds are that Strunk will come by tonight?"

"Small." Sue turned her face to return the kiss. "Probably didn't see the judge today. Why? What do you have in mind?"

"Well, the longer we wait, the more likely Strunk will show up, right? So, since I'd like a little lovin'—" She kissed Sue again. "I thought I'd see if I could convince you to participate now." She smiled.

"I'm in," said Sue.

"Wait here. I want to do something special." She went to her bedroom and stood in her closet considering what she could wear. She wanted to put on something special for Sue. For fun.

"Should I be worried?" Sue asked from the other room.

"No." Alyssa considered the dresses stored in the back of the closet. As she reached for her red dress, she heard a sharp ping like metal on metal. *That's not right.* She ran back into the living room.

Her brain registered Sue on her knees in front of the sliders, hands to her head. A giant spider web grew on the glass, moving toward her. Sue raised her arms against it just as the glass shattered and rained down around her.

Chapter Twenty

"Sue!" Alyssa's heart pounded in her ears.

"Get the dogs!" Sue yelled from her position face down on the floor.

Blade and Zero stood near the couch. "Come!" Alyssa clapped and they obeyed. "Okay."

Sue raised her head and Alyssa saw red across Sue's right temple, eye and cheek. Her stomach lurched. "Your head!" *It's just like Vinnie*, she thought. *This can't be happening.*

"Just a cut." Sue inched her way backward out of the broken glass. "We're going. Now."

"Okay." Alyssa was shaking.

Still on her hands and knees, Sue grabbed the leashes from the basket near the couch and tossed them to Alyssa. "I've got my car keys," she said evenly as she rose to a crouch.

Alyssa scanned the landscape through the shattered door and saw only beach grass, golden in the sun. "I can't see anyone out there."

"It doesn't matter." Sue pulled her shirt up to wipe the blood from her face. "Ready?"

"Yes." Alyssa bent to leash the dogs.

"I wish I had a gun." A new crimson line thickened and dripped down Sue's face. "Listen, he may be on the move. Stay here and out of sight. I'll get the car, then pull up with the back door open. The seats are down. Jump in with the dogs and stay flat. Just stay down until I tell you, got it?"

Alyssa didn't want her going out in the open. "No."

"Alyssa, do you understand?" Sue's grip hurt her arm but got her attention.

"Yes, okay." What else could they do? *I let it come to this.*

"Stay here, then." Sue wiped her forehead on her shirt again, then swung through the front door.

Alyssa looked across the front yard and saw nothing out of the ordinary. She watched Sue run to her car then slide in, keeping herself low behind the wheel.

Beside Alyssa, Zero and Blade began to growl. Hackles rose at their shoulders as they looked backward toward the living room.

Just as the wagon pulled up to the porch, Alyssa heard a step in the shattered glass behind her.

He's here. She ran.

"Heel!" She dragged the dogs who twisted and snarled behind her. From inside the car, Sue swung the back door open. Alyssa dove onto the deck, pulling Zero in first, then Blade. The second dog's feet had barely left the ground when she screamed, "Go, go!" The sudden acceleration rolled Alyssa and the dogs across the car's deck. Gravel spit against the open door, until she reached across and shut it.

"Stay down!" Sue ordered, piloting the car down the driveway.

"He was in the house," Alyssa breathed, terror coursing through her. She felt her body racked with the convulsive attempt to get air and prepare for further flight. "I heard him behind me."

"Did you see him?" Sue asked. The tires squealed as she negotiated the curve onto the road.

"No." Alyssa's lungs sucked more air. "I couldn't see." *I should've looked, then we'd know who he is.* She lay on her back, staring at the ceiling of the car.

"Okay," Sue said, her voice angry. "Okay. We're done fooling around."

Alyssa heard a click from the front and felt the smack of a small, solid weight onto her stomach. Sue's cell phone.

"Dial nine-one-one," Sue said, "and tell them everything. Find a place to meet the cops. Melanie, Strunk, whomever. We have to get you somewhere safe."

Sue was right. Alyssa hadn't confessed everything, and look at what had happened—Sue bleeding all over, a gunman in her house. Any of them, all of them, could have been killed. Her fingers punched the emergency number. *What could be worse than this?*

Jail. She paused before pushing the send button, and thought again of the night she'd spent there, the matrons' hands on her body, the filthy floors and dull green walls, the stench of bodies and disinfectant, the ugly intimidation from the other inmates. She wouldn't go there again, certainly couldn't live there. She couldn't stand it.

"Hey, are you dialing?" The car rocked as Sue rounded another turn.

She thought of what Marcus had said about her career being over. Just staying out of jail wasn't enough. She wanted to keep working. She wanted her life back.

"Dial the phone, damn it!"

And her plan to catch the bastard the other night had worked, sort of. If they'd been ready, they could have gotten him.

She clicked the phone off. She wasn't calling the cops. Not now. She wanted Covington's head on a platter.

200

"Where are you going?" Alyssa asked.

"Away. And I'm trying to make sure we aren't being followed." Sue's voice sounded strained, as if delivered through gritted teeth.

"Are we?"

"I don't see anyone yet."

Alyssa pulled herself into a sitting position. "Then keep heading north."

Sue shook her head violently, and Alyssa realized she was trying to shake the blood from her eye. "Call the police!"

Sue rolled the car through the stop sign that marked the center of Radley.

"Look, Sue, go north, to Glen Arbor. It's far enough away and there's a big grocery there. We can clean and cover your cut. Then we can talk about what to do."

"Alyssa! He shot at you." Sue growled her words, whether from pain or anger, Alyssa couldn't tell. Her stomach twisted with renewed fear, but she willed herself to stay focused.

"No, Sue. He shot at you. He's not following us now, you said so yourself. I have to think. Please."

"This isn't a dog-training exercise. Or just a burglary accusation. You need protection."

"I need time to think," Alyssa insisted. "Please. Our plan worked perfectly. Don't you see—he came to us. If we'd been ready—"

"You're crazy!" Sue shook her head hard and wiped her eye. "What am I doing here?"

"You can leave if you want," Alyssa said.

Sue burst out, "I'm not leaving. You're too completely nuts to be left alone."

"Just a few hours, so I can think this through."

"How about Melanie's?"

"No. I can't go to anyone else's house and involve them." She leaned forward and looked at the blood dripping onto Sue's shirt. "You don't need a doctor, do you?"

"Yes," Sue said. "Good idea. I probably need stitches. An emergency room. Something. The closest hospital is where Delia was, right? South?"

The tone of her voice made Alyssa suspicious. "They'd call the police, wouldn't they?" Sue didn't answer. "Would they?"

"Yes, yes! Help for me and help for you, too. This has got to stop."

"Look, I can't think like this, racing up the coast, you bleeding, my ears still ringing." Alyssa paused. Sue had been hurt because of her. She deserved to know. "There's more that I haven't told you. Please go to Glen Arbor. For just a few hours. So I can tell you the whole story. Then, I promise, I'll listen to what you have to say."

"You'll go to the police?"

"I'll think about it." *No promises*, she thought. "Please. You said I could trust you."

"Okay." Sue wiped her cheek against her shoulder. "Tell me where you want me to go."

Sue drove them into Glen Arbor shortly after 8:00 p.m. The sun was nearing the horizon, but tourists still filled the streets.

"The pharmacy's that way." Alyssa pointed into town.

"We're talking first." Sue headed north a few more blocks until the road ended looking over Lake Michigan. Like it or not, Alyssa was going to talk to her now or she was going to the police. Sue turned. "What the hell is going on? Why won't you go to the police? It's not just that woman who shot your dog. Is it Strunk being an ass? What?"

"I want to tell you, to explain it all. But not like this." Alyssa swung her head to watch a car pass slowly. "I have to concentrate." She gripped Sue's hand. "I have to be safe, to know everyone else is safe."

"Let's go to a motel."

"No!" Alyssa shook her head, then raised her hands to cover her eyes. "They know what the car looks like. The police and . . ." She shook her head again. "No. Somewhere where they can't find us, just for the night. So I can breathe. So I can tell you."

Sue sighed. Alyssa's panic had grown in the twenty minutes it took them to drive there. Maybe she deserved a good night's rest.

"Please."

"Shouldn't we at least call someone? Let them know we're okay?"

Alyssa didn't raise her head. "No one will come by. No one will even know it happened until we call the police."

Sue touched Alyssa's cheek gently. "So you will call the police? I'll stay right with you, I promise."

"Okay." Alyssa raised her head. "Tomorrow, okay? Let's just find somewhere to be together tonight." She smiled and grasped Sue's hand. "You really are okay? There's a lot of blood."

"It's mostly stopped. It'll be okay." Alyssa reminded her of herself when she was a kid, so afraid of losing her father after her mother died. He'd stayed with her, taken her for quiet safe time in the woods. "What about the woods, Alyssa?"

"What do you mean?"

"Well, the tent and my old bag are still in the car from before the fire. And we never pulled yours out. We can probably get whatever else we need in town, if I can charge it." As she spoke, Sue liked the idea better and better. "You know the area. Where can we park the car out of sight and hike into the woods? No one would track us there. You'd be safe and we'd be alone."

Zero stood in the back of the wagon, thrusting his head forward to lick Sue's cheek.

"Okay, the *four* of us would be alone." She pushed him backwards next to Blade. "What do you think?"

Alyssa thought for a second. "The Port Oneida Historic District. I did some training with tracking dogs there once. It worked because not a lot of people go there and the woods are thick. There's old barns and stuff, someplace to hide the car."

"Good! Good," said Sue with a smile. "The sun sets at about

ninc-forty, and another twenty minutes or so until full dark." If she got Alyssa focused on something else, even for a while, it might help her calm down. "Can you get us some place in that amount of time?"

"Yeah." Alyssa nodded tentatively. "I think so." She blinked, then smiled a little. "Yes." Her voice gained strength.

Sue put the car in reverse. "Let's go."

They stopped at the grocery store, where Alyssa bought gauze, butterfly closures, four deli sandwiches, two six-packs of water, a flashlight and dishes and food for the dogs. Then they headed north along the coast of Lake Michigan into the flat valley of the historic district.

As Sue drove, Alyssa explained that the federal government had purchased a block of historic farms and homes as part of the National Lakeshore, hoping to restore the buildings before they collapsed. She knew of a dilapidated barn that would hide the car. From there, they could head into the woods.

Alyssa looked at the fields surrounding them, outlined by high dunes covered with trees and brush. "I trust you, you know."

Sue put her hand on Alyssa's thigh. "I know."

"Somehow, the woods should be scary. But my home has been so much scarier." Alyssa hated the way Covington's people had violated her home.

"The woods are beautiful at night. And no one will find us. Tomorrow, you'll do what has to be done."

"Which is?" Alyssa asked.

"Don't you know?"

"No. Not yet. I mean, it's Saturday. I'm supposed to teach puppy class, but Marcus told me to stay away." She pointed to a little-used road that crossed through the heart of the valley. "That's your turn."

They wound around a small hill until a graying, tilted barn appeared.

"There," Alyssa said. "We can hide the car there."

"You want me to put my car in *there*? It's falling down!"

"Right. So no one will look there."

Sue insisted Alyssa and the dogs get out before she maneuvered the wagon between the tilted support beams. The dogs explored the nearby field as Sue pulled the tent from the back of the car. Alyssa watched the horizon.

"I haven't seen another car and it's after eight-thirty," Alyssa said. "No one else will be up here tonight."

"Are you sure you won't just go to the police tonight?"

"No." Alyssa pulled a sleeping bag from the car. "Not until we've talked." She didn't want Sue to hear this story for the first time from some cop. She needed to look her in the eye when she told it. She tossed the sleeping bag to Sue.

It hit her and fell to the ground.

Was she going to be difficult?

"For the record, I don't like it." Sue looked grim.

"Okay." Alyssa threw up her hands. "For the first time in days, I feel safe. I can think without someone trying to fire me, frighten me, frame me or kill my friends. I just thought it might be nice to talk and spend one last quiet night together before all hell breaks loose. Just one night!"

Sue stared at her, chewing on her lip. Then she bent and picked up the sleeping bag. "Okay, but I'm not happy about it."

"Fair enough. I'm not happy about calling the police. But we can figure it out."

Sue picked up the tent and one grocery bag. "This would be a lot easier with a backpack. You owe me one hell of a complete explanation." She marched away.

Alyssa led Sue and the dogs northeast across the base of the valley and up the forested side of an ancient dune.

The hard ground grew more sandy and shifted under their feet even as the air grew darker. At one point, Sue leaned forward from behind to touch Alyssa's back, pointing to the umbrella-shaped plants whose soft green leaves stretched like a giant tarp across the woodland floor. "May Apples," she said. "Up here they open in July. I loved watching them open when I was a kid."

The dogs wandered through the plants, sniffing.

Eventually they left the trail, marching east along the northern coast of the peninsula. As they walked, Sue drew Alyssa's attention to black cherry trees, clusters of grapevines thick enough for Tarzan to swing on, and a giant oak exploded by lightning. The shadows grew longer as they walked.

"You love the woods, don't you?" Alyssa asked.

"Yes. My parents shared that with me." They took a few more steps. "I don't ever want to leave here again."

Alyssa's heart fluttered a bit, but not from the exertion of the climb. *Of course*, she reminded herself, *that doesn't mean she'll stay with me. I may have to go.*

Finally, they followed a small deer path over a hill and into a clearing where the last rays of the sun shone brightly. Alyssa examined Sue's pale, sweating face. "We can stop here," she said.

Sue sat on the short grass and the dogs dropped to their sides nearby, ready to nap. Sue dug into a grocery bag and offered Alyssa a bottle of water.

"No, thanks. You drink it. You don't have very good color."

Sue downed the water without stopping.

Alyssa sat beside her and in silence they looked out from the dune. From here they could see the lake in the distance, over the tops of the trees. The water glistened dark under the purple sky, the Manitou Islands outlined by the setting sun.

"No haze today," Alyssa remarked, then felt guilty. Sue was covered in blood and she was talking about haze. "We have about twenty minutes of light left. Let's clean you up." She jumped to her feet, pulled the sleeping bag from its case and spread it on the grassy hilltop. "Sit." She grabbed the bag with supplies.

"Alyssa," Sue began, but Alyssa stopped her by placing her fingers against Sue's lips.

"How's your head?"

"Look." Sue pointed to the wound. The slice across her forehead gaped but did not bleed. "It stopped."

Alyssa winced at the parted flesh. "This is horrible. Look at you." She could barely stand to look at Sue's beautiful face smeared with dried cracking blood. Her hand slid from Sue's cheek to her saturated shirt. Then she reached across her lap into the grocery bag. She pulled out a clean white T-shirt. "It's a man's, but it's clean. Okay?"

"Okay." Sue peeled off her own stained shirt.

Alyssa couldn't take her eyes from the places where Sue's skin had been stained by flowing blood. "Here." She opened a gauze pad and dampened it with water. She wiped the area around Sue's collarbone where the blood had settled. "No sense in getting your other shirt dirty too."

"Mmm," Sue replied.

Alyssa drew the cloth forward across Sue's chest. She dabbed and circled, occasionally rewetting the cloth, until most of the blood was gone.

Alyssa pulled herself forward onto her knees to get more height as she brought the cool cloth to Sue's face. She touched the soft spot of her temple and Sue jerked away from the coolness, then closed her eyes and sighed as the compress soothed her.

"Is this what it's like?" Alyssa wiped along the grain of eyebrow and into the creases there. "Loving a cop?"

Sue opened her eyes. "Cleaning wounds? I think that's what it's like to love anyone. Cleaning up the wounds, helping them heal."

Yes, Alyssa thought, wiping Sue's cheek and jaw. Cleaning up the wounds. They could do that for each other.

"Did you love your ex a great deal?" Alyssa asked.

"A great deal," Sue said, without shifting her eyes. "Or I wouldn't have committed to her."

Alyssa nodded.

"However," Sue said, "I learned that the person I loved didn't really exist. She lied to me and I loved a deception. When that became clear, it ended."

Alyssa's stomach tightened. She hadn't told Sue the whole truth. Would this end too?

"Are you afraid?" Sue asked.

Alyssa paused, staring at the chestnut curls that sprang one by one from her hairline. "Of loving you? No." She drew the cloth down the bridge of Sue's nose toward her upper lip, trying to act braver than she felt.

A half-smile slid across Sue's face. "I think I should be afraid of loving you," she said, "but for some reason I'm not."

Alyssa stopped her ministering. Sue loved her. She'd said it casually, just slipped it in, but there it was.

Alyssa dropped her hands into her lap. "This happened because of me."

"Yep. I'd say I fell in love with you because of you." Sue smiled again, broader this time.

It broke Alyssa's heart. "Not that," she said. "Your getting hurt."

"I kind of like that part," Sue said. "After this, you can't object to my being a cop because it's dangerous. I never got shot at when I was on the force. Not once. But when I started seeing you, well." Sue frowned, stretching the gash in her forehead

"Don't make faces," Alyssa said, "or you'll open that thing up again." She watched, but only one small bead of blood popped up. She opened the peroxide and cleaned the cut. "And I never objected to your being a cop."

Sue reached toward her. "Alyssa, do you want to have a family?"

"Someday," she replied, taken aback. Right now that was the last thing on her mind. "I guess. I haven't thought about it much. What made you think of that now?"

"Watching you. Moms are always cleaning up wounds. My mom wanted lots of kids, but she got sick not long after she had me."

Alyssa stretched three butterfly closures across Sue's forehead and leaned back satisfied. "I suppose it would be great to come here as a kid."

Sue pulled her sideways off her knees so that their hips rested together, Alyssa's back against Sue's raised knees. "We can bring kids here, if you want to. But first, we have to get everything else cleared up."

Here it comes, Alyssa thought. *I'll tell her, and she'll see I'm not the person she thinks I am. And it will end.* Her neck stiffened.

Sue stroked her hair. "Will you tell me? Why are you so determined not to let anyone help you?"

"Do I have to?" Alyssa's stomach lurched again.

Sue looked at her, her eyes brown pools. "I love you, you know."

"Don't say that!" It made Alyssa feel even more guilty.

Sue wrapped her hands tightly around Alyssa's biceps. "Why can't I love you?"

Alyssa wished she could hide. But she wouldn't. Not anymore. "Sue, that man called me yesterday. In the woods—he made that noise to test me. And to lure you. You should have heard him gloating."

Sue sighed and gave her a squeeze. "I'm glad I didn't, and I'm sorry you had to. We know better now."

"You don't know it all." She sighed and began her story.

Chapter Twenty-one

"The short version is this: I used to work as publicity manager of Covington Enterprises, a low-profile private research and development facility. Very successful. We had lucrative contracts for testing the toxicity of airborne chemicals and some general household products, primarily using animal vivisection. I had the CEO's complete trust and earned lots of money."

Alyssa stared at her hands, shadowed in the dimming light. "Rodney Covington hired me right out of business school, told me how talented I was and promised that he could train me to be the best. I believed whatever he told me. So when animal advocacy groups began to ask questions about the labs, I did my job. Even though these weren't general protests, but specific accusations of illegal procedures, I put my reputation on the line for him. I defended him like—" She smiled. "Well, like his little guard dog."

She shook her head. "I was such a fool. But then a friend got a tip and came to me. I thought I'd shut them up once and for all, so I went into the labs myself one night, when no one was around to steer me away." She winced against the memory. "The friend told me to look for medium to large dogs, hunting dogs and shepherds, depressed, and maybe even—" She paused. "With one ear cut off."

"Oh, God," said Sue, making a face.

"These were the signs of stolen pets, they told me. And they were there. Stolen dogs, pets, in their labs. They did it to cut costs." She felt Sue's hands slip around her waist, but she didn't look up. "So I stole one dog. A big German shepherd. As proof."

She waited. *There it is. I'm a thief.*

When Sue said nothing Alyssa decided she might as well finish. "I called Covington, gave him a chance to explain. I hoped . . . I hoped somehow it wasn't true. But of course, it was. He lied to me, used me, then threatened me. He had a small, loyal staff to cover it up. No leaks. Except me." She paused.

"So, he called the police and saw that I got charged with stealing the dog. I went to jail. Late the next day, my attorney explained everything, I agreed to testify, and charges were dropped." Alyssa shook her head, remembering. "Then the real nightmare began. The press picked it up, made Covington a public example of corporate greed. He tried to stop me with threats, and I called the cops, but they couldn't find anyone or prove anything. The calls weren't traceable. Covington claimed innocence the whole time, but the fines and bad press ruined the company. He still had a lot of his personal investments, but he'd been a bachelor all his life. The company was all he had. He didn't take it well, to say the least."

"I'm surprised they didn't get him for stalking," said Sue.

"No evidence." Alyssa looked up. "I tried to reason with him. The last time I saw him, he cried. He said he had treated me like a daughter and I had betrayed him. That I was an evil child and deserved to be punished, after all he'd given me." She shivered. "He kind of went off the deep end."

Sue laughed lightly. "Kind of!"

"Anyhow, that's how I got Vinnie," Alyssa added. "He'd been stolen, had a tattooed ear cut off. They couldn't find his owners. I had to adopt him. After all, if I hadn't defended Covington as long as I did, who knows how many dogs might have been saved?"

"When did all this happen?"

"A little over a year and a half ago. In Chicago."

"Is the other stuff you told me related to this?"

"Yes." Alyssa took a deep breath. "They never caught the caller or the woman who shot Vinnie in the park. So I ran. I dropped my first name and started using Alyssa, mostly so anyone doing a Web search wouldn't connect me to the news articles. I just wanted to leave it all behind me. I figured Covington would get over it. But evidently he didn't."

They sat in silence for a few seconds.

"So, do you hate me?" Alyssa's stomach felt queasy.

Sue laughed, just one chuckle at first, then harder. "You are nuts sometimes. You think I'd hate you because you rescued an animal in distress? My God, Alyssa, that's all I've seen you do since I met you, try to save people and animals from distress."

"But I stole someone else's property."

Sue kissed her forehead gently. "That might not have been the smartest way to go, but give yourself a break, Alyssa. I'm sure everyone else did. The prosecutor did."

"I don't know . . ." It seemed too easy for the guilt she felt. Her parents hadn't seen it this way. And Marcus had always said any blot on her reputation would ruin her. "If it gets out in town, everyone will think I'm connected to these burglaries. After all, I did steal before."

Sue massaged the tension twisted into Alyssa's neck muscles. "If you told the whole story, most people would dismiss it. It's become a nightmare for you because you kept it locked up."

"Like living in the closet," Alyssa said. She felt as if she were seeing herself for the first time. "I never did that. Just told people I was gay as soon as I figured it out."

"Then you handled that better than I did."

Alyssa shifted her weight to draw herself closer to Sue, to feel her strength against the full length of her body. "But this. I thought if I just disappeared, Covington would get on with his life. I went to dog school and things have been great. It was peaceful living in Radley, working for Marcus. Then—"

"The burglaries started," Sue finished for her. "And you met me."

"Yes. Both disruptive." Alyssa smiled, tapping her finger against Sue's chin. "One much better than the other, however."

"I'm glad," Sue said, kissing her fingertip. "Why didn't you go to your family?"

Alyssa hadn't anticipated this question. She turned her head and studied the dogs, both sleeping on a sandy patch of ground. "I couldn't go there. My father was furious with me for exposing Covington when I could have continued in what he considered a great job. Honoring corporate loyalty and all."

"Really?"

"He just didn't get it. He's old-school." Alyssa sniffed, the anger fresh. "He always told me my good grades and college were a waste of money for a girl. That I should just get married."

"Wow. Your mom?"

"My mother didn't say anything. I don't think she knew how. Ever. I won't end up like her."

"Not possible," Sue said and kissed her again.

"I didn't want this." Sadness and anger frothed upward and Alyssa let it burst forth. "Maybe I just didn't try hard enough with my dad. I always wondered if I had just acted more like he wanted me to, if he would have loved me more."

"No, Alyssa. He probably fought with you because you frightened him or made him see his own failings."

"Well," Alyssa said, "I sure did that to Covington. Enough that he's still fighting me. He's got someone shooting at me." She couldn't stop the shudder that ran through her body. "How can you love me if I'm so terrifying?"

"You aren't terrifying at all," Sue murmured, brushing her lips against Alyssa's hair. "You're smart and dedicated and honest and brave. All of that is incredibly sexy, especially to a cop."

"An ex-cop." Alyssa kissed Sue lightly.

"A future cop," Sue said, kissing her back.

"The once and future cop."

Sue's mouth covered Alyssa's this time, tongue light against her lips, but Alyssa held them closed just a few seconds, to tease. By the time Sue's tongue found hers, Sue was hungry, diving into her, pulling her close.

"So, what's your real name?"

"Deborah Alyssa Norland." Alyssa kissed Sue's cheek. "I always liked Alyssa better, but my parents insisted I be called Deb."

Sue's hand slipped under Alyssa's T-shirt. "You created a new you. Way to go." Her lips moved against Alyssa's ear. "I told you I'd never been shot at before."

Alyssa shuddered. "Uh-huh." Sue's hand felt so good.

"Somehow that, and knowing I'm with a woman who sticks up for what she thinks is right, makes me hot." Alyssa felt Sue's tongue trace the outline of her ear and sparklers went off inside her. "You ever been naked in the open air?"

"No!" Alyssa laughed. "This is a park. A family playground."

"We're family and I want to play." Sue nibbled her collarbone gently.

Sue's lips felt so soft on her shoulder. She rubbed Sue's hair. They were alive. Sue didn't care she had stolen dogs. And the dark air felt warm. "I've always wanted to be naked outdoors."

Sue lowered Alyssa onto the sleeping bag. "Let me play."

Alyssa felt her bra being undone, then slipped up toward her neck along with her shirt. The cooler air made her aware of the skin on her breasts. "Oh." She smiled. "Nice."

"Try this." Sue lifted her wrists until they rested in the grass above her head. "Don't move. I don't have handcuffs yet, so this is just practice." She grinned.

"You're wolfish when you make love."

Sue raised her eyebrows. "You ain't seen nothin' yet."

Sue's tongue pressed heat against her breast, and when she pulled away, the wetness in the evening air left a cool trail on Alyssa's skin. "Oh." She marveled at how having her hands over her head seemed to make her skin more sensitive.

"Fresh air helps out a lot," Sue said from somewhere near her belly button, "if you know how to use it."

Alyssa lifted her hips and felt the rush of cool air between her thighs as Sue pulled her pants down. She had never felt so open, so exposed.

Sue's lips brushed below Alyssa's waist. "You put the sunset to shame. I love you."

A cop and a poet. Alyssa wanted to spend her life right here. She felt Sue's chin against her thigh, then her tongue warm, in exactly the right spot.

So fabulous, she thought, before the white heat clouded her brain.

In the first light of the sunrise, Sue pulled her arm from beneath Alyssa's head. No need to wake her.

She crawled out of the tent and greeted the dogs in a whisper. They had slept the entire night. She checked the dogs' leashes and found them still tight on the stakes. She didn't want them following her into the woods.

Sue glanced into the tent, where Alyssa still slept, her hair glinting copper in the early sunlight, her face uncreased. Sue wanted to spend the rest of their lives together.

But even more than that, she wanted Alyssa alive.

Alyssa's confession of the night before worried her. What had happened in Chicago, the threats, people taking shots at her still, over a year later. Covington was clearly crazy and obsessed.

Alyssa shifted inside the tent.

Sue hated to admit it, but she just couldn't protect Alyssa from someone like Covington and his hired gunmen. And as much as she wanted to help Alyssa solve this problem herself, she needed more help than Sue could give her.

Sue rubbed her temples. If she went to the police and told them the whole story, Alyssa would be protected. Alyssa might never forgive her, but at least she'd be safe.

If Sue just did what she asked, she might keep Alyssa's love. But she knew for certain she'd be risking Alyssa's death.

Tempting, that chance at love.

Alyssa had made Sue promise to take responsibility for keeping Zero safe. She should at least do the same for Alyssa.

"Love you, Alyssa," Sue whispered as she pulled her cell phone from her belt. "I promised I'd do my best to help you, and I'm sorry, but this is it."

She kissed her own fingertips and pointed them toward Alyssa, then zipped the tent shut. Alyssa did not stir. Sue rose, told the dogs to stay, and began to walk down along the trail.

"Alyssa, wake up."

Alyssa opened her eyes and saw Sue lying just outside the tent, profiled against the thrilling blue of a cloudless sky. Alyssa slid her head through the flap and lay on her stomach.

Sue raised her hand and cupped her cheek.

Alyssa loved the solid feel of that hand. "Life is so funny," she said. "In the middle of all this other crap, this wonderful thing has happened." She kissed Sue's palm, then rested her head there again.

"I don't want to lose you," Sue said.

"No, you won't."

"I'm serious."

She sounded it. "Wait." Alyssa pulled on her jeans and shirt, then stepped out of the tent to sit beside Sue. "I'm serious too."

"Good." When Sue looked at her, Alyssa thought her eyes looked worried. She'd never seen Sue look like this. "I want to help you,

216

Alyssa. To keep you as safe as you want to keep the dogs. And I want you to live the life you're meant to live."

Something was up here, Alyssa could tell. "You'll help me beat Covington."

Sue sighed. "That's just it." She ran her hand through her hair. "I don't think I can. God knows, I wish I were a cop, but I'm not right now. And you need more protection than I can give you." She took Alyssa's hand. "I called the police."

Alyssa felt like someone had plugged her spine into a wall socket. "You did what?"

Sue tilted her head and Alyssa twisted to look behind her. Two state troopers stood near the trees, their hands at their sides. She spun back to Sue.

"You bitch!" She pulled her hand from Sue's and hit her on the shoulder, hard. Alyssa's ears roared with the rush of blood to her face. Sue had betrayed her. "Is that what last night was about? Fuck me into oblivion and then fuck me again by calling the cops? Are they going to arrest me?"

"No, ma'am." One of the officers had moved toward them. "Just questioning. We need to take you back to Radley now."

"Just a minute." She turned back to Sue. "I trusted you."

"If Covington is still after you," Sue said, "I can't protect you. You wouldn't leave a dog as exposed to him as you've made yourself. I won't do that to you."

Alyssa's mouth felt like ice. "How could I have been so stupid?" She rolled her eyes. "Stupid, stupid idiot," she said to herself. "You did it again, trusting some sweet-talker until you got screwed." She looked at Sue. "Did you have fun? Get what you want? Sex, power? What was it?"

"Stop, Alyssa." Sue reached for her hand.

"Don't touch me." Alyssa willed herself not to cry.

"I did this because I love you," Sue said. "I couldn't let you risk your life."

"Well, you want to be a cop. Isn't that risking your life? Isn't that

217

what your ex couldn't live with? Isn't that why your mother made your father quit the force? You don't want anyone else to control you, so why should you try to control me?" A whirlwind of emotions unbalanced her and her words rushed out. "You promised you wouldn't leave me. Well, how much more complete could abandonment be? You might as well not be here. I'd be better off if you weren't." Alyssa stood. The sunlight threw long harsh shadows through the trees. "You say you want me alive," she said, quieter now. "For what?"

"I love you."

"Right." Alyssa's mouth twisted with anger. "Well, I won't have you."

"Ma'am." It was the cop again. "We have to go now."

Alyssa stepped toward Sue. "I have to go now, Sue, or these cops you called will cuff me. Too bad you don't have your handcuffs, Sue, or you could do it for them. You're a meddling liar. I knew it the night you broke into my house, but I let you convince me otherwise."

She shook with fury. *When will I learn?*

Sue stood too. "That's not fair and you know it. You need help."

"Next time someone shows up saying, 'Trust me, trust me,'" Alyssa said, "I will run like hell."

Sue leaned close but did not touch her. "Don't kid yourself."

Alyssa's heart felt like some part of it had torn. "I'm not surprised your partnership failed because you're a self-centered liar."

Sue's hand shot out and grabbed Alyssa's. "I do not lie." Her voice was a sharp whisper. "Look in a mirror if you want to see the person you're afraid to trust."

Alyssa felt as if her brain would freeze solid. She had nothing left to say. She pulled her hand from Sue's and walked past the waiting officers toward the path.

"Let's go," she said to them. She thought she heard Sue call her name but she did not look back.

Chapter Twenty-two

The sky's last rosy streaks had faded into black. *Nowhere near as nice as last night's sunset*, Alyssa thought. Of course, everything had changed since last night.

"Okay, the silence is too much for me." Melanie rose from the Adirondack chair beside Alyssa's. "And I'm getting chilly. You two want to head in?"

"No." Delia shook her head. "Go ahead, Melanie. Your family's in there and it's Saturday night. You shouldn't be out on the back porch with us. We'll watch the dogs."

Nestor, Zero and Blade all slept in various positions near the chairs.

"I don't know." Melanie nudged Alyssa. "It's not official protective custody or anything, but I feel like I should keep an eye on this one."

Alyssa tried to smile. "I'm being held prisoner."

"Hardly." Melanie picked up their empty coffee cups and headed for the porch door. "Strunk's case against you is even weaker now. He'd have put you in jail if he could. And heaven knows, you'd be safer there."

"I could go home," Alyssa said. She felt so exhausted, it took effort to breathe. She wanted to be alone. It annoyed her to be where people kept trying to cheer her up.

"Not on your life," said Melanie. "You hid all that stuff about this guy Covington from me, so you owe me. I want you here so I can sleep without worrying about you."

Alyssa didn't have the energy to resist. Just for tonight, until she got her bearings again. Until the police caught up with Covington. Until she'd adjusted to not having Sue in her life.

"Holler if you need anything," Melanie said and disappeared into the house.

Alyssa stared at Delia. "Go home, Delia," she said. "You need to rest. Besides, I want to be miserable in peace."

"If you keep sighing like that," Delia said, "you'll hyperventilate."

Alyssa did not smile. Her neck hurt so badly her head throbbed.

"You're acting like the world's ending," Delia said, "when, by my reckoning, you've got a lot to be thankful for."

"I don't feel thankful," Alyssa said.

"That's because you're heartbroken, dear. And pouting."

"I'm not heartbroken," Alyssa insisted. "I'm furious. At Sue for betraying me and at myself for trusting her." She narrowed her eyes. "You'd better watch out too, Delia. No telling how she'll use you. Is she paying her rent on time?"

Delia raised one eyebrow. "Darling, her apartment burned." She blinked. "You are pouting and it isn't very pleasant."

Alyssa swallowed. "That's why I want to go home. So I'm not inflicting myself on you."

"You have so many reasons not to pout." Delia held up her index finger. "First off, you aren't dead. When I heard the police had come to question you and found a bullet in your wall and blood on your floor, well, I didn't know what to think. It was a long night for me."

220

"Sorry about that." It had been a long night for her too. A long, wonderful, warm, sexy night.

"Now you've told this horrible story about the mob in Chicago coming after you—"

"Not the mob, Delia." The whole town probably thought she was a gangster. Great. "One man."

"Who hires hit men. Or women. That's organized crime if you ask me."

Alyssa didn't argue.

"And why you didn't tell us this, I can't imagine."

"I didn't think it was important." She wished she could escort Delia to her truck, but she couldn't find the energy to move.

Delia's eyebrows drew downward into a vee. "Well, I hope you're thinking now. Or are you too busy pouting?"

She wanted to pout, damn it. Just pout a whole day or two and feel lousy about falling in love with a rat. Then she'd be over it. Probably.

Unfortunately, her silence didn't deter Delia, who was ticking off her points, two fingers now raised. "Two. Strunk's no longer in charge of the case since you crossed county and state lines with all of this." She raised a third finger. "Three, you've got someone watching out for you, seeing the things you aren't seeing, and keeping you from stepping even deeper into danger."

"Susan Hunter is no longer a subject for conversation." The ache stiffened Alyssa's neck and began to throb in her shoulders.

"I know you're angry at Sue because she called the police." Delia pulled herself forward in the chair. "But she did it for you. She got your predicament out in the open. The police are after Covington now. And you're here safe with Melanie." She paused. "Though I think you'd be safer—and happier—at my house with Sue."

Alyssa summoned all her strength to lean forward in her chair. "Why on earth would I want to be with her? She's shown me her version of loyalty, which is doing things her way, no matter what I think. Who knows what would happen if I gave her that sort of power again? I want to go home." She settled back again. "But staying here is at least staying away from Sue."

221

"She's pacing the floor at my house, dear. She's miserable with anxiety."

"Why?" She looked up into the branches of a large silver maple. "I'm safe here."

"Because she loves you, Alyssa, and you said horrible things to her this morning."

Alyssa started at the bite in Delia's voice. "She told you?" The pain had spread from her skull toward her right ear.

"Not details, no. But she did tell me you made it very clear you didn't want to talk to her. Or be with her. I told her it couldn't be true." She paused, and Alyssa looked at her. Delia's eyes had narrowed. "Is it, dear?"

Alyssa didn't know what was true anymore. Sue had betrayed her trust. Still, she was here, alive and out of danger. Just lonely. And sad.

She did not want it to be like this. She wanted Sue.

"I don't want Sue here," Alyssa said. "I let you bring Zero here. Isn't that enough?" She felt the threat of tears squeezing her throat and forced herself to swallow. "Please, Delia. Go home. I'll be okay, but I need some time to myself."

"All right, dear." Delia stood. "But don't think for one second that I buy Sue's story about your keeping Zero for training."

Delia could really annoy a person. "What do you mean?" Alyssa asked.

Delia bent to kiss her forehead lightly. "Figure out why Sue sent that dog, Alyssa, and why you want him here." Without another word, Delia left.

Alyssa's gaze drifted over to the sleeping dogs. Why *had* she agreed to take Zero? Marcus could train him just as well.

Why had Sue sent her dog along with Blade and Delia in the first place?

As if he heard her thoughts, Zero raised his head and blinked at Alyssa. His ears rotated, listening. Then he yawned and flopped back onto his side, instantly asleep.

Of course. Sue must have remembered what Alyssa had told her

222

Wednesday night, after the fiasco in the woods, about never having unfinished business with a dog. That even if the human stayed angry, the dog just loved.

Alyssa felt the frozen anger that she'd carried all day begin to shift and soften. The regret it had held washed over her. *She wanted to keep me safe because she loves me.*

Another wash of regret, then another. She'd said horrible things to Sue. How could she ever take those back?

She couldn't. *Stupid.*

Alyssa held her head in her hands, massaging her neck. Sue had been right. The one she didn't trust was herself. She didn't believe she could say the right things, or make the right choices to get the right results. So she bit her tongue and ran and let others control her life. And then she got angry and said stupid, stupid things.

She was so tired of being angry. She wanted to be in love.

"Well," Alyssa said aloud, "if that's what you want, you have to get it together. Call Sue and talk it out. Don't cave in and don't be a bitch. There's got to be a middle ground."

She'd do it tomorrow after some sleep.

The screen door opened with a metallic click behind her. "Alyssa?" Melanie said. "There's someone here to see you."

Sue, Alyssa thought, turning.

But standing behind Melanie in the bright light of the kitchen was Samantha Braeburn. Her ivory blouse and plum skirt looked twisted and her eyes seemed glazed. But she didn't look drunk. She looked frightened.

Alyssa stood.

"I didn't know if you wanted to talk," Melanie said.

"Sure, Mel, that's fine."

Melanie stepped aside so that Samantha could exit to the porch.

"I'd like to speak to you alone," Samantha said with a glance at Melanie. "Apologizing is hard enough for me, and I'd rather not do it in public."

Melanie glanced at Alyssa, then shut the door behind her.

"I have to admit this is a surprise," Alyssa began.

Samantha approached her, her smooth face wrinkled with concern. "That was just a story to get me in the house."

Alyssa pulled back.

"I mean, of course I want to apologize. I said hateful things. I even let you clean my carpet." A hand fluttered to her face, then grabbed Alyssa's arm. "They've got Adam and Cal."

Alyssa's mouth dried instantly. Her nerves sprang to life. "Who?"

Samantha shook her head. "I don't know them. I only saw one and he has a gun. But I heard others in the house. He sent me to find you. He said if I call the police he'll kill them both." She shook Alyssa's arm. "They've got my son! I don't know what to do. I don't know what's right."

Alyssa held her, afraid the woman would lose her grip to terror. "Shhh. Or Melanie will hear and she'll call it in." She led Samantha to a chair. "Sit and tell me what's happening. Quickly."

Samantha struggled to gather her thoughts. "I was at the Blue Seahorse socializing a bit when Cal called and told me to come straight home. Something was wrong with Adam." Her fingers floated from her blouse to her bracelets. "So I did, you know, and there was an old man. I'd never seen him before. Cal and Adam were on the floor. They had duct tape on their wrists and ankles."

A chill flushed through Alyssa's body. "Did they tell you why they wanted you to find me?" But she knew.

Samantha pulled a phone from her purse. "I'm to call him when I find you. He wants to talk to you." She dialed quickly. "Please, talk to him."

Alyssa nodded and took the phone from Samantha.

It rang once before a weak voice said, "Deborah Norland. It's been so long."

Rodney Covington. "You fucking bastard."

"Language, Ms. Norland. Besides, you're the one who's been doing the fucking from what I've heard. At least, your sick version of it." His voice sounded as cool and smooth as ever. "First me, now

224

this ex-cop. Perhaps I should talk to her too, warn her how disloyal you are. Or has she already found out? Have you turned on her too?"

"Leave the Braeburns alone."

"When I'm done with you, I'll release them both. But first, I need to see you."

"Where?"

"Come here, alone, now. Tell the mother to stay away and stay quiet until I call her. And not to call the police. If anyone shows up, I'll kill the boy. Believe me, Deborah, I will. I'm dying. It's why they let me out early. I have nothing to lose now. I will kill the boy." He hung up.

Alyssa believed him. She handed the phone back to Samantha.

"What did he say?" Samantha asked, frantic.

"He wants me to go there."

"Go! You have to go. Go get Adam, please!" The woman's nails dug into Alyssa's flesh.

"Samantha, wait. Let me think." Covington would be ready for her and she'd walk right into his setup. But if she ignored him, Adam could get hurt. She had to play his game.

But we'll play by my rules.

She looked at Blade, remembering his extensive private lessons. She could use him. But if she showed up with the dog, Covington would suspect something.

She could leave him in the car with the windows open. Lure Covington outside somehow. Promise him whatever he wanted. The dog would leap through the car window if she called.

Of course, if Covington saw the dog in the car, he might never follow her outside, at least not until he had the dog shot.

But if he didn't see the dog it could work.

"Oh, God, he'll kill my baby." Samantha gagged on her terror.

"No, he won't," Alyssa said. "He wants me."

"You?" Samantha started to sob. "This is your fault?" Her voice cracked with fear.

"Shh. You don't want the Sybesmas to hear."

225

"No." Samantha took a deep breath and stopped crying. "You have to save Adam."

The stakes were so high, Alyssa's head spun. *I can't do this alone.* "You have to get me some help."

Samantha's eyes widened with alarm. "They said tell no one else."

"Not the police," Alyssa said. "You have to go to Delia's and find Sue Hunter." Sue would come.

Alyssa stood and called Zero and Blade. "Take the dogs. Hold their collars." She placed the woman's shaking hands on the dogs. "Take them to Sue."

She wanted to call Sue and explain, but she couldn't risk Melanie overhearing. The conversation with Samantha and call to Covington had been risk enough.

"Tell Sue what's happening. Tell her I've gone to your house. She needs to bring the dogs but stay out of sight. I'll get the men out of the house somehow."

She thought for a minute. They couldn't repeat any of their past mistakes. Not with Adam's life on the line.

"Tell her to do what she thinks is best. Then you stay at Delia's. Do you understand?"

"Yes." She nodded hard. "Sue should bring the dogs and do what she thinks best. Just get my son."

Alyssa tried to look confident. "We'll get them out." She led Samantha and the dogs around the yard to the gate. "Go this way to the car. And be quiet. I have to tell Melanie something or we'll have cops all over the place."

"You're going to get my son?"

"Yes. Get the dogs to Sue, and we'll get Adam."

She watched Samantha walk the dogs to her car.

Alyssa couldn't stand to think of Adam and how frightened he must be. She needed to figure out a way around Melanie instead.

She took a few deep breaths. *Go slow. Remember, you're sad and pouting.* "Come on, Nestor." The pup woke and rose slowly, happy to follow her into the house.

"Hey, Mel," Alyssa called from the kitchen. She hoped she

wouldn't have to talk to Melanie face to face, but her friend appeared carrying a bowl of popcorn.

"Come drown your sorrows in carbs. We have Oreos too." Melanie held out the bowl.

Alyssa managed a sigh. "Nah."

"Samantha's gone?" She put a handful of popcorn in her mouth.

"Yeah. Wanted to apologize. I sent her out the back way. At least she believes I'm not involved in the burglaries." Alyssa forced herself to stand relaxed.

"Big of her," Melanie said, her mouth full. "What'll you do now?"

"I need a walk, okay? To stretch my legs?"

Melanie looked doubtful.

Alyssa needed to distract her. "Please, Mel. I need to think. I have to decide what to do about Sue."

That got Melanie's attention. She swallowed. "Get your butt over to Delia's and talk to her."

Alyssa knew she'd found the way out. "You think?"

"Yes. I love you, but I can't stand your moping, and it's only been a few hours. I can't live with you like this for much longer. Get over there and work it out. Don't just apologize, either. You both did the best you could. Talk it through."

"Advice from the expert," Alyssa said and manufactured another sigh. "Okay, I'll go."

Melanie pointed at her. "But that's the only road trip you're allowed, young lady. I'm going to call in an hour and check on you. No spontaneous camping trips. You're either here or there or in between, got it?"

She grabbed her keys from the counter. "Yes, Mom. I'm gonna go before I chicken out."

"Drive safely," Melanie said.

"Thanks, Mel." Alyssa paused. "You're a good friend."

Melanie smiled and dropped another handful of popcorn into her mouth. "I know. Now go. She'll be there."

Alyssa hoped Melanie was right.

Chapter Twenty-three

In less than ten minutes, Alyssa was driving down the twisting lane to the Braeburns' house. It looked even more impressive in the dark. No sign of the horror going on inside. Just an unfamiliar car in the drive.

She knew that anyone in the house or in the nearby woods could see her approach, so she walked to the porch trying to look brave.

He wants me miserable. I want him outside. No matter what, I have to get him outside to the dogs.

She had calculated that Sue would be about twenty minutes behind her. She looked at her watch. 10:26. By a quarter to, she'd have to trust that Sue was there. Sue knew better than to bring a car up to the house or do anything that would tip off the men inside. So, just like the other night in the woods, Alyssa wouldn't see Sue now.

She rang the bell. *I can do this. In fact, Covington ought to be frightened of me.*

When the door latch clicked she drew herself up to face the man she'd run from for so many months.

But the man who opened the door wasn't Covington. She'd seen this guy before, skinny, with a big Adam's apple. One of the bartenders from the Twelve Point. She didn't remember his name. He smiled and it made her shiver.

"Miss Deborah," he said. "Come in."

He was the caller.

"Adam will be glad to see you," he said. "But not as glad as I am."

She stood looking at him. She should have figured the caller would be here.

"Get in the house." He'd lost his smile. "Be a good girl now and no one will get hurt. Understand?"

"Yes." She stepped in and he closed and bolted the door behind her.

She jumped as he placed his hand behind her neck. "I don't think you do," he whispered, so close she could feel his breath on her ear. "I can help you, if you give me what I want. Do you remember what I want?"

She remembered and nodded. "How will you help?"

"I'll free the boy, the father too. I'll kill the old man if you want. Just let me taste you."

She stood rigid as the tip of his tongue, hard and wet, filled the center of her ear, then left again.

"Taste you all over," he said.

Bile rose against the base of her throat and she forced it down with a swallow. *Think*.

She knew what the men each wanted now. But they didn't know her plan. She still had the edge.

"Free them and I will."

He blew in her ear. "You think I'm stupid. They do too. But I'll show you I'm not. You take care of me first, then I will take care of the others."

"Bring her here, Paul." Covington's voice came from deeper in the house. Alyssa almost felt relief.

"Be smart and play along," Paul whispered again as he grabbed her arm.

The last thing Sue expected to see this evening was Samantha Braeburn driving up to Delia's house. When Zero and Blade jumped from the car, Sue left the house to meet them on the walk.

"Thank heavens you're here!" Samantha said, running down the path, awkward in her high heels. "Alyssa sent me."

"What's happening?" Sue bent to grab the dogs and settle them. "Sit." They did.

"It's Adam. Some men took Adam and one talked to Alyssa on the phone and said she had to meet him."

A ball of fear knotted in Sue's gut. Covington. She felt the car keys in her pocket. "Where are they?"

"At my house." Samantha told Sue what had happened. "She said you should bring the dogs. You had to bring the dogs."

God, she's got some plan again, Sue thought, looking at Blade. *Why hadn't she just called the police?*

"And she told me to tell you to do what you think best. What you think best." Samantha's hair fell into her face. "Don't call the police, please. He'll kill Adam if you do. He said so. He has a gun. He—" She broke off into a sob.

Sue wrapped an arm around her and thought over Alyssa's earlier plans. She'd go to them, pretending to play their game. But she'd play to her advantage.

She wants to use the dogs. Blade sat beside Sue, sleek and fluid. Sue didn't know what Alyssa had in mind, but she understood her part in it. She had to get the dogs there, fast.

"I'll go, Samantha. Go inside and sit with Delia. Tell her what's happening. Keep the phone clear. How long will it take me to get there?"

"Ten minutes."

"If I haven't called you in thirty, call the police."

230

"No!" Her eyes widened and Sue noticed how her mascara had smeared. "They said no police."

"Samantha!" Sue took her wrist and squeezed to get her attention. "If we haven't gotten your boy out by then, we'll need help. Do you understand?"

"All right." Samantha nodded. "In a half-hour." She looked at her watch. "Is that too long? Should I call sooner?"

"No. Thirty minutes."

"Okay."

Sue heard determination there and let her go. "We'll get your son."

"That's what Alyssa said."

"She's right. Now tell me how to get there. Where can I park and not be seen?" She listened to the directions, another part of her brain racing. She had no weapons and no time.

Rodney Covington did look like he was dying, Alyssa thought. His skin resembled dried apricots, wrinkled and orange in the diffuse light of the bedroom. But his stare stopped Alyssa in the doorway. Hard and dark, like chips of slate in a riverbed. His hate made her more afraid than the gun he held in his hand.

"Miss Norland!" Adam's voice drew her into the room. He sat on the bed, hands and feet taped in front of him. She sat down next to him and wrapped her arms around him.

"Adam, you okay?" She felt him nod against her chest. "I'm so sorry."

He looked up at her. "Why?"

"Because she knows she caused all of this," Covington said.

Her lip curled at the sound of his voice. He'd taken so much from her. *It ends now*, she thought.

She swallowed, trying to force submission into her face instead of defiance.

"What can I do?" she asked, careful to avoid eye contact with

231

Covington. She saw Calvin Braeburn on the floor in the corner, his mouth, hands and legs all taped. He slumped against the wall, watching. No help there. "What can I do to make it up? To make it better?"

"Nothing!" Covington strode to her and gripped her chin in his long fingers, yanking her face toward him. He studied her a long time.

She willed her anger to stay down.

"Not frightened enough." He let go of her, then slapped her with the back of his hand, spinning her from the bed.

"Hey!" Adam yelled. "Stop it!"

Alyssa put a hand on the boy's leg. "Stay quiet, Adam. No matter what happens."

He nodded, wide-eyed.

Covington rubbed his hand. "I don't have the strength for the things I'd like to do." He looked at Paul. "Did she bring the dogs?"

"No. No dogs, I looked."

"Pity." He smiled, his lips thin and red within his melon-colored complexion. "We could have started there."

She wanted to scream at him to let the boy go because he had her now. But then he'd know the boy was important to her and hurt him for sure.

"Just don't—" She bit her lip and stared at the floor.

"Don't what?"

It worked. She'd hooked his interest. Alyssa shook her head.

"Touch her," said Paul. "You know women. They tease you, walk around the house half-naked and then tell you not to touch them. She doesn't want anyone to—well, you know. She doesn't want the normal things."

Alyssa froze.

Covington smiled. "Then nothing about her should remain untouched." He sat down on the bed next to her, speaking softly. "Do you know what I mean, Deborah? Do you know what I am going to do to you?"

She stared at the floor. She had to keep him focused, to get him out of the house away from Adam.

"Silent?" Covington sneered. "My God, you're never silent. If you'd been silent and respectful like this, we'd still be friends, wouldn't we? And none of this would be happening." He placed a hand on her thigh, and slid it toward her crotch. "Because this is a just punishment for what you did to me. What you are. Wicked. Unfaithful." She shuddered, and he stood, turning to Paul. "You must do it for me."

She looked up and saw the other man's face lighten. "Yes."

He'd wanted this all along, Alyssa knew. From the first, when he started watching her. She couldn't help shuddering again.

"Ah, she's shivering," Covington said, his voice soft and pleased. "Silence and shivers. I like it. She is already so much closer to showing the proper respect. This will be a good way to teach her the lesson." Covington grabbed her neck and pulled her upright. "Take her."

"No!" Alyssa screamed, but Covington pushed her into the other man, who slid his arm around her waist.

Paul smiled down at her. "I have a gun and a knife. So be quiet. You don't want the boy to see that."

She bit her lip and looked at Adam, who watched with wide eyes. She didn't want him to see anything more.

"What's going on? Is everything okay?"

Alyssa twisted to look at the doorway. She knew that voice. Then Marcus appeared in the hall, a gun in his hand. "Marcus!" She couldn't believe it.

He looked at her without a smile and answered her question before she could ask it. "Your former boss pays well, Alyssa. You should've stuck by him." He shrugged, pulling his pants higher over his belly with one hand.

Covington approached behind her. "You see, Deborah, I've been all around you, all the time, when you didn't even know it. You thought you could run, but you were mine, always." He bent, his mouth so close to her ear she could smell his breath. "I had someone follow you from the day I went to prison. I wanted to take my time and ruin you slowly. First was that damned dog you stole from me." He smiled. "You thought you'd get away just by leaving town and dropping your first name? How stupid. I told them to watch you and then to help you succeed. I had time to help you build a wonderful life."

Alyssa could barely follow him.

"I like that look of confusion, Deborah," Covington said. "There's a delicious irony to it. All this time you thought you had succeeded on your own skill as a dog trainer, but not so. I paid Dixon to hire you and steer clients your way. Once again, I created your success." He leaned even closer, his lips nearly touching her cheeks. "Only this time, I will destroy you. Not the other way around."

Alyssa felt an icicle of fear pierce her throat. She'd had no idea he was this crazy.

He winced and drew back, hunching over his abdomen. "This damned cancer. Four months they gave me and released me early. I had to move faster than I wanted to, but it was worth it to be alive to see it. To see you lose everything bit by bit."

Covington straightened and turned to Paul. "Take her. Now."

"Not here," Paul said. "Not in front of the boy."

Covington considered this. "No, that wouldn't do."

Be smart, she thought. "Not in the dark." She forced a sob, held a hand to her eyes. "Just not in the dark."

"The woods are lovely this time of night. Lovely, dark, and deep." Covington's voice dripped with satisfaction.

Alyssa shuddered again. "No! Please." She sank down, but Paul pulled her up. "No."

"You stay here with them," Covington said to Marcus. Then he addressed Paul. "You bring her. Come on."

She felt Paul hesitate next to her. "You're coming?" he asked.

"Of course I am. I want to watch every second of it." Covington paused. "Don't look so shocked. I'm paying. I want to see her utterly violated. If you give me that, boy, you'll have my gratitude forever. And twice as much cash."

In a few minutes they were outside the house. Covington carried a flashlight and a gun and slowly led them across the yard into the woods.

Paul held Alyssa close beside him. "I can't tell you how glad I am that you're here," Paul said. "To touch you after all this time." He stroked his hand under her shirt.

Her skin crawled.

She stepped high over dead branches as they walked in the dark. She tried to listen for any sound of Sue or the dogs, but she heard nothing. She willed herself not to turn her head and look. Somehow, she knew Sue was there and wouldn't let anything happen to her.

In the shadow from the flashlight she looked at Paul's face, pale beneath sandy hair, skin taut over cheekbones and throat. "You work at the Twelve Point. Why are you doing this?"

"Don't talk to her," Covington ordered. "She's trying to make a connection, talk you out of hurting her. She's a master deceiver."

In response, Paul yanked her even harder. She stumbled over the thick debris on the forest floor. There was no path here.

"Don't tell me what to do," Paul said to the old man, his voice tight and high. "I know what I'm doing."

"Shut up," Covington said. He stopped walking. "Here's a clear space." He kicked a fallen branch out of the way. "Do it."

"You're ordering me," Paul whined to Covington. "I don't like that."

Alyssa's skin prickled as Paul pulled his knife from his jacket and snapped it open. He held it to her throat. "She's frightened now, isn't she?"

Covington's light flashed in her face, and she closed her eyes against it. She felt the flat of the blade press against her windpipe.

"Isn't she?" Paul's voice got higher. "I did this, Covington. I'm the one who watched and didn't touch until you said so. I did what you said and scared her, made her run. Me!"

Uh-oh, Alyssa thought. *He's losing it too*.

Paul pushed her onto the ground between himself and Covington. "You can't order me around anymore!" He continued to rage at the older man. "I did what you wanted. You can't even do this for yourself. You need me!"

"Calm down. She's yours," Covington said. "Enjoy her." He bent and pushed his gun against the back of Alyssa's head. "Take your clothes off."

"No." Paul knelt beside her and smiled. "I'll do it for her." He gripped the front of her polo shirt then slowly sliced it open all the way to the hem.

Alyssa felt the night air rush against her flesh and wanted to curl into a ball. But she had to stay alert. Sue was there, somewhere. She had to help Sue, make a distraction, so she could get closer with the dogs and not be heard.

"You make a cute couple," Covington said.

Alyssa's hand clutched at the pine needles and sand beneath her. "You're a bastard, Rodney Covington!" she yelled, hurling her handful at him.

He yelped and jumped back, dirt coating his face and chest. "I should kill you."

Paul laughed. "Just a little dirt. Nothing to such a big man."

Covington shook with rage, flailing at himself to get the debris off. "I deserve better than this." He wiped his shirt frantically, gun in one hand, flashlight in another.

"There are pine needles on your head, you asshole," Alyssa said, hoping to keep him angry. *Come on, Sue*.

Covington shook his head and pointed the gun at them. "Both of you, get up!" He waved the gun at Paul. "Get her up." Paul yanked so hard she felt like her shoulder might come out of its socket. He held her close, one hand squeezing just below her breast.

Alyssa stood and her heart pounded against her ribs. She'd never seen a gun pointed at her before.

"Move away from her," Covington said.

"You promised she was mine."

"She's more afraid now, because she knows I'm going to kill her. I like this better."

"No!" Paul sounded like he might cry. "You promised! You promised. I waited and watched." He pulled her even tighter to him, the knife in his other hand pressing against her bare stomach. "You can have her after."

Covington wiped at his hair with the flashlight hand, and evidently felt more needles there, because he began wiping himself all over again. "These things are stuck to me. Get away, Paul," he said, still wiping, "or I'll shoot you too."

Alyssa heard a noise in the brush and saw Covington's eyes slide to his left. A blur passed by her and Paul.

"No!" she heard Sue yell from somewhere in the dark.

Covington's gun exploded.

Alyssa slammed to the ground, landing on top of Paul. Pain seared through her right side as she raised her head to see.

Zero had jumped against Covington, knocking the man to the ground. Pain welled from her side, flowing outward across her chest and back. *He shot me.*

Paul didn't move beneath her.

Come on, Sue, she willed silently.

Covington lifted his gun toward Zero, then stopped. He reaimed it toward an approaching noise.

Alyssa screamed.

237

Chapter Twenty-four

As soon as she heard the shot Sue grabbed Blade's collar and broke into a run. *Not Alyssa*, her heart insisted with each beat.

"Stop!" an old man—Covington—yelled. He sat on the ground with a flashlight and a gun aimed at her. She froze, still holding Blade. Alyssa lay on the ground to the right, bleeding but conscious. Next to her lay the bartender, unconscious.

Zero walked up to her, unhurt. "Sit," she said. He did.

"Paul," the older man said, but Paul didn't answer. "Paul Langeland!"

"I think he's out," Sue said. Her muscles tensed as she judged the distances between everyone.

"You must be the ex-cop," the old man said, keeping the gun level as he stood slowly. "The other lesbian."

"Mr. Covington." Sue glanced at Alyssa, who was watching everything. "You're in a mess here."

"I could shoot you now," he said. "It would hurt her." He waved the gun toward Alyssa. "But I need you to help me get them back into the house."

"Why don't you just get out of here?" Sue asked. She needed to talk, to buy time for better position. "Save yourself."

"I have no life left to save. I'm dying. And I want this." He waved the pistol toward Paul. "He screwed it up."

"I'd say you screwed him up. You shot him." Sue stepped toward Covington. They stood about ten feet apart now. She held on to Blade, whose ears twitched at every sound. "You okay?" she asked Alyssa, knowing she wasn't.

Alyssa smiled and raised the hand she had pressed to her side. Sue saw way too much blood.

No time.

"Yep. You shot him. Grazed Alyssa, it looks like, and shot your helper. Why not just cut your losses and get out?"

"Shut up. Pick up him up and get him to the house."

"I need help too," Alyssa said. "I don't think I can walk."

That's a good sign, Sue thought. *She's alert enough to help me out here*. But Sue didn't like the ashen patches expanding on Alyssa's cheeks.

"You'll walk." Covington wiped dirt from his shirt, then swung his flashlight's broad beam toward Zero. "Deborah, can this be the German shepherd they told me you were training? This ill-behaved creature? You are as bad a dog trainer as you were a publicity manager. I'd like to shoot it."

"Shoot the damn dog," Alyssa said. "His behavior's not my fault. It's the idiot owner."

Sue stared at her, but her flare of surprised anger disappeared almost instantly. Alyssa was up to something.

"She can't even handle a well-trained dog," said Alyssa. "It's like she has two left hands. I mean, look at Blade."

Sue looked down at Blade, sitting on her left.

"You haven't changed, have you?" Covington said, shifting his

239

light between the two women. "Still trying to blame others for your sins. I know the other dog is no good either. Marcus told me it's the Doberman he got by in the last robbery. 'No problem at all,' he told me. So much for your training."

Marcus? If he was involved, Sue wondered, where was he?

"No, it's Sue," Alyssa said, "not me." She tried to sit up, but winced and fell back again. "I'm telling you, Blade isn't my fault. He's just wet behind the ears."

Behind the ears. Sue remembered Alyssa saying something about protection training and special hand signals. Highly confidential, not even in the files for Marcus to know. But the dog had to be within six feet of the other person.

"Tell him, Sue," Alyssa snapped at her as if furious. "Even if he is about to kill me, I want him to know that I was better than he thought."

"Shut up, Alyssa," Sue said, playing out the scene. *What is that signal?* "I don't want to waste my time talking to you."

"Screw you, then," said Alyssa. "Go home and pour another two-fingered drink. Drown your sorrows like you always do."

Two fingers . . . behind the ears. Suddenly Sue remembered. "A good idea," she said.

Covington waved the pistol at Sue. "Help her up. She can walk. Then bring him. But don't let go of that dog, or I'll shoot it."

Sue helped Alyssa to her feet, but Alyssa stumbled forward toward Covington.

"I don't think she can do it," Sue said following her with Blade.

"She will or I'll shoot you both," Covington said.

"I can't. I don't want to go back to the house." Alyssa weaved, unsteady on her feet.

"Walk!" Covington shouted and Blade's ears tipped forward.

Alyssa pulled them within a yard of Covington and fell to the ground. "Now!"

"Get up!" Covington stepped toward them as Sue slipped her fingers behind Blade's ears and pressed. The dog exploded with barks and launched like a rocket, over Alyssa and into Covington's chest. The man never had a chance to react.

Covington's screams bounced off the trees, joined by the sudden shrieks of sirens. "Get the dog off! I'll bleed to death!"

Blade held Covington's arm in a firm bite, and the hand hung limp and useless. Sue picked up the gun and flashlight from the ground.

"The release word is 'caviar,'" Alyssa said, barely audible over his screams.

Sue released the dog who came to her and sat. She saw police lights on two cars in the driveway not far behind them and shouted for help.

"Deborah!" Covington screamed. "My liver's failing. My blood won't clot. I'll bleed to death. You'll go to prison forever!"

"Police!" Melanie called from the edge of the woods.

Sue picked up the flashlight and waved it so Melanie could see them better. "Here. We've got three injured. We'll need an ambulance."

Sue heard Melanie radio the message and saw her flashlight move toward them.

"Adam, Calvin and Marcus are in the house," Alyssa said, rolling over onto her back. "Marcus has a gun." Sue could see her stiffen against the pain.

Melanie radioed that information then turned back to them. "Strunk's at the house. Backup's on the way. We'll get them out."

"No, you won't. The boy will die!" Covington said.

"Shut up," said Melanie, bending over him to check his injuries.

"Should you go?" Sue asked. "I can cover this." For the first time she hated the open spaces between here and a bigger town.

"No, not with these injuries and the suspect." She glanced back toward the house, clearly torn. "Not yet."

In the distance, Strunk's voice ordered Marcus to come out of the house without his weapon.

"Poor Adam," said Alyssa through taut lips.

Sue commanded the dogs to lie down, then sat beside Alyssa, intent on distracting her. "For the record, I'd say you're a terrific dog trainer." Her throat tightened at the sight of the blood on Alyssa's clothing.

"For God's sake," Covington said, his voice hoarse and pierced with pain, "arrest her! Shoot that damned dog. It attacked me. I'm bleeding to death."

"Sir," Melanie said, her voice cool and professional, "you are not bleeding to death. So let me advise you of your rights."

As Melanie spoke to Covington, Sue studied Alyssa's face. She lay with her cheek on her arm. Most of her color had drained and her skin seemed translucent and other-worldly.

From the house came shouts, and through the trees they saw men moving in the cruiser's searchlight. All of them strained to see and hear. Then Melanie's radio crackled.

"Got Dixon cuffed and in the car," came Strunk's voice. "Got the kid and his dad too. We're clear here."

Sue felt Alyssa's body relax.

"Okay," Melanie replied, not bothering to suppress her grin. "When that ambulance gets here, send them this way with a stretcher."

"Don't mind me if I don't wait." Alyssa raised her head up slowly. "I hurt like hell and I don't want to spend any more time in this lousy company." Alyssa sat and her eyes opened wide. "Sue, help me walk to the car."

"Are you sure—" Sue stopped when she saw Alyssa's eyes close. "Woozy?"

"Uh-huh." Alyssa nodded.

"I think we'd better wait then. You might pass out if you stand."

"You convinced me," Alyssa agreed, and slid sideways into Sue's lap. "I feel better stretched out anyway."

She must be in a lot of pain, Sue thought. *I won that way too easily.*

Alyssa winced. "Frankly, this is nothing compared to getting ripped up by a guard dog."

"Bitch." Covington spat the word toward them. "You'll pay."

Alyssa lifted her head and Sue felt her tighten against pain. Still she saw no fear in her lover's eyes.

"Language, Mr. Covington," Alyssa said. "And I'm all through paying. We're done. From here on, things will work out just fine."

The next morning Sue returned to the hospital just after 11:00 carrying two bagels and cream cheese in a bag. She'd left Alyssa just long enough to check the dogs, shower and get an update from Melanie.

For the first time ever, she strode through a hospital corridor with joy. Alyssa would be okay.

"Please tell me you brought real food," Alyssa said as Sue entered the room. She had her color back and sat upright in the bed.

"Just what you ordered." She tossed the bag onto Alyssa's lap.

"Thanks."

"I've got more." Sue scooted onto the bed beside her.

"Chocolate?" Alyssa unwrapped a bagel.

"No, news." Sue's hand rubbed the blanket over Alyssa's thigh. "I talked to Melanie. Covington's spilling everything."

"He's admitting it?" She took an enormous bite of bagel.

"Yes and no. Melanie says he hasn't stopped swearing about what a bitch you are and how you ruined his life, and therefore, how you deserved everything you got. He's convinced he's dealing out justice, so he's just telling it all. He's clearly quite crazy. Sorry."

Alyssa nodded, chewing.

Sue shifted closer. "But here's something cool. You know how you figured out how to get past Teddy that night after the fire? That's just how they did it too, more or less. They wore latex gloves against fingerprints. And Covington had provided Marcus with a few house-breaking lessons."

Alyssa mumbled something she couldn't understand.

"Evidently your buddy Covington still had plenty of nasty connections, even after he went to prison."

243

Alyssa swallowed. "I'm not surprised. Where'd they get the information for the robberies? You know, who had what, and where?"

Sue reached into the bag for her own bagel. "Samantha Braeburn."

Alyssa looked shocked.

"Yeah, I know. Surprise." Sue pulled the halves of her bagel apart. "Like you told me, everyone knows she drinks, and when she drinks, she gabs. So Marcus ran into her at the Blue Seahorse a few times, you know, accidentally on purpose. Flirted, bought her some drinks, led the conversation. Didn't take long before he knew pretty much what every summer family keeps and where. So they picked the houses that had links to you."

Alyssa shook her head. "What I don't get is why Marcus got involved at all."

Sue chewed a minute. "Melanie says he did it for money. Covington contacted him while you were still in dog training school, offered him twice his annual income to hire you, help you succeed, then tear you down. Told him he could keep whatever he took in the robberies."

"So the whole time Marcus was plotting against me?" She looked out the window. "Who's got Hendrix?"

Sue patted Alyssa's thigh. Leave it to her to think of the dog. "Some guy from town. Jimmy somebody. Melanie said the dog will have kids to play with and everything."

Alyssa nodded.

"Covington's done for," Sue said, watching Alyssa carefully. "Mel said he won't live a month."

Alyssa nodded and turned back to Sue. "And the bartender?"

"Paul Langeland. I guess Marcus hired him. Melanie said she's known him almost her whole life and never guessed he was such a sicko. A little weird, maybe." She took another bite and chewed. "But then again, you know the profile. The loner type. I gather from Melanie the whole town's gossiping about that."

Alyssa closed her eyes. "I can only imagine what they're saying about me."

"Well, everyone in northwest Michigan knows who you are, that's for sure."

Alyssa raised her hand to her head. "The dog trainer who steals."

"Actually, no. The woman who got shot trying to save the boy."

Alyssa looked at her from between her fingers.

"Seriously." Sue took another small bite. "It's all over television."

"So, no worries. Is that what you're telling me?"

Sue leaned over and kissed Alyssa's cheek lightly. "At least not now. Just get well."

Alyssa smiled, then her face grew serious. "Okay. Then I have something to say."

Sue felt a flutter of anxiety. "Okay."

"Last night, you did it again. You called the police. When I asked you not to. I only wanted you to help me." Alyssa blinked.

Oh, shit. Alyssa probably hadn't forgiven her for calling the cops the first time and now never would. Still, she wasn't giving up without a defense. "Technically, Delia called them."

"But you told her to." Alyssa set the bagel on her lap and crossed her arms. "She told me when she called earlier."

"Yeah, I did." Sue rubbed Alyssa's thigh lightly. "But I had to, both times. And hey, this time you told me I could do what I thought best."

Alyssa smiled. "This time, you're right. I did." She picked up the bagel. "I just wanted to see what you'd say." She took another enormous bite.

Sue slapped Alyssa's thigh gently. "Tease."

"Next time," Alyssa mumbled around her mouthful, "we decide together, okay?"

"Deal."

Watching Alyssa finish her bagel, Sue remembered her first sight of Alyssa, how strong she had seemed, how annoyed Sue had been with her heavy-handed pronouncements.

"I'm glad you're okay, Alyssa," Sue whispered. "Zero still needs a good dog trainer. *I* need a good dog trainer."

Alyssa grinned. "I'm glad to see you've learned something

245

through all of this. Normally, given my current condition," Alyssa continued, her face straight, "I'd recommend you consult my boss, Marcus Dixon. However, I think he's going to be unavailable for a long time. You'll have to make do with me."

"I'll make do with you," Sue said. "In more ways than one."

Chapter Twenty-five

"Tell me again why we're here?" Sue's breath tickled Alyssa's ear as she leaned close enough to be heard in the crowded lobby. "Casinos aren't my fantasy for a Friday night."

Alyssa reached up and patted Sue's cheek, then straightened the collar on her sweater. "I know. But Calvin and Samantha offered the celebration to patch things up. Was I going to say no?"

"I don't know. Are you really comfortable with them?"

Sue looked genuinely worried, so Alyssa kissed her cheek. "She told the cops everything she knew. And she's Adam's mother. I want to help out the healing between her and the town."

"I really love you," Sue said and winked.

Even the wink started the heat within Alyssa. "Thanks for coming. You look incredible."

Sue half-smiled and raised her eyebrows. "Hold that thought until we get back to your place."

"Or we could get a room." Alyssa pulled away and smoothed her garnet-colored dress. "Just the thought of being alone with you is wrinkling my clothes."

"I think I'd like that dress better in a pile on the floor," Sue said.

Alyssa's heat spread. "Stop it, or neither one of us will be able to hold up our end of a conversation."

Sue threw back her head and laughed, and that made Alyssa even hotter.

"Alyssa, Sue, there you are!" Delia waved to them from near the restaurant entrance. Adam ran up and practically leapt into Alyssa's arms.

"Whoa!" Alyssa said, hugging him. Her side seared underneath the bandage but it didn't matter. "You're as bad as Zero!"

Adam glowed with joy. "Mom said Buck could sleep in my bed!" He held up his hand. "High five!"

"High five." Alyssa smacked his palm and he grabbed her hand. "My mom says I should act like a gentleman." He pulled on his black jacket. "'Cause I'm dressed up in a suit."

Alyssa took Sue's hand, and the boy led them like a train to the restaurant.

"Grab on, Delia," Alyssa said as they passed, and she watched Delia hook up with Sue. "Samantha will love this."

They wound through the room to a large circular table where the Braeburns sat chatting with Melanie and Brian. Samantha looked up as they approached and blinked those black-encircled eyes.

"Cool," said Melanie. "Are you a steam engine or a diesel?"

Adam dropped Alyssa's hand and climbed into the chair beside Melanie. "You know about trains?"

"Sure," said Melanie. "We lived near a railroad museum when I was growing up."

Alyssa sat in the chair next to Sue. "Mel, is there anything you don't know about?"

"Not much," Melanie said with a satisfied grin. "Unless you've got more secrets."

"No!" Sue and Alyssa said together.

"Well," Delia said, her voice prim, "I see you two have *that* worked out."

"In fact," said Melanie, "I do have one late-breaking piece of news for you. The cops in Atlanta picked up the woman who—" She glanced at Adam. "The woman you met in Chicago, who dressed up like a cop."

The one who shot Vinnie, Alyssa thought.

"She's wrapped up tight now." Melanie smiled at Alyssa, then turned back to Adam. "I once went for a ride on a steam engine called a four-four-oh."

"No way!"

Alyssa looked around at all her friends. It had been a whirlwind week since it had all ended, full of hospitals, police, reporters and handling the clients at DOGS. This was a terrific change of pace even if it wasn't her usual idea of a good time.

A waiter appeared and poured Champagne into all their glasses.

"A toast," Calvin Braeburn said. Everyone raised their glasses, even Adam. "To Alyssa and Sue for saving our son."

Sue squeezed her arm as she grinned down at Adam.

"I got Champagne too!" he said.

"Yep," Sue said across her. "It's because of the suit."

"Hear, hear," Melanie said, and they all drank.

"Actually," Samantha began, setting her glass toward the center of the table, "Calvin and I also want to share with you a little business venture we've begun."

Alyssa settled back beside Sue. Starting tomorrow, she needed to think about her own financial situation. With Marcus gone, she had no job.

"—and it was Adam, actually, who pointed out the economic opportunity," Samantha finished.

"What Radley needs," Calvin said, "is a new dog training center. Our bank is engaged in securing all the assets of Dixon's Obedience and Guard Services. Dixon seemed willing to sell at a reasonable price. We hope to find someone to buy the business from us. We'd be willing to transact favorable terms to someone we could trust to concentrate on quality one-on-one training. Someone who knows the ins and outs of protection work. Someone who has real dedication to her clients."

Alyssa sat forward, wishing her heart hadn't begun to skip. After all, she couldn't expect—

"Yippee!" Delia's cry drew stares from neighboring diners, but Alyssa didn't care. Was this really happening?

"What do you think, Alyssa?" Calvin asked. "Interested?"

"It's not a gift," Samantha added. "I know how awkward that would be." She smiled. "It's business. All legal and aboveboard."

"Would I get freedom to run it as I see fit?" Alyssa asked.

"Absolutely," Calvin nodded. "You would own it."

"And I can work as your assistant. In a kids' group!" Adam squirmed in his seat. "And maybe when school starts again you can come to my classroom and visit." He turned back to Melanie. "You can come too."

"Nestor will be a giant by then," Melanie warned.

"Cool," Adam said. He took another sip of Champagne.

"That's enough of that, young man," Melanie said, pulling the glass from his hand. "Or I'll have to have you arrested."

"I don't think that would upset him," Brian told her.

Alyssa saw the playful nudge between them.

"You haven't answered the man," Sue said.

"It sounds like Adam has it all worked out," Alyssa said. She looked at Calvin. He didn't look anything like the man who had read the newspaper during his son's dog training class. The terror of the other night had transformed him. "I accept."

"Excellent. We can—"

"Talk about it Monday, Calvin." Samantha cut him off. "This is a celebration."

"Absolutely," Delia nodded, leaning forward to lift the Champagne bottle. "Anyone else besides Adam want another?"

꿏

Alyssa followed Sue into the hotel room and kicked off her shoes. "I'm glad we decided to stay. I had a tad too much Champagne."

Sue clicked on the desk light and tossed her shoes next to the king-sized bed. "I couldn't drive home either." She walked toward Alyssa slowly. "I can't endure another hour with you near me in that dress and not be able to touch you."

Her arms slid around Alyssa, solid and strong, pulling their hips together.

"Then take it off me," Alyssa said.

Sue looked into her eyes and rocked their hips back and forth. "Oh, I will."

This is a fabulous love, Alyssa thought.

Sue smiled. "I know what you're thinking," she said.

"So what are you thinking?" Alyssa asked, enjoying the sway of their bodies together.

"I'm thinking of that move you put on me that night I first came into your cottage."

Alyssa winced. She had almost killed her. "Sorry about that."

"Don't be." Sue bent and nuzzled the side of her neck, licking a long stroke to her shoulder. Alyssa felt her nudge the edge of her dress aside with her chin, then Sue's teeth, gently on the flesh.

"You're the only person who ever brought me to my knees," Sue said, lips brushing hot against her. "I want to return the favor."

"Just no leashes." Alyssa's head fell back as Sue began to kiss the center of her neck.

"No." Her hand cupped Alyssa's breast and her thumb brushed the already hardened nipple. "I'm thinking more along the lines of the element of surprise."

"I love surprises," Alyssa said, drawing a breath and shuddering as desire pulsed through her. "And I love you."

"I love you too," Sue said. "And I promise you're gonna love this." And for the next few hours, she made good on her word.

Alyssa loved every minute of it.

ABOUT THE AUTHOR

Hannah Rickard resides a few miles from one of the Great Lakes where she lives a charmed life. She shares that life with a beloved, three fabulous dogs, the woods and the beach. She writes her best while sitting on the sidelines during her friends' soccer games. Her goal: to live in such a way that people are stunned when they discover she has a Ph.D.

Publications from
BELLA BOOKS, INC.
The best in contemporary lesbian fiction

P.O. Box 10543, Tallahassee, FL 32302
Phone: 800-729-4992
www.bellabooks.com

WHEN THE CORPSE LIES A Motor City Thriller by Therese Szymanski. 328 pp. Butch bad-girl Brett Higgins is used to waking up next to beautiful women she hardly knows. Problem is, this one's dead. ISBN 1-931513-74-0 $12.95

GUARDED HEARTS by Hannah Rickard. 240 pp. Someone's reminding Alyssa about her secret past, and then she becomes the suspect in a series of burglaries.

ISBN 1-931513-99-6 $12.95

ONCE MORE WITH FEELING by Peggy J. Herring. 184 pp. Lighthearted, loving, romantic adventure. ISBN 1-931513-60-0 $12.95

TANGLED AND DARK A Brenda Strange Mystery by Patty G. Henderson. 240 pp. When investigating a local death, Brenda finds two possible killers—one diagnosed with Multiple Personality Disorder. ISBN 1-931513-75-9 $12.95

WHITE LACE AND PROMISES by Peggy J. Herring. 240 pp. Maxine and Betina realize sex may not be the most important thing in their lives. ISBN 1-931513-73-2 $12.95

UNFORGETTABLE by Karin Kallmaker. 288 pp. Can each woman win her true love's heart? ISBN 1-931513-63-5 $12.95

HIGHER GROUND by Saxon Bennett. 280 pp. A delightfully complex reflection of the successful, high society lives of a small group of women. ISBN 1-931513-69-4 $12.95

LAST CALL A Detective Franco Mystery by Baxter Clare. 240 pp. Frank overlooks all else to try to solve a cold case of two murdered children. ISBN 1-931513-70-8 $12.95

ONCE UPON A DYKE: NEW EXPLOITS OF FAIRY-TALE LESBIANS by Karin Kallmaker, Julia Watts, Barbara Johnson & Therese Szymanski. 320 pp. You've never read fairy tales like these before! From Bella After Dark. ISBN 1-931513-71-6 $14.95

FINEST KIND OF LOVE by Diana Tremain Braund. 224 pp. Can Molly and Carolyn stop clashing long enough to see beyond their differences? ISBN 1-931513-68-6 $12.95

DREAM LOVER by Lyn Denison. 188 pp. A soft, sensuous, romantic fantasy.

ISBN 1-931513-96-1 $12.95

NEVER SAY NEVER by Linda Hill. 224 pp. A classic love story . . . where rules aren't the only things broken. ISBN 1-931513-67-8 $12.95

PAINTED MOON by Karin Kallmaker. 214 pp. A snowbound weekend in a cabin brings Jackie and Leah together... or does it tear them apart?   ISBN 1-931513-53-8 $12.95

WIZARD OF ISIS by Jean Stewart. 240 pp. Fifth in the exciting Isis series.
ISBN 1-931513-71-4 $12.95

WOMAN IN THE MIRROR by Jackie Calhoun. 216 pp. Josey learns to love again, while her niece is learning to love women for the first time.   ISBN 1-931513-78-3 $12.95

SUBSTITUTE FOR LOVE by Karin Kallmaker. 200 pp. One look and a deep kiss... Holly is hopelessly in lust. Can there be anything more?   ISBN 1-931513-62-7 $12.95

GULF BREEZE by Gerri Hill. 288 pp. Could Carly really be the woman Pat has always been searching for?   ISBN 1-931513-97-X $12.95

THE TOMSTOWN INCIDENT by Penny Hayes. 184 pp. Caught between two worlds, Eloise must make a decision that will change her life forever. ISBN 1-931513-56-2 $12.95

MAKING UP FOR LOST TIME by Karin Kallmaker. 240 pp. When three love-starved lesbians decide to make up for lost time, the recipe is romance.   ISBN 1-931513-61-9 $12.95

THE WAY LIFE SHOULD BE by Diana Tremain Braund. 173 pp. With which woman will Jennifer find the true meaning of love?   ISBN 1-931513-66-X $12.95

BACK TO BASICS: A BUTCH/FEMME ANTHOLOGY edited by Therese Szymanski— from Bella After Dark. 324 pp.   ISBN 1-931513-35-X $14.95

SURVIVAL OF LOVE by Frankie J. Jones. 236 pp. What will Jody do when she falls in love with her best friend's daughter?   ISBN 1-931513-55-4 $12.95

LESSONS IN MURDER by Claire McNab. 184 pp. 1st Detective Inspector Carol Ashton Mystery   ISBN 1-931513-65-1 $12.95

DEATH BY DEATH by Claire McNab. 167 pp. 5th Denise Cleever Thriller.
ISBN 1-931513-34-1 $12.95

CAUGHT IN THE NET by Jessica Thomas. 188 pp. A wickedly observant story of mystery, danger, and love in Provincetown.   ISBN 1-931513-54-6 $12.95

DREAMS FOUND by Lyn Denison. Australian Riley embarks on a journey to meet her birth mother and gains not just a family, but the love of her life.   ISBN 1-931513-58-9 $12.95

A MOMENT'S INDISCRETION by Peggy J. Herring. 154 pp. Jackie is torn between her better judgment and the overwhelming attraction she feels for Valerie.
ISBN 1-931513-59-7 $12.95

IN EVERY PORT by Karin Kallmaker. 224 pp. Jessica's sexy, adventuresome travels.
ISBN 1-931513-36-8 $12.95

TOUCHWOOD by Karin Kallmaker. 240 pp. Loving May/December romance.
ISBN 1-931513-37-6 $12.95

WATERMARK by Karin Kallmaker. 248 pp. One burning question . . . how to lead her back to love?   ISBN 1-931513-38-4 $12.95

EMBRACE IN MOTION by Karin Kallmaker. 240 pp. A whirlwind love affair.
ISBN 1-931513-39-2 $12.95

DRIFTING AT THE BOTTOM OF THE WORLD by Auden Bailey. 288 pp. Beautifully written first novel set in Antarctica.   ISBN 1-931513-17-1 $12.95

CLOUDS OF WAR by Diana Rivers. 288 pp. Women unite to defend Zelindar!
                                                              ISBN 1-931513-12-0 $12.95

DEATHS OF JOCASTA: 2nd Micky Knight Mystery by J.M. Redmann. 408 pp. Sexy and intriguing Lambda Literary Award-nominated mystery.   ISBN 1-931513-10-4 $12.95

LOVE IN THE BALANCE by Marianne K. Martin. 256 pp. The classic lesbian love story, back in print!   ISBN 1-931513-08-2 $12.95

THE COMFORT OF STRANGERS by Peggy J. Herring. 272 pp. Lela's work was her passion . . . until now.   ISBN 1-931513-09-0 $12.95

CHICKEN by Paula Martinac. 208 pp. Lynn finds that the only thing harder than being in a lesbian relationship is ending one.   ISBN 1-931513-07-4 $11.95

TAMARACK CREEK by Jackie Calhoun. 208 pp. An intriguing story of love and danger.
                                                              ISBN 1-931513-06-6 $11.95

DEATH BY THE RIVERSIDE: 1st Micky Knight Mystery by J.M. Redmann. 320 pp. Finally back in print, the book that launched the Lambda Literary Award–winning Micky Knight mystery series.   ISBN 1-931513-05-8 $11.95

EIGHTH DAY: A Cassidy James Mystery by Kate Calloway. 272 pp. In the eighth installment of the Cassidy James mystery series, Cassidy goes undercover at a camp for troubled teens.   ISBN 1-931513-04-X $11.95

MIRRORS by Marianne K. Martin. 208 pp. Jean Carson and Shayna Bradley fight for a future together.   ISBN 1-931513-02-3 $11.95

THE ULTIMATE EXIT STRATEGY: A Virginia Kelly Mystery by Nikki Baker. 240 pp. The long-awaited return of the wickedly observant Virginia Kelly.
                                                              ISBN 1-931513-03-1 $11.95

FOREVER AND THE NIGHT by Laura DeHart Young. 224 pp. Desire and passion ignite the frozen Arctic in this exciting sequel to the classic romantic adventure *Love on the Line*.
                                                              ISBN 0-931513-00-7 $11.95

WINGED ISIS by Jean Stewart. 240 pp. The long-awaited sequel to *Warriors of Isis* and the fourth in the exciting Isis series.   ISBN 1-931513-01-5 $11.95

ROOM FOR LOVE by Frankie J. Jones. 192 pp. Jo and Beth must overcome the past in order to have a future together.   ISBN 0-9677753-9-6 $11.95

THE QUESTION OF SABOTAGE by Bonnie J. Morris. 144 pp. A charming, sexy tale of romance, intrigue, and coming of age.   ISBN 0-9677753-8-8 $11.95

SLEIGHT OF HAND by Karin Kallmaker writing as Laura Adams. 256 pp. A journey of passion, heartbreak, and triumph that reunites two women for a final chance at their destiny.   ISBN 0-9677753-7-X $11.95

MOVING TARGETS: A Helen Black Mystery by Pat Welch. 240 pp. Helen must decide if getting to the bottom of a mystery is worth hitting bottom.   ISBN 0-9677753-6-1 $11.95

CALM BEFORE THE STORM by Peggy J. Herring. 208 pp. Colonel Robicheaux retires from the military and comes out of the closet.   ISBN 0-9677753-1-0 $11.95

OFF SEASON by Jackie Calhoun. 208 pp. Pam threatens Jenny and Rita's fledgling relationship.   ISBN 0-9677753-0-2 $11.95

WHEN EVIL CHANGES FACE: A Motor City Thriller by Therese Szymanski. 240 pp. Brett Higgins is back in another heart-pounding thriller.   ISBN 0-9677753-3-7 $11.95

BOLD COAST LOVE by Diana Tremain Braund. 208 pp. Jackie Claymont fights for her reputation and the right to love the woman she chooses.   ISBN 0-9677753-2-9 $11.95

THE WILD ONE by Lyn Denison. 176 pp. Rachel never expected that Quinn's wild yearnings would change her life forever.   ISBN 0-9677753-4-5 $11.95

SWEET FIRE by Saxon Bennett. 224 pp. Welcome to Heroy—the town with more lesbians per capita than any other place on the planet!   ISBN 0-9677753-5-3 $11.95

Visit

Bella Books

at

BellaBooks.com

or call our toll-free number

1-800-729-4992